' I have never been good at the ladylike virtues.

'I enjoy the pleasures of the flesh too much! I can't pick and pretend, I like to savour things to the full.' Henrietta grinned. 'In fact, I think the life of a high-class doxy would suit me very well!'

Jonathan frowned, but answered lightly. 'Hardly! I have yet to meet a high-class doxy with your crusading spirit on behalf of the world's waifs and strays!'

'Oh?' Hetta chuckled. 'And with how many high-class doxies are you acquainted, dear sir?'

'That,' he said, laughing, 'is not at all a ladylike question!'

'Which just proves my point!'

'No, no! What you need,' he said, 'is not the life of a high-class doxy, but marriage to a not-entirely-gentlemanlike gentleman! You would shock a conventional gentleman to the bottom of his top boots; it would not do at all. And if he was not in *any* way a gentleman he would merely break your generous heart. So you require a compromise. That is the problem of being an unladylike lady!'

Janet Grace was born in Kent and educated in Staffordshire and at the University of Kent where she studied English and American literature.

Since then she has taught English in schools and to foreign students, supervised a playgroup, fostered disturbed adolescents and taught craft, child development and sex education at a Technical College, before turning to writing.

She is happily married and now lives in a large ramshackle farmhouse in Nottinghamshire with her husband, three children and a menagerie of animals, including dogs, cats, three rats and a parrot.

Previous Title

A MOST UNUSUAL LADY

FOOL'S HEAVEN

Janet Grace

M I L L S & B O O N L I M I T E D
ETON HOUSE 18-24 PARADISE ROAD
RICHMOND SURREY TW9 1SR

First published in Great Britain 1990
by Mills & Boon Limited

This edition 1990

ISBN 0 263 76760 4

Set in Times Roman 10 on 11 pt.
04-9003-78971 C

Made and printed in Great Britain

For Tim, Simon, Cathy and Sam.

CHAPTER ONE

THE click of the closing door sounded startlingly loud in the damp night air. Henrietta paused instinctively on the doorstep but, she thought with bitter self-pity, there was no one to wake and miss her. Only Meggie would care, and she slept in the undreaming stupor of any hard-working servant. Justin Dane was many miles away, and in someone else's arms.

Hardly aware of what she did, for the great anguish of her loneliness tore at her heart, she slipped away from the house—her house, but now so full of the echoes of his broken promises, her foolish hopes—and into the night.

Her thin silk slippers made no sound on the paving stones, and although she once hid in a doorway from a passing carriage, and once heard the rowdy carousing of homeward-bound revellers in a nearby street, most of London slumbered, and she made her aching way unnoticed down to the river.

It drew her blindly. That ever-flowing friend to the broken-hearted, swallowing all agonies into its silent depths. Her thoughts barely formed, without acknowledged intentions, her footsteps whispered on to Westminster Bridge. Halfway across, she drew to a seemingly reluctant halt, her hand dragging along the dank chill of the stonework, and turned to lean over. She gazed down into the slithering darkness beneath her that was the Thames. Darker by far than the strange slate-grey of Justin's eyes, but not as cold. Not as cold.

She almost welcomed the biting chill of the stone as it penetrated the thin muslin of her dress. She pressed her body harder against it, scratching at the stone with her fingernails, crushing her breasts on to the worn surface. She could hardly see the water—the cloud that had blotted out all starlight had brought a steady, defeated drizzle—but she knew it was below. She could sense its sinister flow, silently calling her.

I am so wet anyway, she thought, illogically, it will hardly matter.

The darker black of the bridge's shadow seemed to drop downwards, for ever, as she stretched to gaze over into it. It seemed like a well of black velvet.

Or the soft lining of my coffin.

The thought appeared with chilling clarity, stark in her mind, as if called to her by someone else, someone outside herself. As if a dark, ancient will from the depths of the sliding waters compelled her. Strangely unquestioning, obedient, Henrietta found herself climbing up, scrabbling in the damp to gain a foothold on the slippery stone, struggling to gain the top of the parapet. Soon she would be submerged in the will of the water.

'Stop! For God's sake, stop!'

The voice was not yet close, but it held an imperative note of command, and Henrietta paused, balancing on the stonework, and turned her head, as if waiting at some minor interruption before she could proceed.

Footsteps struck loud on the stones, and the shape of a man loomed from the dark. His face was pale and urgent; his words were an anguished request that cut through the weaving spell of the river.

'Give me your hand.'

Slowly, dazed, she held it out. He gripped it hard, hurting her wrist, and jerked her roughly so she stumbled and fell awkwardly down into his arms.

'Thank God. Thank God. Thank God.'

He was repeating the words over and over, clutching her against him, burying her face in the front of his greatcoat. In a sudden wave of memory the feel and smell of the warm, damp woollen cloth carried her back to her childhood, when her father, fresh in from riding over the Alnstrop acres, would sweep her up and crush her in his arms, banishing her tears.

Henrietta stood a little straighter, and pushed her face away from this stranger who held her. The deadening spell of the water was withdrawing its clinging fingers from her mind. It was then, in contrast to the rough, masculine, wholesome smell of his coat, that she became horrifyingly aware of the stench of the river. The true message of the river, the stink of rotting waste, of murky, foul unidentifiable things, of putrid corruption, of filth and of death. Her mind conjured a vision of her soft white body in the oily waters, rolling with the tide over the worm-oozed mud. She began to shiver uncontrollably, her whole body shaking under the thin cloak.

'Come. You are in no state to be alone.' The voice was low, stern. 'I have a carriage waiting. I will take you to my lodgings and my housekeeper shall make you a hot drink. Come.' Then, as she shook her head and tugged against his hold, 'Don't be a fool, girl. *I* have no designs to harm you. You are safer with me than you are with yourself.'

She had neither strength nor will to argue, and drearily followed as he led. A carriage was waiting near the end of the bridge, and carried them in silence back to a modest house in an unfamiliar street. The man hastened her inside and up the stairs, and she went, her misgivings dulled by apathy, into a book-lined study. The room had a rosy glow, lit as it was only by the flickering red of the banked-up coals in the fire. Her rescuer abruptly vanished, in search, he said, of his housekeeper.

Left alone, Henrietta sat huddled close up to the fire, her arms tight about herself. Eventually, as her clothes began to steam, and the warmth to penetrate her body, the long, racking shudders died away. The lassitude of emotional exhaustion overtook her. Her tense fingers relaxed their clutch on her arms, and she curled back in her chair, letting her eyes drift incuriously around the shadowed corners of the room.

The chairs were draped with Indian shawls, their exquisite rich colours glowing in the firelight. A carved wooden elephant stood more than knee-high at the end of the sofa, his trappings gloriously decorated in gold, silver and—her gaze paused—gems. It must be coloured glass and pieces of mirror that winked to reflect the flames. The intricately carved table also spoke of exotic eastern origins, as did the strange paintings on the wall beside her; and the shelves upon shelves of books that covered the far walls spoke of an intelligent and learned man.

A twist of curiosity pierced Henrietta's apathy. She wanted to see the face of her rescuer in the light. What kind of man could he be, who returned from India to walk the streets of London in the small hours, then thought nothing of rescuing a stray, despairing female and waking his housekeeper to tend her? He certainly had not seemed mad or vicious. He had spoken like a gentleman.

Voices, scuffled footsteps, and the door opened. The plump lady, looking aggrieved in her crumpled lace nightcap, patched slippers and voluminous dressing-robe, eyed Henrietta sharply, then pointedly ignored her as she shuffled forward with a laden tray. The man entered behind her.

'We will have it down by the fire, please, Mrs Stockwell, then you may retire again. I am sorry to have disturbed you.'

Grunting as she placed the tray, with its big jug of steaming hot chocolate and a plate of small cakes, down on the hearth, Mrs Stockwell surged over to the door before she replied.

'I never object to obliging *you*, sir, but there's some I don't doubt are no better than they ought to be.' And, with a disparaging sniff, she withdrew.

The man was young, or younger than she had thought, thirty perhaps. Not much older than she was herself. She had realised he was tall; now as he reached with a taper to light the candles on the mantelpiece she could see the muscular strength of the broad shoulders beneath the immaculate cut of his dark olive jacket. Surely a gentleman.

He threw the end of the taper into the fire and turned to face her.

'I feel we should introduce ourselves.'

He smiled at her, squatting down to her level, and she looked across, into his eyes.

Justin's eyes.

The colour drained from her face as she stared. There was no mistaking that curious slate-grey, the colour of mountain scree in rain, or storm-swept seas, with the fringe of thick, thick dark lashes, and the fine-drawn sallow skin. These were eyes that had haunted her dreams—and her nightmares.

'You are a Dane. A Dane of Thwayle,' she said.

He studied her tense, pale face thoughtfully. 'I am,' he replied. 'Though I am not always proud to acknowledge that fact. My name is Jonathan. Jonathan Dane.'

He watched her, waiting.

At last she looked away, and drew breath. 'Henrietta. Lady Henrietta Cairshaw.'

'Ah!' He nodded, surveying her gravely. 'I realised as soon as I came close to you that you were not the person I sought, for your hair is too dark, but I thought you were more than you seemed.' He touched her hand. 'I am glad I was there.'

She gazed back at him, her vivid blue eyes huge in the white of her face, and her dark hair, freed from the hood of her cloak, drying into an unruly mass of curls, glinting in the candlelight, full of black shadows.

'Justin never mentioned you. I never met you. Why?'

'So it is my cousin Justin you have met. I cannot felicitate you on your acquaintance with my family. I would not choose to introduce anyone to them myself.' He spoke lightly, but his words held bitterness. 'As to why he never mentioned me. I have been in India many years, and I doubt I have been much in the thoughts of my family. But tell me of yourself and your family. Should I know the name? You will find that my absence abroad has made me sadly ignorant of who I should and should not know.'

He was pouring the hot chocolate as he spoke, and handed her a steaming cupful. She cradled it in her hands and leaned her face over it, breathing in its sweetness.

'I suppose,' she said softly, slowly, almost as if to herself, 'that you should know what this life is that you brought back from the river. I suppose you could claim that.'

She still did not look up at him. The irony of her situation, driven to the river by memories of those eyes, only to find them gazing at her as she was snatched from its brink, filled her mind with an edge of hysterical laughter, hedged her about with the unreality of nightmare.

He sipped his drink without comment, waiting for her to continue. With a small shrug of resignation at this quirk in the incomprehensible workings of fate she began, in a low monotone, to speak.

'I will tell you then, Mr Dane, who I am. I was born Henrietta Ferdinand, the middle child of Lord and Lady Alnstrop. My two brothers and I grew up almost entirely at Alnstrop House, for my father hated town life. We were very, very happy.

'When I was ten, my father had an accident while hunting. He died very slowly, over many months, and my mother never recovered from the shock and strain. She was always an invalid afterwards. My brother Robert succeeded to the estates when he was just fifteen. He did his best at parenting John and myself, for my mother could not be much troubled with our worries.'

Her face unexpectedly softened into a very sweet smile.

'We tormented poor Robert dreadfully, always up to something hair-raising, and he would be torn, half disciplining us, half joining in, leading us on, for he always had the best ideas, if he would but tell us them. We adored him. As I grew older, I always knew how to coax him into giving me what I wanted. That is how I persuaded him to let me marry Edward, although Edward was thirty-five, and I only seventeen. I was looking for someone safe and secure, another father. Edward was all of that. He was a dear, fond husband who treated me like precious porcelain. He died of a fever when I was twenty-four. We had no children. I returned to live at Alnstrop with my brothers for a year, then came back to town. I have a house here, Edward's house.'

The expressionless little voice paused, and Henrietta sipped at her chocolate. Suddenly she drank it all down, and pushed the cup towards Dane. She frowned. Her voice hardened.

'Then I met your cousin, Justin Dane. So handsome, so exciting, so different.' Her words were full of anger and bitter self-mockery. 'He promised marriage, of course, and I believed him. Lived in my little fool's heaven until I was the last to know that he had found someone younger, a great deal richer, and even more gullible. They were married last week.' She stared down at her tense fingers, then quickly glanced at him. 'That is why you found me on the bridge. A sordid, silly tale, hardly worth the telling.' She fixed her angry gaze upon the fire, hunching a shoulder against him.

Without comment he handed her her cup, refilled from the jug of chocolate.

He pondered, and when he spoke his voice was concerned.

'Could you not return to Alnstrop now? Surely your brother——'

Her voice was again bitter.

'My brothers both married at about the time I met Justin. John and his wife are cruising around the Mediterranean in the pride of John's heart, his new yacht, Gannet II. I receive the occasional scrawled letter. Robert is at Alnstrop, and yes,' she sighed, 'yes, I could go to him, any time. And I love his wife dearly. But . . . I could not face their happiness. They are so filled with delight in each other, and their son, my godson Henry . . . I could not bear it now.'

'No.' He gazed thoughtfully into the glowing coals. 'No, I can see that . . . Well, if nothing else, I can apologise for my cousin, and assure you he is not worth a minute of your misery. The Danes are not.' He paused. 'There is but one of my family I would wish to spend time with . . .' His voice had dropped to no more than a murmur ' . . . and she may not even be alive . . .'

Henrietta scowled, deep in her own unforgiving thoughts.

'I have learned to hate the very name Dane. To think that once I dreamed it would soon be my own. How I despise myself. If there were no other man alive I would not marry a Dane.'

She leaned forward and took a cake from the tray. Suddenly she was hungry, and the torpor that dulled her mind was beginning to clear. As she ate, she broodingly studied the man who had rescued her. The likeness to Justin was strong, but the differences were there. Justin's hair was as dark as her own, but this man's was a lighter brown, perhaps bleached by years of tropical sun. His face was thinner, the bones finer, the lines that marked it those of thoughtfulness, laughter, and eyes narrowed against the sun. Unlike Justin, whose face showed the lines of discontent and dissipation, and the long years of self-indulgence.

He turned from watching the fire to return her look, and for some while they studied each other with a strange detachment.

'Tell me something of yourself,' Henrietta found herself asking, surprised at the words as she spoke them, at her sudden need to know. 'Why do you so dislike your family, why were you in India, and...' she paused, frowning at a memory, 'who was it you were seeking when you found me?'

He shifted to sit cross-legged on the hearthrug, and shot her a brief, disclaiming smile.

'It is a long, involved and dreary story. I think I should be taking you back to your home, rather than boring you with my life, don't you?'

'No. No, please talk to me. I have been so unhappy. It is my own thoughts that drown me. Fill my mind with something other than myself and my misery. Please. Or alone at home I will not be able to face the visions that fill the darkness.'

He frowned, studying her, then shrugged a little, nodded, and smiled.

'Fate must have intended our meeting. Was I sent to make amends for my cousin, do you think? It is ironic...I have spent so many hours searching, hoping to find Laura, to make amends to her for her treatment by our family...and then to find, instead, you! I cannot think our meeting is just a random chance, can you? Whatever reason may say...'

His voice drifted away, then he leaned back to rest against the chair across the fire from her, his long legs, the buff pantaloons smudged with dirt from the bridge, stretched casually across the hearthrug. It was as if the strangeness of their meeting had brought them as close as friends, or family, or lovers, the patterns of formality dissolved.

'Prepare to be confused, then,' he began, his voice matter-of-fact, settling to tell her a story. 'I hope you have the knack of remembering family relationships. But I think women are better at such things, certainly my aunts always knew exactly who was related to whom and how.

'The story really begins with my great-grandfather, Lord Grimsett of Thwayle, who had four sons, known collectively as "The Grandfathers". They were, by all accounts, the wildest, most ill-disciplined, bad-tempered, erratic and violent of the Dane family to terrorise the Thwayle estates, and many miles around, for many a century. And that area—in the furthest reaches of northern Yorkshire—was never noted for its saintliness.

'Quite early in his life, my great-grandfather made his will, the will that gave all the problems. For he specified in it that all the monies not directly tied into the estates should be equally divided only between those of his direct descendants who, at the time of his death, were living under his roof in family harmony, had reached the age of twelve years, and had done nothing to disgrace the family name.

'The situation was absurd, of course. "The Grandfathers", dissolute and impecunious gambling addicts, and very greedy, all returned to remain under the gaunt, decaying roofs of Thwayle Castle, and wait for great-grandfather to die.'

Dane laughed, with a flash of real amusement.

'He lived to be ninety-six. Meanwhile, of course, "The Grandfathers" had married, and were bringing up families of their own. The first was Grandfather Bentley. I never knew his wife, for she died in childbirth, but she left him with my two evil-tempered uncles to bring up, who in their turn grew up, married and produced my cousins Bentley and Frederick. They, with the unspeakable Justin, made my childhood such a time of misery.'

At the mention of Justin's name, Henrietta had frowned, but, 'I met Bentley, I think. Justin took me to meet him once, for isn't he now the head of the family?' was all she said.

'Yes, the present Lord Grimsett, though it makes me laugh to see him.' He paused.

'I'm sorry I interrupted,' she said. 'Go on.'

'You are *sure*?' He raised one dark eyebrow in mock surprise. 'Well, then there was *my* grandfather, old Carlton. His wife, dear Grandmama Alathea, produced him two sons: George, who emigrated to America, wise man that he was, and thus leaves our story; and Philip, my father, who sadly neglected to do so. My father and mother both died of a putrid fever when I was very small, and I was left to the care of Grandmama Alathea. She was the saint in the household of sinners.'

Dane paused again in his tale and smiled up at her quizzically.

'*Can* you follow it all, or are you dropping asleep from the tedium?'

Her smile was singularly bright and sweet, he thought, as he watched it leap her face into life.

'No, indeed. I am faint, but pursuing, and have no doubt that the meaning of it all is soon to be revealed to me! Please, carry on. We have two more grandfathers to trace yet, and no doubt one of them,' her smile died, 'had the misfortune to produce the father of the unspeakable Justin.'

'Yes, but it was not the next one. Grandfather Victor produced only a daughter, my aunt Alice, and although she married a distant Dane cousin, from across the county, Grandfather Victor never recovered from the shame of this failure, and died while I was in short coats. Alice doubled the failure by dying while producing yet another girl, my cousin Laura, and she came to live, with me, under the care of Grandmama Alathea.

'Then lastly there was Grandfather Horace. He produced a horde of quite horrible uncles, Horace the younger, Victor the younger, George, Charles and Hector, besides the aunts, Anne, Mary, Elizabeth, Caroline. Fortunately they were not themselves so prolific. Horace never married. I believe his temper was so violent that no one would have him.

'Victor produced but the one son who survived, who was, as you may have guessed, my cousin Justin, though his dutiful wife produced him stillborn infants until she died of exhaustion. George's first wife had no children, and although he later married again and had a bulging nursery, none of his brats was old enough to affect the story.

'Charles and Hector killed a man in a public house brawl. They fled the country to escape the law, and I believe they followed George to America. Whatever, they were effectively eliminated under the terms of the will. Two of the aunts married and left home; only the wispy ineffectual aunts Anne and Mary stayed to housekeep.

'So there you have the world of my childhood. Great-Grandfather confined to his rooms, but none the less making his ferocious presence felt everywhere. The two surviving grandfathers, Bentley and Horace, both evil-tempered martyrs to their well-deserved gout, and fighting always for the interests of their own surviving offspring, the uncles, and the three favoured cousins, Bentley, Frederick and Justin.

'Then there was Grandmama Alathea, little Laura, and myself, the unwanted ones. Melodramatic, but true. We occupied the east wing. It was cold and running with damp, and great yellow fungi grew out of the wainscoting. We would pick them and spread them in the corridors for the maids to slip on. We tried to keep out of the way of the family, but it was necessary to appear for meals and lessons.'

Dane paused, his face bitter before he turned away to hide his expression. Henrietta, always quick to sympathy for the sufferings of others, was imagining his childhood with growing horror.

'Grandmama Alathea died when I was fourteen, and Laura was ten.' He kept his voice very level, she noticed. 'The damp and cold had always made her ill. Aunt Anne had died earlier, so there was only wispy Aunt Mary left to spare us any time. Of necessity, we cared for each other, myself and Laura. The married aunts and uncles conspired to dislike us and put us down.

'When I was seventeen, I awoke one morning to be told to pack my bags: the carriage was coming to take me on the first leg of a journey to India. I had barely heard of the place. Knew no more than its name. I was to work for a businessman acquaintance of theirs. When Laura kissed me goodbye, she told me that she had overheard the uncles state that not only would I be disqualified under the terms of the will, and would thus inherit nothing, but would be certain to die in the tropical heat. She begged that I would endeavour not to die. That is the last time I saw her, as I was swept off, leaving her alone in that dreadful household.'

Dane stretched, and shook the chocolate jug, but it was empty.

'So that is how I went to India. As to why I hate my family——'

'Isn't that enough?' Henrietta cried, aghast at this tale of a devastated childhood. By comparison, her own had been idyllic.

'Oh, no. There *is* more—if you care to hear it.'

She nodded, her gaze at him intent.

'I did not find out all of this until I returned from India, and set about visiting Laura, the only one of my family for whom I cared. She was a sweet, shy, affectionate child . . .

'Well. After I left, my other aunts, one by one, died, and the family became steadily coarser, more drunken and violent, with only poor abused Mary left with Laura to be despised and ignored.

'The uncles took to organising long gambling sessions, bringing in anyone they could find with something to wager, and losing vast sums themselves. Girls were brought in from the villages, the cousins and uncles sharing in the sport, while Mary and Laura, so I heard, shivered and hid in the east wing.

'Then one day a certain Count Vilnius, a gambler whose name sounds as evil as doubtless he was, came to join the card-play. He remained some weeks, apparently, entranced both by the play—where he won steadily, and disastrously for my family—and by the very youngest of the girls brought up to the castle for their amusement.

'When he declared he was leaving, his winnings were so vast it was quite impossible for my family to honour them. He told them he would be happy to discount them all in exchange for the gift of Laura. He had glimpsed her creeping timidly down to the kitchen to collect her meals. Did he know she was cousin to Justin, Bentley and Frederick? I don't know. Certainly none of the family cared to recall the fact. She was fourteen. A very young fourteen. He was perhaps fifty, maybe more.

'The uncles agreed almost at once. It was, after all, a godsend. They lost their debts, and she lost everything, including of course, her share of Great-Grandfather's fortune. Count Vilnius left with her that night, and she has not been seen since. I have been trying to trace her, and it was she for whom I was searching. I believe he abandoned her on the streets of London.'

The silence stretched so long that the split and tumble of a shifting coal, the sudden leap of flame, was startling.

Henrietta's thoughts jumbled in turmoil, mixed with disconnected surges of emotion. Fury boiled in her at Justin—that she could ever have loved a man who had once been party to such a deed—and contemptuous scorn at Bentley, now Lord Grimsett, whose prim, mean, tight little mouth she had never liked, certain it betrayed the man behind. Oddly, no part of her doubted the story. What she had been told of the Danes tonight was only the other side, she realised, of the close, self-interested family she had met through Justin. Pity swelled in her for the child Laura, and outrage on her behalf.

'The entire Dane family are despicable,' she burst out, passionately. 'Despicable! It would seem impossible, and unforgivable, that a child should be treated so. I *had* thought it only Justin who lied and exploited, who deserved every woman's contempt. But it is all, *all* the family, *every one*! By God, I could curse every man with the name of Dane!'

Even through the heat of her impassioned outpouring, she caught the flicker of hurt in his eyes. She paused, surprised. The eyes were so like Justin's that a part of her rejoiced to see the pain, wanted to inflict pain. But this man was not Justin. His thin, sensitive face was not Justin's face. It was with shock that she saw she had the power to hurt this stranger, and the realisation pierced her anger with a strange confusion.

'Laura must be found,' she said.

'Yes,' he replied, gravely. 'I will find her. But now I am going to take *you*, if you will direct me, to your home.'

CHAPTER TWO

NEXT morning, Henrietta slept deeply and late, but a little before noon she began to stir. Meggie, who had been creeping about the closet sorting clothes, smiled grimly to herself, and slipped out to order freshly made tea and toast. Henrietta half heard her leave, but her waking dreams were a nightmare confusion of strange meetings, oddly intimate conversations, wicked grandfathers, dying aunts, lost cousins, and the terrible stench of the rising river tide over the mud.

He had done what she had asked, this stranger from the night, this Jonathan Dane, she realised resentfully as she pulled herself up on the pillows and blearily opened her eyes. Her mind was no longer full only of her own misery. The total dreary despair that had engulfed all her thoughts of her life and future since Justin's last visit had curiously lifted, as if the night's events had been a turning point, a release.

She was confused, ashamed, angry; gnawed by an irrational resentment that some chance-met man, some mere stray cousin of Justin's, could have effected this change in her mood, could have frayed her protective pall of misery. This resentment fuelled her broodings on Justin, and helped to fill her with an unwavering hatred of the family Dane. But her thoughts were also, unbidden, venturing outward, puzzling over Dane's search for Laura.

When Meggie returned with the tray, she found her mistress sitting up, scowling, and thus looking better than she had for many weeks, for she lacked the uncaring apathy that had dulled her every expression since Justin's departure.

'Well, Miss Hetta, I don't *pretend* to know what you've been about. Quite a turn it gave me, coming in here to find your clothes, that I had put away myself, all damp and crumpled on the floor, the front of your muslin all smeared with mud. Where *had* you been, Miss Hetta, and never a word to me?'

Henrietta transferred her scowling gaze to Meggie's face and made no answer, but allowed herself to be fussed with plumped pillows, tucked napkin, and neatly arranged tray, while she thought rebellious thoughts about the sort of maid who had been with her so long that to her she would always remain just 'Miss Hetta', and who would probably continue to call her that, she reflected crossly, even when, or if, she ever reached the status of grandmother!

'Well, Miss Hetta? It's no good you thinking you'll get away with not telling me all about it, for no peace will you get till you've put my mind at rest. You drink that tea now, while it's warm. Haven't we been through enough together, one way and another? It's too late to start thinking you can't trust your Meggie now. When I think what I went through over that wretched Justin——'

'Meggie! Enough! All right! Though how I ever allowed you to turn from such a sweet and biddable maid to such an old dragon I do not know! Sit down. I'll tell you about it.'

'Yes, miss, and so you should. Gallivanting off...!'

Meggie settled herself self-righteously on the end of the bed, disapproval and curiosity fighting openly in her expressions, but as Hetta's extraordinary story progressed, reluctantly at first, and shamefaced over the episode on the bridge, but with growing outrage as she told the story of the girl Laura, Meggie's mouth hung ajar in horror, distress and amazement.

'Then he brought me back in his carriage,' Hetta concluded, with a dismissive shrug and a sniff. 'He put the horses to and drove it himself, for he would not wake his man again, so I had no chance to ask him all the questions I have been burning to ask about his search for this poor child. Can you imagine anything so wicked? It defies belief, except that I could believe *anything* of a Dane.'

She sipped her tea, deliberately ignoring Meggie's speechless, open-mouthed outrage, and the rebukes she knew would come.

'I wonder how he hopes to trace her? It must be over ten years now since this Count Vilnius took her. It should surely be possible to trace *him*, unless they have both vanished overseas. I wonder from which country he came, for the name is never English.

'That poor, poor child... well, she is a grown woman now, of course. To think *I* thought *I* had been badly treated by a Dane! She *must* be traced, *must* be rescued and restored to her rightful level in society.

'Think, Meggie, only think. Now you have heard the straits *I* was driven to by contemplation of Justin and the wrongs he did me—all those lies and broken promises. Then imagine this child, so young, so innocent, and so betrayed by all her family, those double-damned Danes of Thwayle. Could anyone possessed of heart and conscience not wish to trace her? I cannot ignore her. I intend to do everything in my power to try to find her, yes, whatever you may say, and, if all the Danes hate me for it, the better I shall like it!'

Hetta finished defiantly, and she drained the last of the tea from her cup.

'So, Meggie! What *do* you think?'

'Oh, miss...oh, miss, to think of you, out there, well, it doesn't bear thinking of. That you should have felt that way and me never known. You should have come and told me, miss! You should never have done what you did!' There were tears in Meggie's eyes which she dashed away impatiently, while Hetta shrugged, shame-faced, and would not meet her eye. 'And to think I should ever feel thankful to some strange man for taking you off to his house in the middle of the night . . . well, what Lord Alnstrop would say, I just don't like to think. As for that poor girl, and the way her family treated her, a proper heathen lot they must be. It just doesn't bear thinking of. And I can't see why you *should* be thinking of it, for it doesn't seem to me that it is any of your business. Though I must say,' here Meggie paused, dabbed her eyes and scrutinised her mistress, 'you *do* look a deal better for it.'

Unexpectedly, shakily, Hetta laughed.

'He is to drag himself from his search for his cousin to call this afternoon, to see how I do. I must get up. Find me something suitable to wear, Meggie. Perhaps that old blue dimity would do.'

When Jonathan Dane arrived at the neat white town house behind the wrought-iron railings, he was welcomed by an affable, elderly butler, and escorted upstairs to the back parlour. It was a small, cosy room, with a fire blazing. The girl he had rescued, distraught and bedraggled, from Westminster Bridge, was sitting with her feet curled up under her, on a sofa near the fire, reading. She uncurled reluctantly, and got to her feet.

'Come in, Mr Dane. Though I must confess I take no pleasure in calling you that. It was good of you to spare the time to call.'

'My dear Lady Cairshaw, you may call me whatever you prefer.' He took the hand she offered so coolly and unsmilingly, with a brief, formal bow. That strange, casual intimacy of the previous night had not, he thought with an unexpected regret, survived the light of day. 'I trust you are fully recovered from your ordeal last night?'

'Sir.' She coloured, but faced him squarely, her voice quiet and determined, if a little reluctant. 'I hardly know how to apologise for the trouble I caused you, but I do wish to thank you.' She took a breath. 'For your tact, forbearance and kindness; but mostly for doing what I needed more than anything else—filling my mind with thoughts of someone worse treated than myself. Please, sit down. I have asked for tea to be brought.'

He watched with quiet amusement as she curled up on the sofa again, unconsciously tucking her feet up like a child under the blue dimity skirts. She clasped her hands in her lap and regarded him earnestly.

'I wish to know more of your search for Laura. I have thought of little else since you spoke of it last night. How did you know where to begin? What have you done so far? What ideas do you have for the future? There are so many things I want to ask you.'

Dane sat down opposite Henrietta, but paused before he spoke.

'Certainly I can tell you more of what I have been doing, though I must beg you to regard what I tell you as confidential.' He paused, made uncertain by her formal reception of him, combined with this unexpected interest in his problem. 'We were both perhaps unusually open in our confidences last night.'

He cocked a querying eyebrow at her. She thought with embarrassment of her self-pitying little life history of the previous night, then her thoughts flew guiltily to her morning's confession to Meggie, disclosing all his confidences.

'Naturally you can rely on my discretion, sir,' she replied, a touch haughtily.

He had not missed the flit of expressions across her face.

'But it was necessary to confide...?'

'Meggie is the soul of discretion. We have shared countless secrets.' Her tone was defensive, despite, or maybe because of, the smile she caught lurking in his eyes. 'Anyway, she had found all my damp clothes, covered with dirt from the bridge, so I had to tell her something, and the truth *is* usually easiest in the long run.' Henrietta glared defiantly. 'She was most distressed.'

'I am not surprised.'

He broke off as the tray arrived, and Henrietta poured tea for them both, and handed him his cup.

She slid unsure, sideways glances at him as he sipped the hot drink, uncertain of herself before this poised, self-assured man, angry at him, because it was he to whom she had, last night, so vulnerably exposed her emotions.

His jacket, a rich chestnut-brown, displayed the lack of ostentation and the perfect fit which marked it as being from the hand of an expert; the buff-coloured pantaloons were spotless; the Hessians gleamed. He might have lived abroad, but he was well versed in English good taste. He caught her eye, but if he was aware of her reluctant approval he made no sign of it, or of noticing the faint blush that coloured her cheeks. He lowered his cup and, after a moment's frowning thought, seemed to come to some positive decision, and began quietly to tell her of his search.

'It was my cousin Bentley who told me what had occurred. He has, as you know, inherited the title now, and married a good lady from Berkshire. I think he has learned to be horrified at what was done, though not to the extent of making any push to trace Laura himself. However, he was happy to give me information and wish me good fortune.'

Hetta snorted. 'A fine head of the family, I must say.'

He shrugged dismissively.

'I expected less. He was able to tell me that when he went through his father's papers after his death there was a letter from Laura, dated some months after she had left Thwayle Castle. In it she begged for money to help her leave Count Vilnius. She was then in rooms in a place called White Cocks Alley, in the East End of London. There seems no doubt that the letter was never answered.

'I have been to White Cocks Alley, and asked for news up and down the length of it, for Bentley had destroyed the letter and forgotten the number of the house, but no one would remember anything in a place like that, whether they actually knew it or not. However, I don't give up hope. Although much of the population of such an area is transient, there are also many who have the misfortune to live out all their lives there. I believe I can find someone who will remember twelve years back.

'It is all a question of gaining the trust of someone there, for, although they will tell you anything you wish if you pay enough, there is no guarantee it will be true. But someone who had known Laura and cared about her, perhaps one of the other unfortunate girls working to survive in a similar situation—they might tell me if I could gain their trust. So far they have merely resented my questions, and...' he paused and smiled wryly '...the fact that I bring them no custom.'

'No custom... these girls...' she paused and blushed a fiery red '...you think Laura is working the streets of London as a... as a whore?'

He was disconcerted by her outraged bluntness, but answered coolly.

'Lady Cairshaw, I must be realistic. What choice of future do you imagine there is for a young girl, seduced, brought to London, then almost certainly abandoned when her so-called "protector" tired of her. Why do you imagine my thoughts flew to her when I saw you on the bridge last night? I search the streets at night, and frequent the haunts where the prostitutes gather, because I have few other options. She can hardly be a seamstress, for I know she could never set a stitch without a bloodstain, and even if she were, it is doubtful if she could support herself. The majority of such poor women must supplement their income on the streets.'

'But Count Vilnius! Perhaps she is still with him, settled in some European capital, raising a family of young Vilnii? Surely it is possible?'

'I wish I could believe so. But, no. Naturally I tracked him down immediately. He was killed seven years ago in a duel, out on the Essex marshes. The man who killed him was defending the honour of his sister, a child of thirteen. There had been other, earlier scandals. It seems almost certain that he had parted from Laura within two years of her leaving Thwayle, possibly earlier.'

'Poor child,' Hetta said quietly. 'Poor lonely, desperate child. I can well understand why you worry for her life and her sanity. But perhaps she went into service?'

'It is possible, though less easy than you might think, I believe, with no references or experience. It is even possible she is married and settled with some honest citizen, which is why I feel I must move with some discretion in my efforts to trace her. I would not wish to be the unwitting cause of wrecking any new life she might have built up despite the past. That is why I have not risked the public exposure of advertising for her in the newspapers.' He sighed. 'Sometimes it all seems so hopeless, yet I feel I cannot give up.' He placed his cup back on the tray. 'But I have bored you long enough with my family problems.' He made as if to get up to leave.

'No, wait. Please. You say that you feel you could learn more from the girls who work on the streets around White Cocks Alley?'

'Yes, I am sure of it, but I have yet to gain their trust. I would guess many of them do not easily put their trust in men. They would speak to another woman . . . But no matter. There is a public house, the White Cocks, that I have yet to visit. Perhaps I will have more luck there.'

'I could help.'

Dane looked sharply at Henrietta. Her expression showed an anxious but stubborn determination, and his heart sank.

'There is no possibility of a lady such as yourself becoming involved with such people as inhabit the area around White Cocks Alley. None at all. It would be totally unsuitable.' He saw the hurt in her face at his rebuff, and the defiance, and spoke on conciliatingly. 'Naturally I would appreciate hearing any ideas that you might have—further areas to investigate, perhaps?'

'They would talk more easily to another woman,' she said, obstinately. 'You said so yourself. I could come with you, even play the part of such a woman myself.' She registered the horror and anger in his face. 'I want to help to trace her. I feel I need to. I was driven to that bridge last night by the heartlessness of Justin Dane. She was driven away from her home by the heartlessness of all those other Danes, those cousins and uncles. It cannot be *just* a coincidence that we met, you and I. I believe I was meant to meet you and help in your search, for who else would share your determination?'

'Lady Cairshaw, thank you. I appreciate your offer and the fact that you care. But, no. No. Never.' He stood, and a warm smile took away some of the harshness of his words. 'I promise you I will call, in fact, I will come tomorrow, if I may, and keep you informed of my progress. And you will stay here by the fire, and continue to recover from your ordeal of last night, and your unsettled spirits. Perhaps in a day or two you might like to come out for a drive?'

Hetta's brother Robert, Lord Alnstrop, might have recognised the set of the chin, and flash of the eyes, but Jonathan Dane merely reflected appreciatively on how quietly she now took his refusal to countenance her absurd suggestion. Indeed, he put the making of it down to some continued disorder of her senses, from which she would doubtless soon recover, as he bowed over her hand and took his leave.

CHAPTER THREE

'MEGGIE! We are going out.'

'Out, Miss Hetta?'

'Out.'

Henrietta flung out of the closet, where she had been discontentedly surveying her clothes. Across the room the wardrobe door swung open on its hinges, evidence of her unsatisfactory rummage through the contents.

'I need to look different, Meggie, and I need to look vulgar. I need a wig, I think, which will mean my own hair cut shorter so I can wear it comfortably; but my main worry is the clothes.'

She paused, and chewed on her finger, frowning.

'Whatever are you up to, Miss Hetta? You've had that look in your eye ever since that Mr Dane left yesterday. There's something you're planning, and I dare swear it's mischief.'

Meggie stood, arms akimbo, surveying her mistress with dubious disapproval.

'Don't *you* start treating me like a child, Meg, for I won't stand it. Tell me, when I give you old clothes of mine that you don't wish to wear, where do you sell them?'

'Miss Hetta...'

'Where?'

'Well, it depends, but Petticoat Lane mostly. Monmouth Street used to be the place, and it still has a good range of boots and shoes, and Rosemary Lane, that's Rag Fair, is good. But Petticoat Lane is the best in my opinion. But why, miss? What do you want with such places, when you can buy everything so fine? And what is all this talk of wigs?'

'Send out to find a hackney, Meggie, and fetch your wrap. We are going to Petticoat Lane.'

The raucous, vibrant turmoil of Petticoat Lane astonished Hetta. She clutched Meggie's arm with a laugh of exhilaration as they fought their way through the throng of people.

'This is an amazing place. Whyever have I never visited it before? You keep all the fun to yourself, Meggie!'

Meggie sniffed.

'You keep a tight hold on what you're wearing, Miss Hetta. You blink, and you'll find half your clothes vanish from your back. They'll end up on the stall down the street, where you'll have to stand shivering in your shift to buy 'em back.'

Hetta giggled, but then spoke impatiently.

'*Do* stop disapproving, Meggie. You had your say in the hackney, and I shall take no notice. I have quite made up my mind. I'll teach that oh, so patronising Mr Dane to dismiss my help out of hand! What if what I mean to do *is* unsuitable? Jumping off Westminster Bridge is "unsuitable" too. At least this has given me the determination to stay alive and find the girl. Don't you care about that?

'If my parading as Haymarket-ware just for a few days can bring that girl back from the streets for ever, then how *can* I stop to count the cost? Finding her is too important. You *know* you have always supported me in what I do, and I especially need you now. Come, now, tell me. Whatever shall I wear to be accepted as one of the Cyprians of White Cocks Alley? Come, let's look around and you tell me what you think.'

Everywhere were clothes. The street was full as far as the eye could see, with racks and rails of coats, jackets and dresses, trestle tables piled with oddments, boxes and loose piles of boots and shoes along the pavements. The door to every house stood wide, displaying rooms within jumbled with yet more: scarves, shawls, handkerchiefs, every sort of linen and whitewear, hats, bonnets and feathers. Every side alleyway was hung throughout its length with clothing, from gentlemen's finery, to the coarse breeches in drugget or corduroy for the working man.

People jostled and pushed. Maidservants, and the occasional footman, carried bundles of fine clothing, given as perks, or in lieu of wages, and touted them at the different stalls, haggling for a better price. Young gentlemen stood, fingering the cloth of the jackets, giving the coat off their back in part-exchange when they had selected a more fashionable garment. Sharp-eyed Jews wheeled hand-barrows of clothes, collected round the streets of the capital, shouting for passage through the throng, and vanished into back rooms to sort their bundles. Quick-fingered children scurried underfoot, darting to escape a kick or a curse.

Hetta pushed her way through to several racks of peculiarly garish dresses, her face lighting up as she contemplated the shimmering purples, glowing puces, rich mustard-yellows and one voluminous gown in the bright green of fresh limes, ornamented with vast embroidered flowers in silver and gold.

'Just look, Meggie. Isn't it truly magnificent?'

She held the gown against herself, and pranced a quick pirouette. The vast, red-faced woman who ran the stall surged a little nearer, and watched her with a beady eye.

'It seems to me, Miss Hetta,' Meggie began with grudging interest, 'that if you are to do this as you say, you've a need to think clearly. You'll never persuade anyone you're a common drab from the streets, no matter what you wear, and that's a fact. One look at your face, and it's plain you've never had a sniff of real hardship.

'But somebody's little fancy piece, the Cyprian choice of a gentleman who keeps you in a bit of style, well, that's possible. There's many a girl from a respectable home who makes an early mistake, and they don't all end up so badly. But I'm not happy, miss, unless you have a gentleman as is there as your protector. If you could only persuade this Mr Dane to pose as your gentleman friend, why, then you could ask your questions unbothered by other's attentions.'

'Huh! Oh, I'll grant you, it's a sensible idea, Meggie.' Hetta considered the matter reluctantly. 'If only my brothers were not married and settled, John would have been game to help me... But you're right, it would have to be this man, Dane. Though I hate to ask him, and how I could persuade him, I don't know. No matter, I'll consider that later. Let me decide now, who I shall be! I need a character to play, a convincing role, if I am to perform this charade successfully.'

She had hung the green dress back on its rail as she talked, and now stood, oblivious of the jostling people, nibbling at her finger, deep in thought.

'I shall keep my name as Hetta, for it hardly matters, and I think...oh, I think my parents ran a grocer's shop in...yes, Tunbridge Wells. I cannot say I am from Thwayle, like Laura, for I know nothing whatever of the country or speech of such people, but perhaps my mother was from the north, and so I could claim that Laura is my cousin.

'I left Tunbridge Wells for love of a handsome face and a red coat, but he soon left me, and rather than follow the regiment I have stayed in town, and am now supported by a new man, fresh back from India—*if* I can persuade the wretched man to support my story, of course—who is very generous to me at present, so I could claim that I have no wish to transgress and offend him.'

She paused, with a frown of concentration, then smiled. 'However, having sent money back to my ageing parents in Tunbridge Wells, after many years when they probably believed me dead, I have heard back that my cousin Laura is a similar disgrace and shame to the family, having run off with a certain Count Vilnius twelve years ago, when no more than a child. I want to meet her again, and heard she once lived near The White Cocks, so I am out to discover her whereabouts. What do you think, Meggie, will it serve?'

Meggie giggled.

'It's amazing, miss. I don't know how you think of it all. I could almost believe you then.'

'Good. Now help me choose the sort of clothes our Hetta, the grocer's daughter from Tunbridge Wells, might wear to delight the heart of a supposedly lusty gentleman from India!'

When they eventually found a hackney to take them back to Hetta's house in St Dunstan's Street their arms were laden.

Hetta had insisted on the embroidered lime-green. 'I know it is just what she would have chosen, and I cannot wait to wear it!' Also several other dresses, in bright colours and loud stripes, and shimmering, transparent gauzes. Meggie, involved now in the whole charade, had insisted on low necks, and front-opening bodices.

'Good heavens, why?' Hetta had asked.

'Easier for a gent to undo, of course,' she had replied, phlegmatically.

'Meggie! The things you do think of!'

And they both suddenly collapsed in helpless laughter over a pile of elderly whalebone corsets.

They had also purchased shawls, ostrich feathers, and a splendid chestnut wig.

'You wait, Meggie. I shall look quite amazing.'

'Oh, I've no doubt at all about that, miss.'

Meggie was resigned by now. Well, she knew it was outrageous, but there was no doubt it was doing Miss Hetta a power of good.

* * *

It was late afternoon when Jonathan Dane made his second visit to St Dunstan's Street.

He had been telling himself, as his carriage juddered over the cobblestones, that it was probably best if he made his polite farewells during this visit. There was really little point in prolonging the acquaintance. She was so adamant in her dislike of his family, it was doubtless an unkindness to irritate her with his presence. She certainly seemed over the shock of that unhappy night, and, if some of her ideas were still irrational, it was surely no more than an irritation of the nerves. No doubt her intentions were good. It was a pity to lose the friendship, for he could not deny she had a certain attraction—he frowned—but it would probably be for the best.

Esther would definitely *not* be pleased if she heard of the night-time meeting. She was a stickler for the proprieties, and even, he suspected, a little inclined to jealousy, though he quickly stifled that unworthy thought.

The butler smiled a welcome and took him once again to the back parlour, but it was empty, and Dane surprised in himself a twinge of disappointment. Her blue dress, he remembered irrelevantly, had exactly echoed the blue of her eyes. He paced the room, studying her possessions with a frown. He spun round, smiling, as the door opened, but it was merely the maid.

'She won't be but a moment, sir, she wanted to change.'

Dane nodded, and was turning away, but the girl, with an air of earnest bravado, continued. 'Please, don't discourage her, sir. I know it seems the height of foolishness, and so I told her myself at first, but I've come to see that it's just what she needs. Truly, sir, it's doing her good. But she will need you, and I'm relying on you, sir.'

Puzzled, he was about to reply, but she had bobbed a curtsy and withdrawn before he had the chance. He had set aside a copy of *The Ladies' Magazine* and was absentmindedly flicking over the pages of *Marmion* when the door opened yet again.

Dane let the book fall unnoticed on to the sofa as he stared, outraged, at the vision that confronted him.

The lady wore a green silk dress of garish opulence, its gold and silver flowered embroidery glinting in the firelight as she moved. The neck was cut exceedingly low, and she had dispensed with the modest fichu, leaving the white swell of her breasts to rise, round and inviting, from the ruffles of gold lace. A silver-gauze shawl was draped loosely from her shoulders. Her chestnut hair, mounded high on her head, was topped by three nodding white ostrich feathers, and she smirked and tittered at him from behind a matching white ostrich feather fan. Only by the great blue eyes did he know her for Henrietta.

She twirled around, her face alight with defiant laughter and mischief, and sank into a deep, deep curtsy at his feet, flirting wicked little pouted kisses up at him over the top of her fan. 'What do you think, sir? Would I seduce you?'

She held up a daintily imperious hand for him to raise her to her feet.

He continued to hold her hand in his as she stood close before him, smiling provocatively up, those absurd feathers bobbing and dipping above her. The warm subtle sweetness of her perfume filled his head. Horrified, he could not turn his eyes from hers, and it seemed an eternity before he began to breathe again, drawing a long, ragged breath, then forcing himself to breathe normally.

Angrily, he pushed the fan aside and, taking her chin, pushed her head roughly one way then the other, staring at her. Then he drew his hand back hastily. He released her and turned away. 'Your hair! What have you done to your hair?' He was furious to hear his voice shake a little.

She laughed, well-satisfied with the effect of her costume, and waltzed across to sit down on the sofa.

'We have cut it short, at least, Meggie cut while I gave directions. It's not possible to wear this wonderful wig over so many curls of my own, so they had to go. It's not important. Everyone has short hair nowadays. But, tell me! Do I look seductive? Would I entice you to wicked ways? For, you see, Meggie persuaded me to write a role for you into my story. *I* was set to go on my own to search for Laura, but Meggie will be happier if I have the protection of some man, and, after all, Laura is your cousin... So if you will only be so good as to assume the role of my protector, I can ask all the questions necessary and remain unmolested!

'I am to pose as a grocer's daughter from Tunbridge Wells; now, of course, steeped in wicked ways. Meggie and I gave *excessive* thought to just what a shopkeeper's daughter with a taste for high-life would choose to wear to delight her newest gentleman friend, just back from India! Did we get it right?'

She seriously expected him to answer, he realised, playing this like a ridiculous game of charades. He was angry. Almost uncontrollably angry. Angry at the strength of his own response to her ludicrous fancy dress, angry at the way he could see this charade was taking him. Angry that he had ever confided Laura's story, and stupidly involved her in his search. Why ever had he been such a blabber-mouthed fool?

'I suppose...' his look was contemptuous '...that were I the sort of man who is attracted to street drabs it is possible I would find you of interest. But I am not, and in Lady Henrietta Cairshaw I find such behaviour crudely vulgar.'

His words were very cold, but the qualm that he felt as he watched all the happiness drain from her face merely strengthened his rage.

She pulled off the wig with its tall feathers, and flung it on the sofa beside her, ruffling her fingers through her own short-cropped curls with the casual unconcern of a boy. He glowered as he looked at the ravaged head, but she was not regarding him.

'It should not be necessary to point out to you,' she remarked, with a coldness to match his own, 'that vulgarity was exactly the impression I aimed to achieve, so I am naturally delighted you judged our efforts to be a success. I intend to put that success to the test tomorrow night, in the White Cocks public house, in an effort to gain news of Laura.' His head shot up, his face furious, but she allowed him no chance to speak. 'I *would* appreciate your assistance, for, as I said, you form a necessary part of my story. Listen.'

Ignoring the icily disapproving silence, Henrietta outlined the life-story of Hetta, grocer's daughter of Tunbridge Wells, as she had invented it in Petticoat Lane, and concluded defiantly, 'However, should you find yourself unable to help, naturally I shall carry on alone.'

He argued with her. He argued with her furiously, with cold sarcasm, with anguish, endlessly repeating the absurdities, the risks, the probable futility of what she planned.

She jutted her chin and outstared him with those great blue eyes, shrugging off his arguments, insisting that she could not ignore the plight of a child who had been treated so by—and she almost spat the words—the Danes of Thwayle. She knew what his family were like. *She* would recover from them, and she intended to save Laura also.

'You fool. Obstinate fool! All that happened years ago! She is no longer a child.' Dane spoke loud in frustration. 'She would be twenty-six by now! And this is all futile, for she is undoubtedly dead.'

'Then we shall find out,' Hetta retorted coolly, 'and honour her grave.'

He could not move her, whatever he said. At last, exasperated, he pulled his watch from his pocket and regarded it impatiently.

'I have to go. I am taking a lady to the theatre tonight, and cannot disappoint her.'

'How pleasant,' Henrietta responded cordially. 'And what are you to see?'

He frowned, and shrugged irritably.

'*King Lear*. Esther—that is, Miss Wanhope—expressed a great desire to see *King Lear*. I have had some problems acquiring tickets for a night when both she and her father are free to accompany me.'

'Miss Wanhope?' Hetta's voice was a query. 'I don't believe I know the name.'

'There is no reason why you should.'

He meant to stop there. His private affairs were no concern of this impassioned eccentric. But something impelled him to speak on.

'I met Miss Wanhope in Madras.' Dane's voice held, he hoped, cool reproof. 'Her father is a missionary preacher, and she accompanies him to assist in his work. She is a most estimable young lady. She is accounted very beautiful,' something prompted him to add, 'and has honoured me with an understanding of intent.'

'I beg your pardon? I fail to understand!'

Hetta looked genuinely perplexed.

Dane replied stiffly, angry at himself once again for further committing his confidences to this woman.

'I asked Miss Wanhope to marry me while we were in Madras. She, understandably, of course, did not wish to commit herself until after her return to England and a chance to see something of London Society. But she did not wish to rebuff my offer entirely. So she kindly gave me an understanding of her intention to reconsider my offer at a future date.'

His look was so haughty that Henrietta dared offer no comment beyond, 'Well, congratulations, Mr Dane,' and she kept her mixed thoughts on the nature of Miss Wanhope's behaviour to herself.

'And now, I must certainly go. Lady Cairshaw, I will come and discuss this further with you tomorrow. I would like your word that you will do nothing rash before we have spoken again.'

Hetta walked up to where he stood by the door, and laid a hand lightly on his arm to detain him.

'You must learn to call me Hetta now, whether you like it or not, or you will spoil all; and I must call you Jonathan. After all, we *are* to act the part of lovers!'

He glared at her.

'Don't worry,' she smiled contemptuously, 'we merely share a wish to trace your cousin. There will be nothing to jeopardise your relationship with Miss Wanhope, of that you may give her my *heartfelt* assurance! I am sure she must be as anxious as you are to see this poor abused girl found, and such a wickedly un-Christian injustice remedied.

'Don't forget now. Tomorrow we go to the White Cocks. Please be here, for I would wish your protection, but make no mistake; I will go whether you are here or not.' She rang for Hodgson to show him out, then held out her hand. 'Goodnight, *Jonathan*.' She smiled. 'Enjoy *King Lear*.'

He bowed stiffly over her hand, made as if to speak, then closed his mouth angrily on the words and abruptly followed the butler downstairs, leaving without a backward glance.

CHAPTER FOUR

HETTA paced the room, and anxiously nibbled the tip of her finger. She glanced once more in the glass. She was again wearing the green dress, the wig and the ostrich feathers, but she had a white shawl instead of the silver-gauze, for the night was cold, and had thrown a black taffeta domino over everything.

'You *will* tell the staff it is a masquerade party? I can't have them worrying. I would not put it beyond Hodgson to contact my brother if he suspected the truth.'

'I have already told them so, miss.'

'Where *can* he be? It is almost nine. Meggie, I do believe he is going to desert me. He is not going to come. It is only to be expected of a Dane, of course. Only a fool would rely on them. I should have *known* he would not arrive. Well, he need not think he will deter me like that.' She scowled furiously. 'Send out for a hackney, Meggie. Tell Hodgson I was mistaken, we meet up at the Wilsons' house. I will redirect the hackney later.'

'Oh, Miss Hetta, are you sure you should? Alone? You can't blame Mr Dane for not arriving——'

'Oh, can't I just?'

'—for you know he did not like the idea from the start. You pushed him into it——'

'So? That means I can ignore him, doesn't it? Well, so I shall.'

'Oh, Miss Hetta. You shouldn't go out alone. Wait! I could come with you.'

'No, Meggie, that would alert everybody! And there is no time for you to change. Order the hackney, I shall leave now.'

With a last tweak at the ostrich feathers, and a coy flutter of the fan into the mirror, Henrietta defiantly drew the concealing domino close about her and sailed downstairs to the hall.

'Only Meggie need wait up,' she announced to Hodgson. 'Just leave a candle by the door when you retire.'

'Yes, m'lady,' the butler replied dubiously, and moving out to the kerb he gave the directions for the hackney. Hetta only waited until the hackney had rounded the corner before she called to redirect the driver.

'To the White Cocks, if you please, at the end of White Cocks Alley.'

If she thought of it at all, Hetta had expected the White Cocks to look something like the Alnstrop Arms in the village of her childhood, a long, low, welcoming building, with a cheery landlord, a dark panelled taproom, rich in wafted memories of alcohol, and a couple of cosy private parlours for hire.

She had not envisaged this vast building of grimy brick, three floors of windows, their paint cracked and blistered, then a jagged jumble of dormers above, thrusting crazily up through the soot-blackened roof-tiles. A board painted with two white cockerels, in menacing attitudes, hung above an archway which plainly led through to the inn-yard, so, pushing down her fears with a ferocity born of rising panic, Hetta sauntered through.

An ostler was busy with horses and a carriage, whistling tunelessly through his teeth as he set straps and tightened buckles. A couple of torches burned, for the light had quite gone from the late evening sky. Rows of windows looked down into the yard, and innumerable doorways and passageways opened out from it, some light and welcoming, others, black as the waters of the river.

Hetta shuddered, then, remembering her purpose, moved over to the ostler in what she hoped would pass for a suggestive lounge.

'And where might a girl like me sit for a friendly drink, would you suggest, for I am a newcomer to the neighbourhood?'

The man straightened his back, and ran a knowing eye up and down her body, lingering on the way her skirt hitched up at the ankle.

He nodded, unmoved at his assessment. 'You'll not be welcome in the main tap, for he keeps that for respectable custom, but there's a back room the girls use regularly, and rooms upstairs, if needed. Through that way. Don't worry, the gentlemen'll know where to find you.' He grinned, spat on to the cobbles, and returned to his horses and his keening whistle.

Her spirits somewhat buoyed at successfully passing this first test of her masquerade, Hetta took the passageway the ostler had indicated, and found herself in a stone-flagged corridor, with wall-panelling painted a drab green, and various doors leading from it. Only one, further down, stood ajar, however, so she ventured to it and looked inside.

It was certainly the right place. The low ceiling was decorated with ornate whorls of flaking, smoke-stained plaster. The walls were papered down to the dado in a rich maroon and gold stripe, now much smeared, while below, a dark brown paint covered the walls and most of the dirt. Stained wooden tables and chairs cluttered the floor. At the far end of the room, a polished wooden counter ran chest high, and behind it rows of bottles crowded the shelves.

The bar did not only serve this room, for the passage behind the counter ran round, Hetta discovered as she walked over to it, to serve the main tap, and other private parlours also, judging from the noise that came through.

This room was quite quiet. In one corner a couple sat, the girl perched on her partner's knee, holding a tankard from which they both drank, pushing and giggling for turns. Two other men sat at a desultory card game at one of the tables, three girls leaning on their shoulders, vying for their attentions. Four other girls sat moodily, staring into their glasses, making spasmodic, muttered conversation. Only one, leaning up against the bar, looked around as Hetta entered, and grinned at her as she crossed the room.

'New round 'ere, ain't yer?'

Hetta nodded, leaning her back to the bar as she surveyed the company. 'Well, it don't seem as if there was too much to hurry this way for,' she countered. 'Place is like a morgue, ain't it?'

The girl grinned again. 'Dog fights tonight. Out the back.' She gestured with her head. 'You want some noise, you go out and watch the fighting. Me, I'd as soon stay here with a glass o' geneva.' She raised her glass to Hetta. 'Good health, lady.'

A man had appeared behind the counter, white linen shirt-sleeves rolled up to reveal sinewy forearms, a stained and smeared white apron over his breeches.

'Who's yer friend, Em'ly?' he asked cheerfully. 'And what're yer drinkin', luv?'

'The name's Hetta.' She shot him a glowing smile, but her thoughts were whirling. What should she drink? She would have to ask for something. She had never touched gin, but had heard much of its ruinous effects on the populace. Should she order a glass regardless? Then a sudden memory floated up from her childhood, of her grandmother chuckling over a clutched glass and claiming, 'You can't beat a glass of shrub. No, my dear, you can't beat a glass of shrub.'

On impulse, she found herself saying, 'A glass of shrub for me tonight, if you please, good sir!'

'I'll have to mix you up a jugful,' he warned.

'A jugful,' said Henrietta recklessly, 'will do me just right!'

She and Em'ly stood watching as the man busied himself with squeezing lemons, mixing the juice with sugar syrup, and rich Jamaican rum. The smell was uncannily redolent of Grandmother and childhood.

When the jug was mixed, and Hetta had paid, by common consent she and Em'ly drifted to a table and sat down. They talked, and bit by bit Hetta allowed Em'ly to draw from her snippets of the life history of the grocer's daughter from Tunbridge Wells, and learned in return that Em'ly had come down from the north, near Manchester, when her widowed mother had died, and there had been nothing there to keep her.

'But that's past 'istory, ain't it? I was no more'n fifteen then. Learned a lot since then.'

She shook her head solemnly over her glass. They were sharing Hetta's jug of shrub now.

'If you come down from up north,' said Hetta carefully, eying Em'ly hopefully, 'then I dare say you know my cousin Laura. She came down from those parts; and with a count, no less; and she . . .' Hetta paused for emphasis ' . . . she was only fourteen.'

She waved at the barman to mix another jug of shrub. It was strong stuff, and seemed to be cementing their friendship usefully.

'Laura? I never met no Laura.' Em'ly paused, and drank reflectively. 'Oh, I dunno, though. A long time ago, you say?'

'Oh, a long time. All of twelve years. Though I did hear she ended up in these parts with this count of hers. I would dearly like to see her again. But there, like you say, it's past history. No one would remember her now.'

She paused hopefully, for there was no doubt that her words seemed to have awakened a memory in the recesses of Em'ly's mind, but at this point a surge of people entered the room, squeezing in until it was filled with sweating bodies and raucous shouts.

'Dog fight's over,' commented Em'ly laconically, and hitched up the mud-spattered, flounced hem of her dress to display a length of bony calf and ankle in grubby white clocked stockings. 'Now perhaps we can earn a living.' She looked speculatively into the crowd of people. 'But that Laura—I reckon I do remember something. She's not round here now, of that I am sure, but I reckon she was. I'll let you know if I remember.'

Several men pushed past their table on their way to the bar, nodding greetings to Em'ly, eyeing Hetta with knowing, appreciative glances, but several more girls had entered with them, and Hetta sighed with relief as they all moved on. She felt suddenly very frightened, very alone. If only Em'ly would remember about Laura, then she could make her excuses and go!

A fat, red-faced man had surged up to their table, very drunk, but inclined to be cheerful, for the right dog had won. Beads of sweat stood out across his forehead, and over his nose and thick upper lip, as he leaned forward and, with his stubby grimy fingers and thumb, took hold of a pinch of the smooth white curve of Hetta's breast.

'That I like!' he said firmly, then, as she flinched away, 'And coy. I like that too!' He spread himself into a chair. 'Come, sit on my lap, my girl, for we must become better acquainted.'

He swept a great arm about her, pulling her over to him. His breath was hot on her neck. Oh, God, what could she say? How could she deter him? Surely she would not have to go through with this? What had she done? Suddenly, out of desperation, inspiration came.

'Oh, sir, you're too kind, sir, but I have a gentleman friend who is so jealous.' She began to pull away. 'I'm expecting him here, and if he were to find me with you, why, there'd be hell and the devil to pay!'

'But he isn't here, is he?' the man declared with undaunted good humour, and the irrefutable logic of the drunk. 'So we shall have a little fun together. No man should hog a treat as good as you all to himself.'

He dragged Hetta firmly on to his lap, and, taking her glass, helped himself to shrub.

'By God,' Hetta hissed to Em'ly. 'Jonathan'll kill me. Wouldn't you like this one?'

Em'ly shrugged. 'You'll not turn his mind while he's in that mood. Make the best of it. Who's to say your Jonathan will come?'

The man tossed back the last of the shrub, and rubbed his mouth on the back of his hand. He leaned forward, nuzzling his face into her breasts, fumbling at her bodice with awkward fingers.

'Come on,' he said hoarsely, 'we'll find a room.'

Jonathan had been angry before he even set out for Hetta's house.

Esther had been primly, coyly flirtatious. With him—but also with several other eligible men at the tedious afternoon gathering they had attended. She had then insisted on being driven around to look at some sights before he delivered her home, and, although he knew he should have been pleased, he was worrying about what Henrietta might possibly be contemplating. He found himself being terse and irritable.

Esther, making it plain she was putting this down to jealousy on his part, took it all with arch good humour and congratulated herself on her success. She would not, however, allow him to mention his search for Laura.

'I wish you had never told me *anything* about your dreadful cousin. I can't think why you did.' She paused to prink up her artfully arranged blonde curls, and rearrange the pink ribbons of her bonnet. 'After all,' and she giggled coyly, 'it is not a polite story for a nicely bred lady to hear. I know Papa would be quite horrified to hear of such things, and never expect me to think of them. He says a pretty girl should think only pretty thoughts. Don't you think that a charming sentiment?'

So Jonathan had mentioned nothing of his meeting with Hetta, or of Hetta's ridiculous plans, and had found that for the first time he had, quite unintentionally, a secret from his love. This also made him angry, for he had hoped to share all his thoughts with her.

He was late home, and slow to change. He defiantly sat down to eat the supper Mrs Stockwell had prepared, thinking that Hetta deserved to be made to wait, for she should not have such crack-brained ideas, and certainly should not inflict them upon him. He did not arrive at St Dunstan's Street until ten in the evening, his arguments to dissuade her from her folly ready mustered.

The news of her departure fanned his anger with alarm. The thought of her stupid, courageous innocence set down among the villains of the White Cocks...

He sped the chaise through the streets at a reckless pace, urging his horses on, as increasingly hideous scenarios loomed up in his raging imagination. My God! How could she dare? His panic and fury consumed him.

It was not hard for the whistling ostler to identify the chestnut-haired girl with the white ostrich plumes, and point the way for this tall, dark man with the blazing fury in his eyes, though he did spare a commiserating thought for the girl before turning back to his horses. She had been quite a looker.

Dane paused in the doorway of the red and gold room, rocking on the balls of his feet, ready to fight he knew not what; then he saw those damned ostrich feathers, dipping and waving at a table down near the bar. Roughly pushing his way through the press of people, his heart hiccoughed and pounded as he watched the great beery man, on whose lap she sat, slobbering his face into the silky whiteness of her breasts, then rise to his feet, dragging her after him, his intentions clear in his red, panting face.

'No, sir, truly, my Jonathan will kill me!' He heard, as he arrived behind them, and also heard the fear in Henrietta's voice.

'You're damned right he will!' Dane snarled, grabbing her by the arm and swinging her round to face him. His hand came up and hit her a resounding slap across the cheek.

He had not meant to do it, and when he saw the relief, then shock and pain, that crossed her face, it almost sobered his rage, but then she tossed her head at him in contemptuous fury, and it was easy to continue his anger.

'Hey!' The thwarted red-faced man barged back between them. 'This lady's spoken for.'

'Precisely.' Dane's voice was cold. 'And I am the one who spoke. I suppose she didn't mention she was here with me? No? Oh, you can't trust a woman. Do you find that? Tell them one thing, they'll do the opposite. I suppose she's been making up to you, has she? Leading you on? Giving you false hopes?'

The red-faced man, having blearily assessed how much taller and fitter and angrier this man was than himself, now shrugged a little sheepishly, and took a step back. Em'ly pulled him down beside her.

'There's more bottles than one jist waiting to be uncorked, don't you know?' she said, and leant over to loosen his cravat. She winked at him and jerked her head at Henrietta and Dane, still eyeing each other furiously. 'You don't want to get caught in the middle o' that!' She raised her voice and called to Dane, 'Go on, sir, you show 'er. You show 'er what for!' And she giggled helplessly, lying against the fat man's shoulder.

'How dare you?' Hetta hissed at Dane. She twitched her arm, as if to shake off his grip, but he continued to hold her, his left hand clamped on the soft skin of her upper arm, his right hand flexing and clenching into a fist at his side.

'How dare I? By God you have a nerve, Henrietta. To come flaunting yourself down here as a common drab... To be rescued from such a situation... And after I had ordered you not to venture out without me——'

'Don't speak to me like that! What right have you——?'

'I shall speak to you in any way you deserve, my girl, and treat you as you deserve too. If we are to play this ludicrous game, then we will play it my way, and if you act like a drab you'll get punished like one.'

Her chest heaving with fury, she raised a hand to hit him, but he caught her wrist with ease and twisted her arm behind her, crushing her against his body. Tears started in her eyes as she struggled against him, and she could hear Em'ly and the fat red-faced man both egging Jonathan on.

'Give 'er a taste of who's master, that's the way!'

Desperate, she looked up into his face, and gazed at his anger, her lips quivering.

Without warning he bent his head, and suddenly he was kissing her, crushing those soft, yielding lips with all the brutality of the fierce possessive fury that gripped him.

Reeling, she dimly heard the jeering cheers of Em'ly, but she felt drowned in his rage and could barely breathe. But she felt the change in him. When the punishing anger became an aching hunger, and his kiss became quiveringly tender, and her body leapt in a dizzying, yearning response.

Abruptly he let her go. Avoiding her eyes, he sat down on her empty seat and swung her roughly on to his lap.

'As you have begun this charade, we will play it out,' he said tersely, and waved to the waiter to refill the jug.

Outraged with shock at her treacherous response to him, Hetta sat silent, every fibre of her body resentfully aware of his arm flung with casual proprietorship about her waist, the shift and flex of his thighs beneath hers, the pressure of his body as he leant forward to pour the drinks.

The interruption seemed to have distracted the ardour of the red-faced man, for he and Em'ly stayed in a happy haze of rum and lemon to share the next jugful. Conversation of a sort began to flow, and after a while Hetta managed to join in, exclaiming with forced lightness to Jonathan, 'And would you believe, Em'ly here thinks she remembers my cousin Laura. You remember, I told you? The one from up north. Perhaps I'll find her yet!'

'No, it weren't me as knew of 'er.' Em'ly paused. 'Jist wait a minute.' She paused again, for thought, while her companion nibbled and kissed his way up her arm. 'Sarah!' she announced triumphantly. 'It was Sarah once had a friend called Laura, though I don't know if she came from up north.' She beamed, well pleased with this feat of memory.

'Which is Sarah?' Hetta asked quickly, for the man was now showing signs of impatience again.

'She's not been down for quite a while, luv.' Em'ly was being pulled firmly away. But she did have rooms at Mrs Crabbe's place in Lockchain Terrace. Try there!' And with a perky grin Em'ly took her man's arm, and they fought their way through to the door.

'Come on. We're leaving as well.' His voice was cool, the bonhomie of his talk with Em'ly and her companion instantly gone.

Dane set Hetta on her feet, but he kept his arm firmly about her as he led her out, and Hetta, though she would not have admitted the fact, was glad of it. The touches of the other men made her shudder now, and the shrub was making her dizzy, her footsteps uncertain.

As they reached the cold night air of the yard, and Dane hollered for the ostler to bring out his chaise, Hetta reeled unsteadily against him.

'I am sorry,' she stated with careful dignity. 'I am unaccustomed to the shrub,' and was startled when he suddenly looked down at her and began, inexplicably, to laugh.

She had no idea why he laughed, unaware of how his fury had evaporated in his overwhelming relief at bringing her out of her folly unscathed, and how, compared with this, finding news of Laura seemed oddly unimportant. Strangely, for she knew she was angry with this man, laughing seemed a good idea. When the ostler waved off the two of them, she was hooting like a cockatoo with abandoned mirth.

She felt sobered by the time they reached St Dunstan's Street, sobered and ashamed. She slid sideways looks at Dane, confused by the memory of what had occurred between them, but when he spoke his tone was cool.

'I will call tomorrow, if I may?'

'You will not go to Lockchain Terrace without me? You could spoil all if you alarm this girl. It should be me who speaks to her.' Her voice was tense, and she laid a hand on his arm. 'I will go without you if you will not promise.'

'Don't threaten me, Henrietta!'

But his renewed spurt of anger was brief. It seemed there was a strange, indisputable inevitability about their relationship. It was pointless to fight this whim of the fates. He sighed. It was not what he would have chosen, and he paused, looking gravely down at her in the darkness. He felt he was sealing some unknown pact, committing himself to he knew not what.

'I will call for you at eleven tomorrow. We will go together.'

'Thank you. Oh, thank you.'

Her fury, shame, resentment, all were abruptly forgotten. Her smile was suddenly as bright as a child with a present, and on impulse she kissed his cheek, as she had always done her brothers'.

Silently he handed her down, and saw her safely into the house.

CHAPTER FIVE

HETTA'S sleep was wreathed in nightmares, endless stone-flagged, green-walled corridors stretched bewilderingly about her, and she knew she must search for and reach a place she was terrified to find. Later there were hideous men with vast red sweat-beaded faces and pudgy, intrusive fingers, and she could not escape the foulness of their hot breath on her face. She woke shaking in the darkness of her room and sobbed quietly in the uncomforting emptiness of her bed.

She slept again, eventually, and was dreamlessly oblivious when Meggie woke her at half-past nine, flinging back the curtains on to thin autumn sunshine, and presenting a huge steaming cup of chocolate. Meggie had heard all that had occurred, and given vent to her horror, the evening before, as she had helped Hetta to bed.

'Dear Lord, Meggie, but I have a headache. That shrub of Grandmama's has a kick like a carthorse. Pull the curtains closed, do.' Meggie looked disapproving, but pulled shut the curtain that would cut the sunlight from the bed. 'You were right, Meggie. I should not have gone alone. I was never more frightened and disgusted in my life than when that dreadful man mauled me about and tried to take me out with him. It would have been worse had the shrub not dulled my senses. And, though I hate to say it, I was never more relieved to see any man than I was to see Jonathan.'

'Jonathan now, is it, miss?'

A sudden memory had made her mistress frown.

'Well, it has to be, doesn't it, Meggie,' she said, crossly, 'for how else can we convincingly play our parts? It is no good grumbling. Yes, I have admitted that I was wrong to go alone, but if he will help, and be seen to protect me...' She paused, uneasily considering this prospect, then spoke on with a brisk, uncaring determination. 'Well, then I can trace his cousin, of that I am sure. Why, look at the success I had last night. The very girl I talked to——'

'Knew someone who was not there, who might have known someone years ago, who might have been called Laura, and if she was, might have been the one you are looking for.'

'Oh, Meggie! I thought you supported me.'

'Well, so I do, Miss Hetta, but there's times when you do try a body's patience with your goings on.'

She stumped off into the closet, and made a noisy show of sorting clean linen to express her anxiety at her mistress's gallivantings.

Hetta regarded her broad back view with affectionate exasperation. The shy country girl from Alnstrop village, who had obeyed her every word with wide-eyed devotion, had become over the years something of a protective tyrant, but Hetta loved her dearly.

'Meggie!' she called. 'Another of my gaudy dresses, if you please. Something that will convince this Sarah, if we find her, or Mrs Crabbe the landlady, at any rate, of my supposed profession. Mr Dane has oh, so kindly agreed to call for me at eleven. But...' she frowned '...however shall I get out of the house without Hodgson and the rest of the staff thinking I am still in masquerade costume?'

When Dane arrived to collect Henrietta he was met with an apology from Hodgson, for Lady Henrietta was not ready yet, and would he kindly step upstairs.

Today she was curled up on the sofa. She flung aside her book and jumped up as he entered, greeting him with a self-consciously carefree babble of chatter, but refusing to meet his eye.

'I'm so sorry I'm not ready. I had chosen a most wonderfully hideous red and gold striped satin to wear today, truly impossible, it should be just the thing to convince these people we are to visit, but it just needs a little alteration. Meggie is doing it for me. She is quick with her needle, and she should be done very soon.'

Dane was accustomed to Miss Wanhope, who, he reflected, was frequently over an hour late for engagements and never offered him an apology of any sort. He refrained from making any of the comments that sprang to his mind on Henrietta's choice of costume, and, responding more to the anxious defiance in her tone than to her words themselves, he spoke gently.

'It is not important,' he said.

She was wearing a loose mantua, in cream and powder blue silk with a design of delicate oriental flowers, flung about her with a casual, crumpled unconcern which, unwillingly and to his surprise, pleased him.

He thought of the delicate porcelain perfection that had always attracted him to Esther, that remote, immaculate, fair beauty that, in the torrid heat and garish colours of India, had seemed to set her apart from other women and give her the fragility of a nymph, the command of a goddess.

A single blue ribbon threaded Henrietta's roughly shorn curls. His dark brows snapped together as he regarded her. She had curled up on her sofa again, and was waving him, with careful nonchalance, to a chair, but he remained standing, for there was something he had steeled himself to say.

'I owe you an apology, Lady Cairshaw. I am deeply ashamed of my behaviour last night. There was provocation, but . . . but I should never have . . .' He paused, and struggled for words, but he found he could not mention to her now the things that he had done. 'I should not have reacted as I did,' he compromised, stiffly. 'I am deeply sorry.'

He had expected an outburst. That she would reproach him, fly out at him, argue with him, justify herself, but she did none of those things, and, breaching all his defences, left him speechless.

'If I am to be fair,' she said slowly, reluctantly, 'you have nothing for which to apologise. I behaved abominably.' She had stood up, facing him, and now, taking a deep breath, she spoke determinedly to a point a little over his left shoulder. 'I have realised that I should never have left here unattended as I did, and that in doing so I put you in an impossible situation.

'You'—he could almost see her grit her teeth to say this—'you behaved with considerable aplomb to extricate us from the situation, while still extracting the necessary information about Laura. Thank you. It was a masterly piece of impromptu acting. I congratulate you.' She paused, then, 'Could we put it behind us now, and work together to find your cousin, as friends?'

Relieved at having spoken, she now looked him earnestly in the eye, holding out her hand solemnly, as if they were two schoolboys sealing a pact.

He stifled the absurd, irrational surge of disappointment that came with her words. If she chose to consider his unforgivable actions of the previous night as necessary acting, he was, of course, thankful. And if they were to be tied together in this search, then friendship was the only way to succeed. Taking her hand, he forced a smile.

'As friends!' he said.

Meggie called then—the dress was ready—and with a smile she left him.

To his amazement, she was back in less than twenty minutes, a long blue pelisse pulled tight around her to cover as much as possible of the dress, and a bandbox in one hand.

'The wig,' she hissed at him, gesturing at the bandbox, then sailed ahead of him out to the chaise.

'I could wish you had brought a closed carriage,' she remarked as they turned the corner from St Dunstan's Street. 'No matter, we must stop somewhere out of the way and you must help me adjust the wig.'

He turned to her in some alarm.

'Is that essential? Surely it is not necessary to wear it?'

'Why, of course it is. I must appear to be the same girl who talked to Em'ly, and this is my most effective means of disguise. I do *hope* to have a life after we have found Laura in which I will not be instantly recognisable as Hetta of the *demi-monde* from Tunbridge Wells!'

'Are you quite certain you wish to go on with this? It would be disastrous for you if you were recognised. And after last night...'

'Mr Dane... Jonathan, last night is what has made me quite determined. Can't you see that? I was frightened, and utterly repulsed by the attentions of that man.' She saw his hands tighten on the reins so his knuckles showed white. 'But you arrived in time, and I can treat it all as a charade. Laura was given to a man like that. Given body and soul. Nobody came to her rescue just in time. She had to learn to live such a life permanently. *If* she did learn to live so, for I am certain I could not do it. I would sooner die. But, even more than before, I must find her. Can you understand that?'

Dane shrugged and frowned. 'Perhaps.' All his emotions seemed confused and untrustworthy. He hardly knew what he felt.

'Stop here!' The road was running between high-walled warehouses, and although carts and wagons rumbled in and out of an entrance further down the street, where they were was quiet. 'Just a moment, while I put on my wig. Here, take this.'

She took off her bonnet, then fumbled to untie the ribbon from her hair, but it tangled in her curls. Looping the reins on his arm, he had to untie it for her, his fingers soft in the bouncing curls. He thought of Esther's neat silky ringlets, framing her face. He had always wanted to twine them around his fingers, but he would not presume to do so. She hated her hair to be touched. Hetta had pulled the dreadful high padded wig from the bandbox, and was tugging it on to her head, pulling it straight and tucking errant black curls underneath the mass of chestnut.

'Will it do? Straighten it for me, please, for I'm certain it cannot be right; and is all my own hair hidden?'

He poked and prodded dubiously, but was surprised into a burst of laughter when she then produced an impudent little straw bonnet with a vast bunch of vivid red cherries decorating one side, and perched it on top, tying it under her chin with a generous bow of scarlet ribbon. She chuckled at him.

'Henrietta, you are an outrageous baggage!'

Their unexpected intimacy surprised him into the exclamation, and he knew it held more admiration than reproof. She had unbuttoned her pelisse, and pushed it open to display her gaudy stripes beneath—the frills, flounces and ribbons.

'You look quite magnificently appalling!'

'Thank you, sir,' she said demurely.

We are both enjoying this impossible game, he thought with startled recklessness, and laughed. She smiled up at him naughtily under her lashes.

'I am glad you like it, for I chose it just for you! You may drive on!'

With a flourish she settled herself back in the seat.

Lockchain Terrace proved to be a mean-looking row of red-brick houses, probably not more than fifty years old, but already showing signs of shoddy building, with cracks in the brickwork and warped window-frames. A pinched front door stood central to each house, with a tiny fanlight over, and, apart from a tiny area each side to give light down to the basement, they opened directly on to the pavement. They stood three storeys high, the sash windows on each floor a little smaller than those on the floor below, and the roofs were low and flat behind a cement-topped parapet.

On the opposite side of the street were ranged an assortment of small shops, a grocer's, a milliner's and a coffee shop, then a small workyard behind a high wall, which seemed to specialise in making and repairing barrows, handcarts and donkey and pony carts, judging by what could be seen through the wide-open gates.

'Let me down, Jonathan,' Hetta said. 'I will ask in the coffee shop for Mrs Crabbe's.'

Uncertain why, he swallowed his instinctive protest, and let her go.

She was back in moments, just as half a dozen small boys materialised, as if from the cracks between the snaggled paving slabs, all hopeful of earning a few pence by holding the horses.

'Number three,' she smiled up at him, triumphantly.

He jumped down, and handed the reins to the boy who had clutched off his cap when Henrietta approached.

'Which shows it pays to be a gentleman,' he grinned at the boy, who flushed awkwardly under his grime. 'Walk them up and down, if you would, until we come back.'

The boy nodded importantly, and set off with measured steps, while Jonathan hurried to join Henrietta, already knocking at the door of number three.

'Do you never wait to be assisted by a gentleman?' he asked, half exasperated, half amused.

She looked surprised.

'Why yes, sometimes. But other times I get impatient. I want to hurry on and make my own decisions. I never managed to become the sort of female who waits demurely for a man to do things for me.' She laughed at him. 'Life is too short to just stand about looking fetching! But there, you see, no one has answered my knock, so now you may knock for me with masculine firmness, and no doubt you will command an answer.'

He did too. No sooner had he lowered his hand from the door-knocker than the door flung open to reveal an irate lady. Her apron was grubby, her cheeks veined with red and purple, her lank grey hair was escaping from its pins, and she scowled at them impatiently from over the tiny head of a damp, mewling baby.

'You'll have come about the room, I suppose. Well, you'll have to show yourselves up, it's the top floor, left hand side. If you want to take it, we can talk about terms when you come down. I'll be in here.' And with an irritable jiggle of the miserable baby Mrs Crabbe vanished behind the door to the left of the hall.

Dane had raised his hand to knock, to call her back, but Hetta stopped him.

'Come on, I want to look at the room.' She set off up the narrow stairs. 'Come on!'

He regarded her with alarm, but she had already rounded the first landing, and he had no choice but to follow.

The room was larger than he had expected, with a window looking out on to the roof-tops of the shops opposite, and a smaller room leading from it that looked over the backyards and across to the rear windows of another, similar terrace. The smaller room was empty, but the main room contained a large bed, a chest of drawers, a table, much ringed and stained, and a sofa filled with horsehair that had at some time formed into independent-minded lumps, and was now creeping out to escape through the seams.

'Yes,' said Hetta, 'I think it will do.'

Jonathan, who had been peering down into the street to see the fate of his horses, turned abruptly to face her.

'And precisely what do you mean by that, my girl?'

She raised a haughty eyebrow at his familiarity, but he outstared her, in her garish red and gold striped satin, and her bobbing bunch of cherries. Abruptly, she chuckled.

'I know, I know, I get what I ask for. As for what I mean, I mean that this room will be ideal for me. I want you to take it, in your name, as if you are setting me up here for your convenience. Don't you see? I now play the part of your little kept fancy-piece. I will be ideally placed to discover more about Laura, but have the benefit of your protection. Word will doubtless creep out from the White Cocks that you are both jealous and violent; I shouldn't be disturbed!'

He flushed, and frowned at her, but she merely grinned back at him. She would not let him anger her today. She knew, with a curious certainty, that if they worked together they would find Laura. Alone they would fail. They needed each other. Maybe he was just a little slower in appreciating that fact. Or in appreciating the way she intended to set about her search! She grimaced as she bounced on the bed and listened to the protesting creaks of the wooden frame.

'It is doubtless alive with bedbugs!' he remarked savagely; then, with an effort at reasonableness, 'But why do you feel the need to be here at all? We don't even know that this Sarah is still here.'

'Oh, Jonathan, I can't continue to creep in and out from my house with my wig tucked underneath my arm. I can't permanently hide from Hodgson until I have on my pelisse. Hodgson was with my father, then my brother at Alnstrop, for years before he came to me. If he thinks all is not well with me I swear he will send to Robert, and I do not want Robert here at present. He should be with his wife, not chasing after his sister.

'Also, I should be glad of an excuse to leave my house for a little while. It is a house full of memories. Painful memories. They are memories that I think I will learn to live with eventually, but not yet, and I would be glad of a little time away.

'I will tell the staff that I am going to friends, that I wish complete rest, and they are to hold my mail until I send for it. Meggie can come with me; the little back room will be perfect for her. Even if Sarah has moved away, it will be much easier for us to trace her if I am living here, and take the role of a member of the *demi-monde* permanently. There, you must admit the plan has a great deal to recommend it.'

She had not intended such a long outburst, or to give him so many reasons. They might have agreed to work as friends. That did not mean she had to justify herself to this man. Irritated with herself, she jumped off the bed, and went over to him, regarding him impatiently from under the ridiculous bonnet.

'It is an absurd plan, Henrietta. This is no place for you. You as good as admit that your brother would forbid it——'

'Oh, no. It is just that he would worry. He could hardly forbid it. And, Jonathan'—she looked him squarely in the eye—'I will come here, with or without your approval.'

'Just as you went to the White Cocks! I thought you had learned your lesson.'

'This will be much safer than that.'

Her chin had tilted up in a way he was learning to recognise. Why, he thought, was he not angrier? Why this vague stirring of anticipation?

'You leave me with nothing to say.'

'I know!' The cherries on her bonnet bobbed. She was flaunting her role at him, deliberately playing up to her hideous stripes. 'You must learn to give in to my whims gracefully, my dear, sir, as poor Robert had to...' she paused '...but then, like him you must promise to be there to pick up the pieces when all collapses in disaster!' She chuckled, and spoke as her impulsive self. 'Oh, *do* just smile and say you will do it!'

'Henrietta'—he frowned at her, and drew breath—'you are the most wilful, ill-disciplined, outrageous, unprincipled, manipulative baggage it has ever been my misfortune to meet!' He glared at her, but she was chuckling irrepressibly, and he reluctantly smiled. 'I will take the room for you'—her face lit up—'on one condition.'

'Yes?'

'You must allow me to refurnish it for you, and pay all your expenses.' She frowned. 'I can do this and it will be entirely in character with the parts we are playing. I am, after all, accustomed to exotic eastern opulence. I shall demand it here.'

She eyed him thoughtfully. He looked very determined on this.

'It will be such an expense.'

'Expense,' he said firmly, 'is of no consequence whatever.'

'Is it not?' She was suddenly interested. 'Then what happened to the poor boy who was sent to be disinherited and die in the tropical sun?'

He smiled and shook his head. 'It is a long story, that I will tell you some other time. But I can assure you, the poor boy refused to die, and learned the ways of business very profitably. Now, do you accept my condition?'

She gave him a long, thoughtful stare, then smiled up at him charmingly.

'Thank you, sir. I accept.'

'Good girl. So you too have learned to give in gracefully!'

She laughed again, and he thought for a moment that she was going to reach up and kiss his cheek, as she had done the previous night. But she did not. She held out her hand.

'A bargain, then.'

'A bargain.'

Dane went downstairs to root out Mrs Crabbe and arrange to take the rooms, while Hetta wandered about on the bare floors wondering what she would need to bring, and what Jonathan would deem it necessary to provide for her. She lingered for a while on the landing, hoping someone would emerge from one of the doors and she could start a conversation, but nobody did; the house was quiet.

Then the door downstairs opened, and she heard Jonathan come out, making his farewells to Mrs Crabbe. Hetta ran down to join him. They stepped out on to the pavement, and Dane, through his fingers, gave a piercing whistle that brought the small boy back down the street at a run, the two bays trotting obediently behind, while three small boys tumbled out of the chaise and on to the pavement, hopefully unobserved.

'Little monkeys,' Dane remarked, but he sounded unperturbed, and handed pennies to those hopefuls, as well as sixpence to the puffing youngster in the checked cap. He handed Hetta up before springing up himself and waving the boys clear.

'Well?' said Hetta. 'Did you take the room, were the terms satisfactory, did you find out anything about the other tenants?'

He waited until he had negotiated the corner at the end of Lockchain Terrace, where a coffee stall on a wooden cart had halted, and its burly owner was dispensing cups of coffee from vast copper vats to passers-by prepared to part with their pennies. The bays regarded the enticing smell of coffee with dark suspicion, but Dane manoeuvred them firmly past and set them away down the street at a sharp controlled trot.

Hetta watched with approval. She liked a man who could handle horses well. Her husband Edward had been competent but cautious, and Justin had been too impatient, startling the horses and jabbing at their mouths.

Her brother Robert had a real way with horses, and her brother John too, though he was reckless, and it seemed that Jonathan knew very well what he was about. She smiled.

'Yes, I have taken the room,' Jonathan began. 'Though I put on record for you now that this is not what I think proper, or suitable or acceptable in any way, and if I did not think you quite capable of moving there without me I would not have done it.'

'I know, Jonathan,' she said, sympathetically.

He glared at her.

'I ought to write to your brother and inform him you are suffering from an unbalanced mind,' he said bitterly.

'But you won't.'

He shook his head resignedly.

'It must be my mind that is unbalanced, but, no, I won't. The terms I negotiated are acceptable, and I have paid one month in advance. I told her we would be arriving in three days' time, but that I will be moving in some furniture before that. She will see it up to the room when it arrives. These few days should also enable you to settle your affairs at St Dunstan's Street to your satisfaction. And, oh yes, there *is* a girl there called Sarah. She is Miss Sarah Battey, and that noisome child your new landlady was clutching so unwillingly to her bosom belongs to her. I wish you joy of the acquaintance!'

'So she is there! Oh, Jonathan, I know we will trace Laura eventually. I knew taking this room was the right thing to do.'

'Huh!' Dane grunted, but he looked at her sideways, and found himself smiling. 'And shall I pull up here,' he asked, 'or are you returning to Hodgson in your wig and cherries?'

'Oh, Lord, I had quite forgotten. Here!' She pulled off the bonnet and handed it to him while she took off the wig and ruffled up her curls again. 'Never mind the ribbon, where is my own bonnet?'

'No,' said Dane perversely. 'You should look as you did when you left the house. I will tie the ribbon if you will hold the reins.'

Surprised, she handed it to him, and sat, head a little bent, while he threaded the ribbon through the dark curls and tied it as nearly as he could remember in the way it had been. His hands were very gentle.

'Thank you,' she said, disconcerted, when he had done, and quickly sat her own demure little straw chip bonnet on top, tying its blue ribbon neatly under her chin. 'Will I do?'

'Very well,' he said, then, 'Yes, you look quite presentable.'

As they arrived back at St Dunstan's Street, Dane remarked, 'I will not see you again until I call to take you to Lockchain Terrace. I have arrangements made with both Esther and her father, and I wish to have some time to make purchases for your room. Is it too much to ask that you will not go back there until I take you?'

'Why, no,' said Hetta with a sweetly innocent smile. 'Naturally I would not dream of doing such a thing.' She chuckled. 'Never fear, good sir. I shall stay demurely here behaving just as I ought, I give you my word. When shall I expect you?'

'Well, it will be Monday, won't it? Shall we say two in the afternoon?'

'That will suit me very well, sir. I will be ready.'

And as Dane drove away, he reflected that she probably would.

CHAPTER SIX

JONATHAN DANE jerked his thoughts back to the words of his host, Sebastian Wanhope. Wanhope was leaning earnestly across the table towards him, obviously awaiting some response.

'Really, sir, really,' Jonathan ventured.

'Yes, it is amazing. To translate the Bible into six Hindustani dialects was achievement enough, but to translate the New Testament into twenty-one dialects...well...it has made an incredible difference to the work of a humble missionary preacher such as myself, an incredible difference.'

'I am sure it has, sir,' Dane remarked, wondering of whom it was that Mr Wanhope spoke.

He had allowed his thoughts once again to stray to the furniture he had been choosing for Henrietta's room. He had been enjoying himself far more than he had anticipated. The chore he had thought to accomplish with feelings of impatient exasperation had become an absorbing game. It pleased him to guess from what he knew of her, and had seen of her house, the things she might like; to imagine the roles they would be pretending, and to impulsively buy things which appealed to him and which he thought would appeal to her.

'You must be speaking of Mr William Carey, Papa. What a remarkable man. I am almost inspired to learn another language in order to emulate his great work.'

Esther Wanhope fluttered a smile and her eyelashes at Dane. Although there were several eligible guests at the dinner party at the Wanhopes' that night, Esther was very prettily devoting most of her attention to Dane. Her dress was, she felt, one of her most charming, in white with tiny ribbon bows of apple blossom pink; and her ringlets, the colour, she had been told, of ripening corn, were caught up with matching tiny bows.

She had a small suspicion that Dane was not affording her, of late, quite the unquestioning devotion she had come to expect. She wished to charm him back to the fold, and also—she slid a warm glance down the table to where young Lord Glenby sat watching her wistfully—she wished to excite the demon of jealousy in a certain hopeful breast. Her plans seemed to be working well, but Dane still showed an irritating absentmindedness at times. She began to make lively conversation to him about their visit that afternoon to the British Museum.

Henrietta had found the time while she waited for Dane's return tediously flat. She informed the household that she would be away from Monday, and for an indefinite period. She told them she needed a change of scene. She cancelled all her engagements, telling her friends the same story, and all those who knew of her feelings for Justin Dane, and her reaction to his recent marriage to a pert little heiress from Lincolnshire, were understanding of her desire for a total break with town life, and refusal to leave a forwarding address. They reflected together that they had known all along that she would take his desertion very hard, and reflected privately on their relief that she was taking her misery somewhere else.

Hetta and Meggie worked together to alter, where necessary, the clothes from their foray into Petticoat Lane, then, in view of what Hetta had seen of the clothes of the girls around White Cocks Alley, they paid another hilarious trip to the second-hand clothes market, and bought a great many more.

'There!' Hetta said, chuckling, as they folded the last of the dresses into a portmanteau. 'There can be no doubt the wretched man ought to be able to imagine he finds me utterly irresistible!'

'Well, as long as there aren't a great many others who feel the same way!' Meggie muttered dourly.

She was torn between excitement at the whole adventure, and anxious doubts over whether she should be supporting Miss Hetta in such a ridiculous scheme at all. She was also not at all sure that she was going to enjoy the privations of life in Lockchain Terrace. She had a strong suspicion that it would involve a great deal of extra work for herself. She sighed gustily.

Sunday saw Mr Dane escorting Miss Wanhope to the church where her father was the visiting preacher. Sebastian Wanhope was touring the parish churches of the capital, giving sermons to raise money for his missionary work in Madras. His rhetoric was fiery and convincing, and the good people of London gave generously to save the souls of the unfortunate heathen.

Esther liked to be escorted each Sunday, so she could sit in the front pew and gaze up at her father with a touching devotion, hanging upon his every word; and she liked Dane to escort her, for his tall dark good looks certainly provided a dramatic foil for her own fair beauty. She had persuaded him to stand with her after the service and help to sell printed copies of Papa's sermon to the congregation, knowing she looked her best dimpling and smiling at the faithful as they handed over their shillings in return for the printed sheets of burning exhortations.

She had smiled a prim invitation at him after he had driven them home, and hoped he would enter the house for refreshment, but, although he kissed her hand with charming gallantry, he pleaded a previous engagement, and departed. She was pouting as she went inside.

She would have been yet more perturbed had she been privy to Mr Dane's occupation that afternoon, for the 'previous engagement' of which he had spoken seemed to consist of transporting various goods from his own house to a seedy establishment in Lockchain Terrace, and the testing of new and sturdy locks and bolts which had, on his orders, been fitted to the door of a set of upper rooms. These seemed to meet with his satisfaction, for he appeared happy to leave his own goods behind in this unlikely place, and returned home looking remarkably cheerful.

By Monday afternoon Lady Henrietta Cairshaw was packed, organised and impatient. Her travelling bags were stacked in the hall; both Hodgson and the housekeeper had full instructions. There was nothing left to do and Hetta was eager to escape. At the sound of carriage wheels she could barely wait for Hodgson to open the door.

Dane had brought the closed carriage, but was driving it himself, clad in a warm, black, caped driving coat, for there was a sharp easterly wind.

'I thought it more discreet to leave my coachman at home and drive myself,' he said quietly to Hetta, as the bags were being loaded.

He was a little apprehensive now, he suddenly realised, both at the enormity of what she was insisting on doing, and the irresponsibility of his support of it; and, more sharply, in wondering what she would think of the changes he had made in the rooms she had chosen. He handed her and Meggie into the carriage and they set off, clattering over the cobbles.

On their arrival at Lockchain Terrace the same small boy as before, with the same checked cap, appeared promptly from the coffee shop. Almost as if he had been expecting them, Hetta thought, and she was certain she caught a cheerful, 'Ow d'yer do, Mr Dane, sir,' as the boy ran to the horses' heads and fondled their noses quite as if he knew them well.

She threw a puzzled look towards the boy, and looked queryingly at Dane, but he just smiled and shrugged a little.

'Someone will collect the bags,' he said. 'Let me escort you both up to your rooms.'

He also had a key to the house now, Hetta noticed, as he showed them inside and, banging on the inner door, shouted 'We're here, Mrs Crabbe. Tell Billy, would you?' Then, 'Come on up.'

He seemed suddenly less assured, and shot her a quick look she found hard to interpret, but he took them upstairs in silence and, undoing an impressive new lock on the door, flung it wide to let Meggie and Hetta into the room.

They stepped in; and Hetta's face lit up with amazement. The unwelcoming room of her visit had been utterly transformed. All the original furniture had gone. A rich, red-patterned carpet covered the floor, and curtains of a matching, glowing red velvet hung at the window. The bed was new, with slender white-painted bedposts, and curtained with a pretty chintz, cream, with a red and green flower design, to give warmth and privacy.

A tall, bow-fronted mahogany chest of drawers stood near it, with a delicate oval mirror above, gilt-edged, and set with two unusual, twined vine silver candlesticks. A matching mahogany table and two chairs were pushed back against the wall, out of the way, while set on either side of the fire stood two large armchairs, unusually deep and comfortable, covered in the red velvet of the curtains, with cushions of chintz to match the bed-hangings, and casually strewn with the most exquisite Kashmir shawls.

The fireplace, a Forest pattern hob grate, had been crusted with rust and contained nothing more than a recent fall of soot and a very dead starling when Hetta had viewed it last. Now it was blacked and shining, a glowing coal fire burning within it, and a large brass kettle hissing gently on the hob. Next to one of the armchairs stood Dane's own glittering, bejewelled elephant. Beyond, in the corner, stood a small writing desk.

Wide-eyed, Hetta ran over to the little room. This too was carpeted, there was a small bed for Meggie, a large wardrobe and some cupboards, and a wash-stand with bowls and ewers set out ready. Meggie was regarding all the arrangements with an expression of agreeable surprise.

Hetta turned to Dane.

'Jonathan, you shouldn't have done it!' she exclaimed, crossly. 'You have made me feel guilty, guilty that I pushed you into so much trouble and expense. It was not necessary. You know it was not.'

He looked oddly disconcerted, uncertain, and gave a little shrug.

'No...I suppose it was not. I'm sorry if you don't like it,' he said, staring down at the pattern he was tracing with the point of his cane on the carpet.

'Why, good heavens,' Hetta surprised herself by speaking with a gruff, impatient reassurance; she had somehow not expected that what she said would matter. 'Yes, I like it very well, and...' she paused, then shrugged as he had '...and thank you.'

She turned away, aware she had been ungracious, and walked to the window, fingering the soft velvet of the curtains. She told herself she was foolish to feel so ill at ease that he had done so much. They had agreed it, after all. It was no more than stage sets for their charade. He moved over to join her, and they stood a moment, staring out across the roof-tops.

'Well, I am glad you like it,' he said diffidently, and held out his hand to her. With reluctant shyness she held out her own; she had not meant to break their bargain. He did not shake hands as she expected, however, but, with a small frown, briefly raised hers to his lips, before abruptly letting it go.

There was a knock at the door, and he moved away to open it. He admitted a gawky, spotted youth bearing the first of Hetta's travelling bags.

'Thank you, Billy. In the small room, if you please.'

Meggie marched back to the little room to supervise this operation, chasing Billy back to bring the rest of the bags promptly. Dane took Hetta's pelisse and suddenly chuckled at his first view of the dangerously low-cut gold and green wide-striped taffeta liberally trimmed with puce ribbons which she had chosen for today.

'When Billy has done, and we are alone, will you take off the wig?' he asked, and she smiled, and nodded. 'Now,' he went on, 'allow me to make you a cup of tea to christen your new abode.'

'A cup of tea? *Can* you make tea?'

'Yes, indeed, o lady of little faith. I have a great many useful skills, and making tea is one of them. Sit down.'

There was, she noticed now as she curled up in the armchair and stroked the glittering elephant, a cupboard that she had overlooked at one side of the fireplace. Dane opened it to reveal tea, sugar, chocolate, crockery, cutlery and a beautiful Wedgwood teapot. He set about competently putting what he needed on to a tray, and moving the kettle further into the heat of the fire to bring it up to the boil. She talked about the room as he busied himself, making amends for her earlier churlishness by praising his choices, and watching with pleasure the small deft movements of his lean strong hands in the firelight.

'How did you set about choosing everything?' she asked, curiously.

He sat back on his heels and smiled at her.

'It seemed to me that perhaps we have both begun to enjoy the parts we are playing, you supposedly craving a rich vulgar opulence, me indulging in the exotica of the east. So I combined something of each, to make our roles convincing, then endeavoured to make it into the sort of home I hoped you would enjoy.'

She smiled at him, heaving a sigh of unexpected contentment. There was a little bookshelf too, she could see now, over by the bed, crammed with titles. Later she would go and browse through them, exploring what he had chosen for her.

She studied the back of his bent head, and the way the brown hair curled at the nape of his neck. She wanted to stretch out and just touch it with her fingertip. It was really nothing like Justin's hair, she thought defensively, hardly like a Dane at all. He caught her eye as he stood up with the tray and carried it over to the table, but did not seem to notice the rise of colour in her cheeks.

He poured the tea and brought her a cup, calling through to Meggie to come also. Meggie accepted a cup of tea, but took it firmly back into her own little room—there was a lot to be sorted, she said. Billy had brought all the luggage and departed, clutching his tip.

'Who is he?' Hetta asked.

'Billy? He is Mrs Crabbe's nephew, but he appears to live with her. A strong and useful lad, if not over-endowed with intelligence!'

'And your other small friend in the street? Which reminds me, what of the carriage, your horses?'

Dane laughed.

'There is nothing for you to concern yourself over. Everything is arranged to my complete satisfaction. I am not a man to set myself up with a lady of pleasure without ensuring all is arranged for my convenience!

'The small boy is called Samuel. His aunt runs the coffee shop opposite, and they have agreed to supply hot meals whenever we request them, to be collected by us, or delivered by the said Samuel. But in addition, Samuel's father, a Mr Perkins, owns the cart repair business. He has some stabling he is not using at present, and we have come to a mutually acceptable agreement over the housing and care of my horses. So you see,' he chuckled and, leaning back in his chair, regarded her with lazy amusement from under his lashes, 'I can be seen to come and indulge my fancy here whenever I wish. Your story will be quite convincing!'

For a moment her heart seemed to stop beating, then to start again in slow painful thuds. That long lazy look made him so like Justin—the Justin she had once found utterly irresistible—that it was frightening. Confused, she looked away, pulled off the role-playing wig, and flung it aside. She took the beautiful Kashmir shawl from the back of her chair and, making as if to admire it, put it around her, covering her shoulders and chest. She knew he was watching her and began to talk about the shawls. 'They are so beautiful. Surely you must want to keep them for Laura, when we find her, or to give to Miss Wanhope?'

'I have others I can give to Laura, if we find her, and Esther is not fond of Indian things.' This was true, but Dane was aware that this dislike did not extend to the highly prized Kashmir shawls. He pushed this awareness firmly to the back of his mind. 'So I would be pleased if you would have them.' He concluded, 'I feel they are necessary stage-dressing, don't you?'

She smiled, more at ease with his matter-of-fact tones. 'Then, thank you, kind sir,' she said.

He stayed, stretched out in the armchair, feet comfortably propped on the fender, till evening. He talked idly, amusingly, of India and his travels there, describing the old man from whom he had purchased the shawl that Hetta was snuggling around herself, weaving stories about the Rajah who had given him the carved elephant, in grateful thanks for some business advice.

'But are the gems real?' Hetta asked, in some alarm.

'So I have always believed,' he replied. 'I love it. It is so wonderfully flamboyant.'

'But you can't leave it here. It must be worth a fortune.' Hetta was horrified.

He shrugged. 'I'd like it to be here. Tell any visitors they are just chips of coloured glass or paste. Look, there are pieces of looking-glass set in with the rest. No one would think it more than a pretty toy. Anyway, it is not important.' And he began to speak of the Rajah's vast crumbling palace, filled with unimaginable riches, and of his journey on the Rajah's elephant.

Hetta spoke too; of Alnstrop, and of visits to other parts of Britain, for she had never travelled overseas. But she was aware that they both avoided speaking of intimate or personal things, and she was relieved. She had just caught a glimpse of things she did not want to face; and there might be more problems for her in this masquerade than just the search for Laura Dane.

He had ordered a hot meal for that evening, and it arrived, carried up the flights of stairs on a large tray by a puffing but proud Samuel. Meggie laid the table for two, insisting on taking her own meal separately in her room, and Dane produced a bottle of wine.

He served the meal himself, noticing how he derived pleasure from watching her appreciation of his planning and care.

'It is absurd,' she said, as they ate. 'I came here prepared to live in some sort of squalor while I searched for Laura. Instead I am spoiled, pampered. Truly, it was not necessary to do so much.'

'Oh, I think it was.' He was carefully removing chicken meat from the bone and did not look at her. 'We have agreed on my role in all this, have we not? I am rich, and wish to pay richly for my pleasure. You will naturally not wish to offend this goose who lays the golden egg, which will explain to Sarah, and any others who might interest themselves in the matter, why you will *not* accept offers from gentlemen friends in my absence. I can assure you, it would be common practice for many women of the type you purport to be to do just that, and you might find it expected of you. I merely give you an obvious reason to decline such gentlemen's attentions.'

He looked up at her now, and his eyes seemed stern. She thought of the red-faced man.

'Thank you, Jonathan,' she said.

He proposed a toast to the success of their quest for Laura, and they clinked glasses over it solemnly, but soon after they had finished eating he stood up to leave.

'Won't you wait while we send for your carriage?' Hetta asked. She was suddenly very loath to see him go, and to find herself truly launched into her new role.

'No. I will go down and speak to old Perkins myself. You will wish to organise things before you settle for the night, I have no doubt. I am sure I have been here long enough to establish our credentials! I will tell Miss Perkins at the coffee shop that the tray can be collected now, so expect someone to arrive shortly. After that, lock the door.'

He looked as if he wished to say more on this, but changed his mind.

'I will not be able to call tomorrow, as I have business in town, but I will be with you again on Wednesday, probably for the afternoon and evening. I will be interested to hear what you have discovered in the meantime.' He paused, then, 'Take care!'

He touched her cheek lightly with his finger, turned, and ran quickly away down the dark stairwell.

Hetta turned back into the glowing red room he had made for her.

'Well, it's nothing like as bad as I'd thought it would be, Miss Hetta, that I can say,' commented Meggie, bustling in to warm bricks on the hob. 'And *this* Mr Dane seems a *proper* gentleman!' Her voice almost held approval.

Hetta curled up in her chair by the fire, and pulled her shawl tightly about herself.

CHAPTER SEVEN

HETTA was up, dressed and bewigged, in good time for her first full day in her new role. She was waiting for Meggie, who had gone over to the coffee shop to buy bread for their breakfast, and standing by the window staring down into the street.

She had been gripped by a moment of panic when she woke that morning, and opened her eyes on to the strange room. Dane's miracle transformation had not reached the ceiling, and the damp-stained flaking plaster above her head was a sharp reminder of the world of poverty and misery into which she had so wilfully plunged herself. She had felt so outraged, so blindly determined to find Laura whatever the cost...had it all just been obstinate folly? She knew well what her brother would say.

And this man, this Jonathan Dane. Why had she been so loath to see him go last night? He was a Dane. He was a man who meant less than nothing to her, who, in addition, had made a point of telling her that he had promised himself to a girl who was as virtuous as she was beautiful. He was useful to her only in so far as he was a necessary part of this charade to trace Laura. Nothing more. But, surely, she told herself, in an effort to be fair, she could not work usefully with him while she continued to despise him for being a Dane. She would treat him dispassionately, as a business partner, she thought, and just turn to him when she needed him, with as little concern as she might feel if she turned to one of her brothers.

That settled in her mind, Hetta had got up and asked Meggie if she thought she had run mad in bringing them to this God-forsaken place.

'Well, yes, Miss Hetta, seeing as you've asked me,' she had said firmly, 'yes, I do. Quite mad. But I'd rather see you with this madness than in the spirits you were before you met this Mr Dane. Run mad you may have done, but your search for this benighted girl is curing you of the malady that that double-crossing Justin left you with, which is nothing but good, and that is the only reason why I'm here with you at all. You don't think I would have let you come if I didn't think it was all for the best, do you? *This* Mr Dane is a proper gentleman!'

'Oh, be quiet, Meggie,' Hetta said crossly.

Looking down from the window now, she saw Meggie finish chatting to young Samuel, and push her way in at the coffee shop door, having picked her way distastefully through the dung, vegetable refuse, and mud that fouled the street. Two girls in cheap cloth gowns, their shawls pulled about them, scurried after her across the filth, and vanished into the doorway of the milliners. Hetta had glimpsed them through the windows there on the previous day, heads bent over their stitching. An old woman, bedraggled in the filthiest of rags, was picking hopefully along the gutter, her bent fingers like twisted claws. Such people never crawled along St Dunstan's Street, Hetta thought, and felt irrationally guilty. Was that how the Lauras of this world ended up?

Hetta shuddered, and went back to the fire, filled with a new determination to play out this role she had chosen—to find Laura before it was too late.

She set about pondering the best way to befriend the other occupants of the house, and Miss Sarah Battey in particular. Should she find reasons to run up and down the stairs all day in the hopes of an accidental encounter? Find an excuse to go and gossip with Mrs Crabbe in order to further pick her brains about her other tenants? Or simply walk over to the door opposite hers across the landing, knock briskly and say, 'Hello, I'm new, who are you?' and risk a rebuff. She had just decided in favour of the last of these options when there was a knock at her own door. Thinking Meggie had forgotten her key, and locked herself out, Hetta ran over and flung it open.

A tired looking girl was standing there. She had long, lustreless ginger-red hair, sharp hazel eyes, a face full of freckles and an upturned nose. A wide-eyed baby was clutched awkwardly in one arm. She favoured Hetta with that look of defiance that was defence in advance against rejection, and announced, 'You're new 'ere, ain't you. I live over there.' She jerked her head towards the opposite door. 'I'm Sarah. 'Oo are you?'

With an unusually broad smile of welcome, Hetta stepped back. 'Come on in,' she said. 'I shall be on my own today, apart from Meggie, for I know my gentleman friend has business elsewhere. I was hoping for some company, and not knowing a soul to ask around. My name's Hetta.'

'Coo!' remarked Sarah, as she entered and surveyed the room. 'Old Ma Crabbe said as 'ow 'e was doin' you proud, and she didn't tell a lie, did she? You've landed yourself a good'un and no mistake.' She wandered around the room, touching the bits of furniture, fingering the materials, opening cupboards; jiggeting the baby on her arm, for it had begun to squirm irritably.

'Shall I take the child?' Hetta offered. 'Come and sit by the fire. I have the kettle hot, and Meggie will be back in a moment with bread for breakfast, if you would like some.'

The girl pushed the baby carelessly into Hetta's arms, and grinned. 'Wouldn't I jist,' she exclaimed, 'for I'm devilish 'ungry!'

Meggie arrived back just then with fresh bread and butter, which she dumped on to the table, covering her disapproving look with an outraged sniff after receiving a warning glare and an introduction to their neighbour from Hetta. 'Well, there's ample for three,' she managed to say, gruffly, 'and I discovered Mr Dane's provided pots of jam in the cupboard.'

'Really?' Hetta ran to look at the row of pots behind the tea and sugar. 'That man is quite extraordinary!' she said, unsure whether she was moved to admiration or irritation.

'I shouldn't complain if I was you,' remarked Sarah. ''Ere, give us the child. I'll feed 'im, that should stop 'is snivellin'.'

She pulled down her bodice roughly, and set the child to suckle, then ignored his little snuffles and whimpers as he endeavoured to feed comfortably, but set about the plate of bread and jam Meggie handed her with ravenous appetite.

In answer to odd queries of Sarah's, Hetta told again the brief story of her 'life'. Sarah nodded sympathetically as Hetta described the handsome young man in the red coat who had lured her away from Tunbridge Wells and her family.

'All the same, ain't they? Look so 'andsome in their red coats; me, I can never resist 'em. But the 'eart that beats under the red coat is as faithless as any other. Knowin' that makes no difference though, does it. Bloody fools, us women. So 'ow did you meet this one then, as is so free with 'is dibs?'

Hetta suddenly chuckled. 'I met him in the middle of the night on Westminster Bridge. He was most insistent in his attentions, and—well, we've seen so much of each other since that he thought he would prefer to set me up here. It's convenient for us both.'

'Lor',' said Sarah, 'but some people 'ave all the luck.'

A steady rain had settled outside, the sky a uniform dark grey, and inside the unhappy baby had eventually dropped asleep where he fed. There seemed no better excuse for making another pot of tea, and staying talking by the fire, but Hetta could feel herself to be nervous as she set to probe Sarah's past, hoping to gain the girl's confidence and co-operation, and then to gain news of Laura. The information emerged gradually, between cups of tea and slices of bread, and, far from being perturbed by Hetta's questions, the girl showed a pathetic pleasure that anyone should show any interest in her at all.

It appeared that she had been born in a village not far from York. Her father had been a tailor, and Sarah, their only child, and her mother, would help at home with the sewing up of garments. Her father had died of some infection of his chest when Sarah was nine, and after that things had been much harder. Village people still brought some sewing work to them, but Sarah's mother had not been a competent seamstress in her own right, and commissions had become fewer. She had died when Sarah was thirteen, leaving the girl virtually destitute. There was no other family that Sarah knew of to whom she could turn. She had sold off the few bits of furniture they still possessed, and used the money to buy her way to London, for it was well known you could make your fortune there.

And here she had stayed. She had met a man on the stage-coach who had helped her at first, initiated her into the rites of that oldest of professions, and supported her for a short while. Then she had stayed for some months in a house run by a Mrs Goldrich, but she had not liked many of the men she met there, and Mrs Goldrich was too greedy with the takings. When a young man offered to take her away with him, she went hopefully. And so the weary tale progressed, from one man to another, one lodging to another, her past a series of abandonments by men who had cared, if they had ever cared, only until they wearied of her. Hetta felt chilled to the marrow as she listened, but Sarah was not cast down.

'Things are bad now because of 'im.' She nodded her head towards the sleeping baby. ''Tis only to be expected. No man wants to stick around when you're caught with one of these, and 'is pa was no different to the rest. But there, 'e's a sickly brat,' she said hopefully, 'and there's always another man to pay the bills when I want to go and find one. Just look at your luck!'

'How do you work, now you have the child?' Hetta asked, anxious in her concern at the girl's plight. This was a world so far removed from her own, and she suddenly felt deeply ashamed that she was here, merely playing at the hardships that were all Sarah's reality.

The girl shrugged, and shook her lank gingery hair back from her eyes. 'Old Ma Crabbe'll take him for me, but only when I owe her for rent, and then she takes extra for doing it. 'Tisn't easy.'

Hetta looked at the pathetic morsel of humanity wrapped in a grubby twist of blanket. 'How old is he?' she asked. 'What's his name.'

'Ooh, 'e must be three months now, more's the pity. I never thought 'e would survive. Puny little thing. 'E doesn't really 'ave a name. Not old enough to want one yet, is 'e?' She laughed.

Hetta stifled her horror. 'I could take him for you,' she heard herself saying. She could feel the icy glare of Meggie's disapproval boring into her back. 'I could take him when Jonathan, my gentleman friend, is not here. It would give you more chance to work, and not pay extra to Mrs Crabbe.'

'Would you do that?' The girl's grin was vast. 'I knew my luck would turn. I knew it. It always does eventually. 'Ey, thank you, 'Etta, and if there's anything I can do for you...'

'Well, there might be,' said Hetta, and at last she felt she could broach the story of Laura. '...so when I learnt from Em'ly at the White Cocks that you lived in this same house where my Jonathan was taking rooms, and that you had known a girl called Laura, well, it just seemed as if it must be meant to be, and that you would know where I could find my cousin. Specially as you both come from up north. I dare say you'd be likely to be friends?' She paused, hopefully, and waited for the moment of truth.

'Why, yes,' said Sarah. 'I certainly knew a girl called Laura.' Hetta breathed a long sigh of relief. 'Just fancy if she was your cousin! But it was a long time ago, mind, years, and I've never seen 'er since.'

'If you could just tell me all you remember of her?' prodded Hetta hopefully.

Sarah leaned back in her chair and stared up at the ceiling, apparently composing her mind for thought. The baby whimpered as he lost the nipple, and began to suck drowsily at his own clenched fist.

'Well,' she began, but the art of telling a coherent story seemed to elude her, and it took many patient questions before Henrietta felt she had learned all there was to be discovered from Sarah. It was not as much as she had hoped—she could not surprise Jonathan by leading him to his cousin tomorrow—but the story confirmed they were on the right track, and there was a further route to explore.

Sarah remembered Laura arriving in the area, a timid slip of a girl with very dark hair, and curious slate-grey eyes, then barely more than a child. She was brought by a much older man, he was maybe fifty, Sarah guessed, stout, with hard black eyes, an olive skin, and black oiled hair. Hetta shuddered as Sarah described the man. He was a foreigner, a count or some such, with such an odd way of talking you could hardly understand him, and with some strange name Sarah had forgotten.

They took rooms in White Cocks Alley, and Laura rarely came out, but when she did she looked pale, tired and bruised. Sarah had had a room in a house further down the Alley at that time, and passed a friendly word or two with Laura whenever she saw her, but the girl was shy, and the Count did not encourage her to socialise. In her own haphazard way, Sarah seemed to have pitied the girl, and to have been perhaps the only one who did.

After some months it became obvious that Laura was expecting a child. As her young body had thickened and swelled into the shapes of womanhood the Count had lost interest in Laura. He took to spending longer and longer periods away, leaving Laura alone and frightened. It was then that she began to visit Sarah at her rooms, confiding her fears and miseries to Sarah's blunt, unimaginative sympathy. Eventually he went for good, leaving Laura with twenty pounds, just sixteen years old, her first child due in four weeks' time.

Hetta found she had her fist pressed to her mouth like the baby as she listened in anguish to this tale, pressing back her own outrage, swallowing on the pity for the pain she knew she would give Jonathan when she told him the story.

Sarah had taken Laura in. She herself had had, at the time, no permanent gentleman friend, but could make ends meet with the custom she found at the White Cocks inn. And there was no one else for Laura to turn to. She had had the child in Sarah's rooms, with only Old Mother Goodby from Saxon Street to see her through. But the baby had been surprisingly strong, a little girl, and, even more surprisingly, Laura had loved it.

They had lived like that for some months, Sarah working and Laura caring for the baby and taking odd cleaning jobs where she could take the baby with her. She had been very low, Sarah said, always talking of dying, her and the baby together, and speaking bitterly of justice, and God's mercy. Then she'd changed. Suddenly seemed to get harder, more determined. She had found a young girl she could pay to take the child at nights, and went out on the streets. But not round here.

She'd insisted on going up the Haymarket, looking for men with more than just the odd coin in their pocket. Said if she must sell her soul, she'd be sure to sell it dear.

It had paid her, too. She met a young man one night, a newcomer to town, out to enjoy the high life. But he had fallen for Laura. Fallen for her very hard. Packed her up and took her away to some lodgings he found for her, her and the baby both. He was rich and he was kind. She had gone willingly. She had tried to keep in touch with Sarah, had written one or two letters, but Sarah could neither read nor write, and soon after moved away to other lodgings herself with a young captain of Horse Guards she had met. She had not seen or heard from Laura again.

Hetta pondered this story, then raised her eyes to Sarah's freckled face.

'But what,' she asked, 'was the name of the kind, rich young man?'

'That,' replied Sarah, 'is what I was jist a-trying to remember.' There was a long pause, while Sarah stared at the flames licking on the coals. 'Jem, she called him,' she mused. 'I know it was Jem.'

'So would his name be Jeremy?' Hetta prompted.

'Sir Jeremy. It was definitely Sir Jeremy. I know 'e came from a good family. But 'is other name...I've forgotten. I'd know it if you said it to me, like, but...' There was another long pause. 'Ban...Band...something like that? No. I don't know. Sorry, 'Etta.'

Hetta was frantically racking her brains for any Sir Jeremy she might know, a friend of one of her brothers perhaps, but she could think of no one.

'It doesn't matter, Sarah. Thank you for what you've told me, and especially thank you for everything you did for my cousin all those years ago.'

'Oh.' Sarah shrugged and grinned. 'Long time ago now. I'd forgotten it. Still...p'raps I could leave the baby with you tonight? Need to get a decent night's work in. Bring 'im round about five?'

Hetta ignored Meggie's sniff. 'Of course,' she said.

CHAPTER EIGHT

DANE arrived at Lockchain Terrace in the late afternoon of the following day. He had hoped to arrive earlier, but once again Esther had delayed him.

She had asked him to accompany her while she shopped for new materials for dresses, and he had done so, watching with increasing impatience as she required yet another assistant to hold yet another bolt of cloth against her while she simpered and asked his opinion of the colour, shade, texture or whatever. He was astounded at his silent criticism, his unusual irritability. He knew that he ought to enjoy such a time with the woman he believed he loved, should be pleased that she cared so much for his opinion, and this awareness added guilt to his irritation.

He found himself wishing heartily that she cared as much about his search for Laura as she did for her choice of clothes. He very much wanted to confide in her, and tell her about Henrietta, but each time he endeavoured to broach the subject she cut him short with increasing annoyance. That, she repeated distastefully, was his own family shame and misfortune; it was not something he should be wanting to trouble her with. He had become silent, and was aware that his silence was resentful, and all her charm during the homeward drive had not entirely mollified him.

His spirits unaccountably lifted, however, as he ran up the staircase of number three Lockchain Terrace, and rapped a fanfare of knocks with his knuckles on the door on the top landing, while shaking the worst of the raindrops off his caped coat.

Henrietta looked as glowing in that room as he had thought she would. The fire was blazing and the kettle murmuring, the rich reds of the furnishing seeming to give off a warmth of their own against the wet greyness of the day outside. He smiled, and relaxed into the warmth as Meggie bustled up to take his wet coat and hat, his gloves and cane. Hetta jumped up to greet him, with a businesslike shake of the hand.

She was not wearing the detestable wig, he noted with satisfaction, and her cropped curls sat like a neat black cap, quite unadorned. The dress she wore was certainly one of her Petticoat Lane acquisitions, but it was in blue, a rich blue that enhanced the colour of her eyes, and she had added a white lawn neckerchief, fastened with a little paste brooch, that discreetly covered her neck and bosom.

She was politely thanking him, he realised, for all the little things she had discovered since he had left. '...and the pots of jam—who ever would have thought of such a detail?—and the coal in the backyard...there is enough to last us all through the winter, I swear! Billy brings it up for us every morning...' She stood, very formal and correct. 'You put such consideration into everything you arranged. Thank you so much!'

He grinned, feeling frivolous, unimpressed by this carefully correct Henrietta, and, settling his face into a mould of exaggerated solemnity, he threw out his chest, put his hands to his lapels, stood, feet apart, and said in deep, sonorous tones, 'It is that careful attention to the fine details, the fine details, my boy, that makes a job well done. If every detail is right, then the job will be done well, and *that* is how you will make your profit!'

She had to laugh, 'Whoever is that?'

'Probably the best man I ever met,' he replied cheerfully, swinging himself over uninvited into one of the armchairs by the fire, and shaking the kettle hopefully. 'I have an immense respect and fondness for him. Joshua

Priestley. It was him that my family sent me to work with in Madras, and they could not have done a better thing for me. He was like a father to me, and taught me everything he knew of business life, and, indeed, of life as a whole. I owe him a vast debt of gratitude. But . . .' and he grinned '. . . he was a terror for the fine details!'

He settled back in the armchair, long legs comfortably sprawled, holding his hands out to the heat. His coat was of a deep blue superfine that gave a bluer than usual tinge to the dark grey eyes, and his cravat, of immaculate white lawn, was held by a plain pearl pin; his fawn pantaloons were spotless despite the weather, and if his Hessians had suffered a little from the rain it was hardly noticeable as they dried.

Suddenly aware of her scrutiny, Hetta looked away. She had remembered, too, the news she had to give him. 'I am afraid that what we can offer you by way of refreshment is a little limited, but tea we can always manage. As you noticed, we keep the kettle constantly simmering!' she said.

'Tea will do admirably. I drink a great deal of tea.'

'Do you? So do I, far too much, I dare say, for our doctor swears it causes sleeplessness, and should not be over-indulged in. But I do so enjoy it! I will make a pot as readily as Astley's horse!'

'Astley's horse?' Dane's voice was incredulous.

'Do you not know of Astley's horse? Well, such must be the deprivations of living in foreign climes! The star of Astley's Circus for many years was a horse who not only danced the hornpipe, but could also make a pot of tea. He would lift the kettle from the fire with his teeth! Here'—she handed him a cup—'I dare say mine tastes better than his, though, even without a hornpipe!'

He chuckled, and held the cup critically under his nose, sniffing dubiously at the rising steam. 'Well . . . I don't know about that . . .' But she merely smiled and refused to rise to his bait.

'So,' he said. 'And how have you fared since I saw you last?'

She delayed her revelations, nervous of telling him such things, and instead made him laugh with her descriptions of her first forays down into the dung-spattered world of Lockchain Terrace, the dubious and unsavoury contents of the grocer's shop, the ready backchat of young Sam and his disreputable cronies, the endless miseries of gossip with Mrs Crabbe!

Then she stopped pacing the room, gesticulating as she talked, enjoying his amusement, and sat on the chair opposite him across the fire. She drew a reluctant breath, and, gripping her hands in her lap, began to tell him all about her meeting with Sarah, and about Sarah's life.

'It was after that that at last I felt I could really begin to ask about Laura.' She paused and regarded him anxiously. 'It seems incredible, but it *was* your cousin that she knew,' she said.

His head shot up. He had been listening to her with idle pleasure, assuming she had no special news, but now he studied her with painful intensity. 'Well?' His voice was rough, and he leaned towards her. 'What is it, Henrietta? Tell me! What did the girl say? Is Laura dead?'

'No. Oh, no, not that I know of. But . . . her story is . . . distressing.'

He shook his head angrily. 'Tell me,' he said.

She told him everything she had learned from Sarah of those months of Laura's life. She tried to keep her recital calm, but the depth of her horror and pity crept into her voice. As she described the Count's departure, and the birth of Laura's child in such squalid conditions, she was aware that suddenly Jonathan was no longer looking at her. She saw his face twist with pain. He had closed his eyes, and turned his face aside, but though he sat quite motionless she saw the glint of tears on his cheeks in the firelight.

Hetta's voice faltered and stopped. She could not talk on. In the face of such anguish she felt pitifully helpless. She thought of leaving him in privacy, indeed she meant to do so when she rose from her chair, but on some impulse she crept to him and crouched on the floor at his side, leaning a little against him, hardly knowing whether she was capable of offering him comfort. He clutched an arm about her and held her shoulders with a grip that was painful. She could feel the tremors that shook him. She crept an uncertain arm about him and stayed motionless, feeling the harsh grip of his fingers, listening to the flutter of the fire, and aching at the soft drop of his tears as they fell on to her arm.

It could not have been long before he pushed her gently aside, pulled a large lawn handkerchief from his pocket and matter of factly blew his nose. 'I am sorry, Henrietta,' he said, and his voice was unexpectedly normal, calm. 'I am sorry, I had no intention of distressing you. Please, tell me the rest.'

She did so, still crouched on the floor beside him, her arms hugged around her knees, while he stared into the fire.

When she had finished he stood up, restless, as if he could not relax while knowing such things. 'Henrietta...' She held out a tentative hand towards him, but he seemed not to see it. 'I must go out... I need to walk... to think. I will be back later.'

He pulled on the hat and coat Meggie had set to dry, and was gone, his footsteps on the stairs dying away into the silence before the final punctuation of the closing outer door.

Hetta curled up in the chair, where he had sat, still warm from his body. His tears were still drying on her arm. She wanted to cry for him, to ease the ache that crushed her heart, but she found her eyes were dry. She curled up smaller where she sat, and waited for his return.

He was back more quickly than she had hoped, in hardly more than an hour, and although he was very wet he seemed composed, even cheerful. He had brought back another bottle of wine, and also a bottle of brandy—'because we need our spirits fortifying,' he said. He poured them each a generous glassful, and took one through to Meggie. 'To warm a few of the cockles of your heart, my dear,' he said to her, and she blushed and giggled at him.

He went to Hetta and took her hand. 'I am sorry, Henrietta. Truly, I had no intention of distressing you. I'm quite composed now. Thank you for discovering so much, so quickly. Come, sit down, and we must think constructively about the identity of this man, a Sir Jeremy who was young, foolish and kindly ten years ago. Have you any ideas?'

It was just at this point that a curious snuffling whimper came from the open bottom drawer of the new mahogany chest of drawers. Dane's head shot around in bewilderment.

'Oh, good heavens!' Hetta exclaimed, 'I had quite forgotten the poor little mite.'

The whimper was growing into a wail, and in Dane's horrified imagination it was suddenly as if it was Laura's child crying, and the slight dark-haired figure who crouched over the drawer to pick it up was Laura herself.

Hetta turned, holding the child. 'Meet Sarah's nameless offspring,' she said ruefully. 'She swore to me that she would not be an hour when she left, and that was early afternoon, for she knew I wanted him gone before you arrived. Men are supposed to have such a horror of babies. Wretched girl, she will have gone to the White Cocks with the money she gained yesterday, and will not now be back until the small hours, I suppose. I am so sorry.' She rocked the child on her shoulder, soothing it instinctively while it blinked and hiccoughed.

'If you will just excuse me,' she added, 'he does need attention.'

She vanished into the small room, and Jonathan sat with a wry smile as he listened to the baby's wails, Meggie's dark muttering, and Henrietta's soft cajoling, coaxing tones.

When she returned the baby was wrapped in a clean piece of blanket, and Meggie fussed about setting milk on the hob, 'For it should be boiled for a baby, Miss Hetta, I do know that.'

Hetta paced the room with the hungry, impatient child, and muttered unseemly things about mothers who abandoned their babies, but, Dane noticed with amusement, kissing and cuddling the baby throughout. He sipped his brandy and watched her, intrigued by this new view of her and, he thought, her seemingly boundless capacity for caring.

'Thank heavens I stayed with Robert and Louisa when my godson Henry was about this age. At least I am not now the complete ignoramus I was about babies. I was never obliged to feed Henry, however. That, naturally, was entirely Louisa's and the nurse's province. Shall we get anything down him with a spoon, do you think, Meggie?'

'Have to, shan't we, Miss Hetta, unless we want to listen to his noise all night, miserable little brat that he is?'

'Oh, Meggie. Shame on you. He can't help being hungry. Is that cool enough yet? Let me try.'

For some minutes Jonathan sat forgotten, watching the baby splutter hopelessly over the spoonfuls of milk, while both baby and Hetta became damper and unhappier.

'Try him with a crust soaked in milk,' Dane suggested tentatively, 'something he can suck.' Then, as they set about this suggestion, 'I am just going out for a few minutes. I will be back directly.' And he hurried off into the night.

The wails from young Master Battey, assailing his ears as he ascended the stairwell on his return, told him that his crust suggestion had not been an unqualified success.

'No good?' he asked, as Hetta turned to him as he entered the room.

She laughed ruefully, but with an edge of desperation. 'It worked until he sucked a lump of bread off and nearly choked himself. Drat that girl Sarah. It really is too bad. I don't know what to do with him for the best.'

With a smile Dane reached into his pocket and brought out a new clay pipe. It had a long, fine stem, and a bowl decorated with the head of a sailor. 'I thought of it while I watched you struggling with the spoon,' he said, a trifle smugly.

Henrietta stared at him over the head of the howling baby with a look of exasperated incomprehension. 'Really,' she said. 'I had no idea you smoked a pipe.' Her tone said that she did not care either. 'It is obviously some Yorkshire eccentricity.'

He laughed. 'No, look. I am sure it will work. Have you a clean scrap of muslin, or some such?'

'My handkerchief?'

He took it and put it over the mouthpiece of the pipe, 'Just in case of any pieces that might choke the child again,' he murmured to himself, then began to pour a little milk into the bowl of the pipe. Suddenly Hetta understood.

'Jonathan,' she said, staring at him, 'your ingenuity is outrageous. Dear Lord, I wonder if it will work!' She held the mouth of the pipe to the questing lips of the unfortunate baby, while Dane, with the warm milk in a little jug, poured it into the bowl of the pipe as needed. The system was not perfect, but it worked, and a great deal more milk descended into the baby than descended on to the towel wrapped around his neck. Hetta was laughing as she watched the baby's satisfaction.

'Little devil for his food, isn't he?' Dane remarked with a certain pride. 'I can hardly keep pace with him at this end of the pipe.'

Hetta giggled. 'To think how silly we must look! The two of us kneeling over this misbegotten infant busily pouring milk down its throat through a clay pipe, it is too ridiculous!'

He laughed as well, then hastily poured again as the pipe-bowl gurgled ominously.

'Well, it worked, didn't it?' he asked, infuriatingly complacent, as he tipped the last of the milk into the pipe. 'It takes a man to sort out these little domestic crises!'

'Well, of all the smug, complacent, self-satisfied——'

'Shockingly tautological!' he murmured, disapprovingly, and abruptly ducked, laughing, as she flicked the milky pipe at him.

'But you really are peculiar, Jonathan. Most men would have vanished at the first wail, and not been seen for a week.'

'But then, I am not most men,' was all he answered.

The child seemed replete, and Hetta sat with him cuddled to her shoulder while he did those windy things that replete babies did, then fell asleep, his tiny fist tightly clutching her neckerchief.

Dane regarded Henrietta's contented smile with sudden apprehension. 'Don't get too fond of the child, Henrietta. You can't do everything for all of the world, you know. And he is very small and sickly.' Dying babies had not been such an uncommon sight in India, and the child's large sunken eyes did not look hopeful to Dane. He did not want Henrietta to be hurt. But she only shrugged gently, so as not to disturb the child, and smiled.

'What of Sir Jeremy?' she asked. 'Have you had any thoughts?'

'Why, yes. I thought I would go into town tomorrow and ask at White's. A few judicious questions might bring a Sir Jeremy to light. Failing that, I will steel my nerve to approach members of my family again. They know most people who are about in society. Bentley is at his town house at present, I know, and I have heard that——' He suddenly broke off, confused.

'So Justin is back in town, is he?' Hetta asked. Her voice was bleak.

'I believe so, yes,' he answered quietly, cursing himself for a fool.

'Yes,' she said with a great effort at unconcern. 'Justin prides himself on always knowing who everyone is, who they are related to, who they might inherit from . . . Yes, ask Justin. He will know.' And she turned to kiss the sleeping baby, hiding her face.

He made as if he would like to say something, but she did not look at him, and he shrugged and spoke of something else.

Later they sent across to the coffee shop for food, and talked of safe, uncomplicated things while they ate. Later still, Sarah returned, inebriated and unrepentant, and took the baby back.

Dane returned to his own house. Despite the excellent ministrations of Mrs Stockwell, it seemed empty and unwelcoming. He had promised to return to Lockchain Terrace as soon as he had news of the forgotten Sir Jeremy. He would make an early start on the morrow.

CHAPTER NINE

'I STILL have my doubts about your being here,' Dane said resignedly, as the chaise approached Streatham.

'Nonsense,' Hetta replied with unabated cheerfulness. 'You have merely brought your concerned sister with you to assist in your search for your cousin. What could be more natural?'

'Apart from the fact that I don't have a sister——'

'He won't know that!'

'And that he may recognise you——'

'No, I have never heard of the man!'

'Or may meet you again in the future——'

'Why ever should he?'

'I would hardly take my respectable sister to meet a man of whom my sole purpose is to enquire into his past excursions into the world of the *demi-monde*!'

'Jonathan, you are simply looking for problems! You must learn to be less bound by the polite conventions of society! What are rules for but to be ignored when it suits you?' She waved an airy hand at his exasperation, and directed his attention to a fine show of autumn colour on a beech tree they were passing. Hetta, like a schoolgirl fetched from the confines of her seminary, was irrepressible in her delight at escaping the noisome world of Lockchain Terrace for the day. Nothing Jonathan could say would dampen her spirits.

Patting his arm consolingly, she continued, 'Naturally you have no interest whatever in Sir Jeremy Blanding's other youthful follies. You merely wish to enquire of him whether he was ever acquainted with our cousin. Anyway I can put him at his ease by explaining that, owing to our own particular family misfortune with Laura, I have an especial interest in helping and reclaiming our fallen sisters throughout London.'

'The dear Lord preserve us!' murmured Jonathan drily.

Jonathan had discovered the name of the man whom they were shortly, without doubt, to embarrass, from his cousin Justin. He had visited White's, and found Justin morosely sitting there, sunk deep in an armchair, a large brandy at his elbow, and the newspaper spread before him.

Jonathan had regarded that face, so like and yet so unlike his own, with a marked lack of enthusiasm, and fought down a surge of anger on Hetta's behalf. His civil congratulations on his cousin's recent nuptials, to which Jonathan had not been invited, were received with a brusqueness that was rude, but Justin, when pressed, had begrudgingly admitted to a knowledge of two men named Sir Jeremy.

One, Sir Jeremy Cornish, was from Northumberland. The other, Sir Jeremy Blanding, had built a new place somewhere beyond Streatham. Neither was possessed of fortune, influence or connections, and thus Justin had no further interest in them. He showed no interest either in why Jonathan should wish to know, but merely retired contemptuously behind his newspaper again, heavy-eyed and frowning. Further enquiries had produced a direction for the inhabitant of Streatham, and Sarah, when questioned, had wondered how ever she could have forgotten; of course his name had been Blanding. It had all seemed so simple.

But Henrietta had, as he had reluctantly known she would, insisted on accompanying him on this next stage of their quest, and somehow he could not refuse her. However, he *had* refused utterly to take her in her guise as a London doxy.

'Not even if I am an utterly orthodoxy?' she had asked jauntily, teasing, for she was alight with their success, but he had refused to be shaken. It would offer an impossible insult to Sir Jeremy, whose help they required.

He had suggested passing her off as his wife, but somewhat to his surprise she had abruptly refused, then argued stiffly of the embarrassment it could cause to Esther were she to meet Sir Jeremy in later years. Jonathan did not trouble to point out to Henrietta her inconsistencies, merely agreeing to her proposed role as his sister, raising an amused eyebrow as she appeared arrayed for the part in a subdued, high-necked lilac dress for driving, and a plain straw chip bonnet over her own hair.

'You had better wear a large cloak and hood over that demurely charming ensemble,' was all he had commented before they left, 'or you will ruin your hard-earned reputation in Lockchain Terrace!'

The day was mild, with a hazy autumn sun breaking through. They had risked the open chaise, for Henrietta had refused to be enclosed any longer. The restrictions of life in Lockchain Terrace were already beginning to wear at her spirits, and she had been longing for escape. She had been silent as they passed over Westminster Bridge, and Jonathan had talked lightly of the fine weather, but she had been quite cheerful by the time the Kennington turnpike was reached. The roads had not been unduly busy and they had made good speed, allowing the horses to take their time over the pull up Brixton Hill, and arriving in Streatham a little after twelve.

'Now, his villa is said to be some way beyond here on the Mitcham Lane,' Dane remarked, drawing the horses to a halt in the middle of Streatham. 'What we need is a suitably informed native to direct us. Hold the reins, would you please, Henrietta? I will go and enquire.'

He was soon back with the necessary directions. The road in question proved to have various new villas strung out along it, interspersed with green fields. That belonging to Sir Jeremy Blanding was set well back from the road, a sweep of gravelled drive leading up to the pillared porch then beyond to the back areas of the house before returning to the far gate. It looked a prosperous house of middle size, asserting just so much of its owner and no more. The hoofs and wheels crunched over the gravel as Jonathan drove slowly in, and as they drew to a halt outside the front door the sound of children's shrill voices and a small dog's yapping could be heard from the garden at the rear.

'It all looks rather respectable,' remarked Hetta, in subdued tones, and straightened her bonnet, then straightened her back. 'No matter, we remain undaunted, do we not?'

A man had appeared from the back of the house, to take the chaise and horses. They ascended the steps to the front door, and Jonathan smiled at Hetta reassuringly. 'On with the fight for the fallen ladies!' he said lightly.

In response to their knock a solemn-faced butler took Jonathan's card and the short note he had put with it, and, leaving them to wait in a small morning-room, vanished into the depths of the house.

The man who eventually came to join them looked what he doubtless was, of solid, middle-ranking respectability. He wore a dark cloth coat over a tan patterned waistcoat. His cravat was neat, but unimaginative. His breeches were of a drab beige, his stockings of white silk, his shoes of plain good dark leather. His face still retained the pink freshness of a boy, his eyes large, pale blue and perplexed, his hair downy fine. It was hard to believe, Hetta thought, that he must surely be approaching thirty, of an age with Jonathan, and the father of all those hopeful children now disporting themselves in the garden.

'How do you do?' he said. 'Miss Dane, Mr Dane. Please, sit down. In what way can I help you? You say that your business is of a private nature?'

While he was debating quite how to begin, Dane found himself forestalled by Henrietta. She leaned towards Sir Jeremy, her movement echoing her expression of earnest concern. 'What we have to ask you,' she said, 'is indeed of a private and personal nature. It is a subject that is rightly deemed unsuitable in the conversation of ladies. But I have put aside that most natural embarrassment in the interests of a greater good for a fellow creature in need of our help, and I am trusting that you will do the same.' She paused, gazing at him with huge, sincere blue eyes, and Blanding coughed self-consciously, looked confused, and made some mutter intended to convey that he would do what he could.

'We have a cousin,' Hetta began again, 'who some years ago, while we were in India, was most appallingly misused by the rest of her family. We are doing all in our power to discover her whereabouts and restore to her her rightful dues from the family. We have traced her through the most heart-rending situations, and have been led to believe that we may have you to thank for rescuing her from one such situation and giving her your aid and support. If this is so then we wish to offer you our sincerest thanks, and beg from you further information as to what you might know of our cousin's present whereabouts. Dear sir, can you help us? Her name is Laura, and when you knew her she was living in White Cocks Alley.'

Dane had to admit she handled the part superbly, looking every inch the determinedly dutiful, anxious cousin.

'Yes, Sir Jeremy,' he added, as their unfortunate host failed at once to make an answer. 'Naturally we appreciate your position, and guarantee you absolute discretion in anything you might tell us, but we would be most grateful for your help.'

Sir Jeremy, who had blanched white, then flushed a deep, painful pink, moved across to the sideboard. 'Allow me first to offer you a glass of wine,' he said, making an obvious effort to compose himself. 'Madeira?'

They accepted, and he slowly poured the drinks then handed them round. Jonathan noticed that he glanced somewhat nervously at the door before he began to speak, as if assuring himself that it was, in fact, securely closed.

'I do indeed remember Laura,' he said, his voice little more than a mutter. 'I don't think I will ever forget her. But you must realise...in my present position...'

'Everything you tell us will be entirely confidential,' Jonathan reiterated.

'Our only interest is in Laura's welfare,' Hetta added.

Blanding sat uncertainly, twirling his glass between finger and thumb, staring down into the red wine. 'I can tell you simply that I have no idea at all of her present whereabouts.' He sighed. 'But it may help you in your search for her to know the events of that year. They do not, however'—he glanced shamefaced at Hetta—'make an edifying or heroic tale. But I will tell you for what it is worth, and you shall judge whether or not any of it will assist you.'

'Thank you, sir,' Henrietta said quietly. Her wide blue eyes were solemn with a genuine, respectful sympathy. He gave her a small, shy smile, and she had a sudden vision of the boy Laura must have met.

'I was just nineteen,' Sir Jeremy began, 'and newly arrived in London. I was a green youth. Unbelievably so, looking back, and unforgivably so too. My father had not allowed me to attend school or university—he feared for my health, as the only child—and my arrival in town was my very first time loosed from my leading-strings. I felt inordinately excited, determined to catch up on all the gaming and wenching I was sure I should, but for my father, have been enjoying for years.

'Gaming was easy; I joined a few clubs, met a few other young and foolish boys. For the wenching I drifted naturally to the Vauxhall Gardens, and also to the Haymarket. It was there that I met Laura one evening, and the pattern of my life changed.'

He paused and looked up. 'Oddly enough, it has come as no real surprise to me that Laura should have come from what is obviously a respectable family. I suspected she was gently bred, even though she would say nothing of her past before her arrival in London, and resented any enquiries. Her likeness to you, sir,' he said nodding towards Dane, 'is so marked that I have no hesitation in accepting your claim of relationship.'

Fortunately he was not looking at Henrietta, and did not notice her look of discomfiture.

'I became enamoured of Laura as soon as I met her, and our meetings became frequent.' He was embarrassed, but spoke on determinedly. 'I visited at her lodgings. The discovery that she had a child was a blow, but I did not see it as an insurmountable problem. I was determined to marry Laura; I wanted to rescue her from the squalor and vice that was so blatantly unfitting for her, to carry her home on my white charger, as it were.' He gave a small, self-deprecating shrug. 'The child would be hard to explain to my family, but I toyed with the idea of passing her off as a young widow, or of finding suitable fostering for the baby.

'She would not have me. She told me I was too young. I believe she knew that it would be impossible to gain my father's consent, and I would be penniless without it; that all my talk was no more than empty bravado. But she swore to me that she did not want to be the cause of a rift between me and my family. That I should not, for her, ruin my own chances of achieving my rightful position in life. I have never met a girl with a lovelier nature,' his voice was wistful, 'or more beautiful.

'So we compromised. I found lodgings where we could stay together and she could live in some degree of comfort. We were very happy for some months, but we were no doubt foolish in expecting to remain so. Two things occurred. I lost heavily at the tables. I should have known better, for the man I had played with was a hardened gamester, but I set to win back my losses. He took me for so much that I was forced to apply to my father for assistance to a tune that frightened me, and nearly gave him an apoplexy. Then, very shortly afterwards, a well-meaning busybody informed my still irate parent that much of my income was presumably going to support my...' he shrugged '...to support Laura. This busy man gave my father our address, and he arrived one morning on our doorstep.

'Well, I don't need to spell out the scene for you.' He gave a small rueful smile. 'I am sure you can imagine it all for yourselves. I can remember saying a great many fine and noble things, of the sort a penniless, idealistic twenty-year-old might say, but I was no match for my father, with his flaying tongue and his tight purse-strings. I managed to leave Laura with two hundred pounds altogether, by pawning my watch and other such expediencies, and I paid some months of the rent in advance. That was all I could do.

'My father had me back home, and my engagement to the daughter of his closest friend announced within a fortnight. I never saw Laura again. I was duly married and settled down. When my father died I sold his house. It had not been long in the family and I had no fondness for it. Besides, I wished to escape the close attentions of my father-in-law on his neighbouring estate. So I moved here and built for myself, and thus you find me.' He leant back in his chair, and drained his glass of wine.

'If any of this sorry tale is of assistance to you, I shall be only too pleased.'

'Thank you, sir, for your confidence,' Dane said quietly. 'And may I thank you again for the kindness you showed my cousin. Two things you could perhaps add, which might assist us. One, obviously, is the direction of the house where you left Laura, in case there is anyone there who still remembers her. But also, do you remember any names of friends of Laura's whom we might possibly trace, apart from Sarah Battey, who led us to you?'

'The address is easy. We lived in Eleanor Street, near the Haymarket, at number twelve. Friends are more difficult. Apart from Sarah, and there she lost touch before long, she kept up with none of her acquaintances from White Cocks Alley. They were a rough lot. And of course there were no other gentlemen friends while I knew her.

'There was a girl though, who lived on the floor beneath us in Eleanor Street. A true Haymarket Cyprian in a way I felt Laura could never be. A great strapping brazen girl, with a laugh that rang through the house, and a tongue to hold her own against anyone. But the friendliest girl, and a heart of—well, almost gold! We would help each other out when the luck had run badly, and she and Laura were certainly friendly. I can see her face so plainly in my mind, a towering girl with a mountain of red-blonde hair. She had a figure of proportions not to be forgotten.'

Blanding smiled at the memory, then caught Hetta's amused eye and had the grace to blush. 'But her name,' he continued hastily, 'no, that I have forgotten. Perhaps you would care to leave me your direction, and if I remember the name of this girl I could send it on to you?'

With this Dane and Henrietta had to be content. They thanked Sir Jeremy Blanding again as he showed them out, and their last view of him as the chaise rounded the turn back on to the road was of his suddenly being engulfed in a swarm of pink-cheeked fair children, very nice in their white pinafores, who streamed round the side of the house in hot pursuit of a small terrier with a doll between its teeth.

'I do think,' said Hetta, 'that we can account him a piece of good fortune for Laura. What a pity she could not marry him. I wonder that she made no more push to do so.'

'Do you?' said Dane. 'Would you have chosen such a callow youth? Besides, as he said, she would have seen it to be an impossibility. He *was* good fortune for her, yes, but he would have been a great deal better fortune had he been older, richer, more independent and more determined. To have allowed himself to be forced to abandon such a girl in such a way...I am sorry, Henrietta, but I become so angry.'

She looked at the tense lines of his face and the taut grip of his hands upon the reins. 'Look, there is an inn ahead,' she said. 'If you would not object I would like to stop for some refreshment.'

He turned to look at her, and smiled somewhat bitterly. 'If in doubt, feed a man, eh?' he asked.

She coloured faintly at his tone, but regarded him steadily as she replied.

'That is right, sir, but I, too, am hungry.'

'I'm sorry.' His smile was rueful now. 'It was always Grandmama Alathea's motto for coping with ill-tempered uncles and grandfathers. "If in doubt, feed a man." But you are quite right, of course. We shall both be better for a meal.'

The inn was small, but comfortable, and was able to provide a private parlour for their use. Dane ordered a cold spread and a bottle of wine, which appeared with commendable speed, and coffee to follow.

'Well, we have another address to investigate,' he remarked with satisfaction, over a plate of cold beef.

'Yes, indeed, and the possibility of a new name also. We have done very well!' They both felt suddenly immensely pleased with themselves. 'Why, I believe we could offer our services at Bow Street. We make a splendid detecting team!' Hetta chuckled.

'And tomorrow——' Dane began with a flourish. 'No, it will have to be the next day, for tomorrow I have an engagement. The day after tomorrow the Cairshaw and Dane detecting team will mount a major investigation into the inhabitants, past and present and future, of that renowned house of ill-repute, the iniquitous, the vice-ridden number twelve, Eleanor Street!'

'Undaunted, we shall unearth and inexorably reveal their every innermost secret!'

They laughed, with mutual satisfaction, and mock-solemnly clinked their glasses together in a toast to their endeavours.

CHAPTER TEN

HENRIETTA sat gently rocking the baby to and fro in her lap. It lay quite still, gazing up at her, its wide dark eyes never leaving her face.

Sarah was talking. She had been sitting in Hetta's room for some while, talking about times past, about Jeremy Blanding and Laura and other people whose names were unknown to Henrietta. Having spurned the pot of tea on the hob, she had brought her own bottle—of gin, Hetta gathered—with her from her room, and had been drinking steadily as she talked. Hetta, having managed to hide her improbable ignorance of the fact that the Blue Ruin, Old Tom or Stark Naked of Sarah's conversation all referred to her gin bottle, had found her attention wandering entirely from her reminiscences. She had developed a muted friendship with Sarah, sharing the food and coal Jonathan provided, occasionally walking out together, and endlessly gossiping. When sober, she could be sharply amusing, but the girl's gin-oiled ramblings were yawningly tedious.

Henrietta's thoughts ran over the events of yesterday, just recounted. Unfortunately Sarah had no knowledge of the house in Eleanor Street. Not that Henrietta had thought she would, but it had seemed worth asking. She might have known somebody who had lodged there.

Thoughts of their investigation led to thoughts of Jonathan. He was, she knew, to spend time with Miss Esther Wanhope today, as he did regularly. She supposed it showed an admirable devotion. It was only to be hoped that Miss Wanhope appreciated his attentions.

As for herself, Hetta was devoting more of her attentions to the baby.

She had seen a great deal of his wizened little face recently. At some time each day Sarah had appeared hopefully, proffering the child. Once, irritated, Hetta had demurred; she was too busy, she had said, and Sarah had shrugged laconically.

'I'll take 'im dahn the White Cocks, then. Leave 'im in a corner, out of the way.'

Hetta had reached out angrily and taken the child in. Certainly Sarah seemed to lack all that Hetta had ever considered to be normal maternal feeling, and Hetta, herself in need of someone on whom to pour her affections, gave more and more care to the loveless baby. She now gazed down at him tenderly, edging her finger into the lax grip of his tiny fist.

He continued to regard her with what seemed an unnatural apathy in one so tiny. She remembered her little nephew, Henry, who lived every moment of his tiny life with gusto, feeding greedily, howling with the fury of total outrage, gurgling with fist-clenching, hair-pulling delight into his mother's face, sleeping with the abandonment of utter exhaustion. This poor mite already seemed to view the world with the resignation of despair.

'What are you going to call him, Sarah?' she asked abruptly.

'Call 'im? Call 'oo?' Sarah broke off her ramblings, perplexed.

'The baby.' Hetta held the child up. 'Your son. What is his name?'

Sarah shrugged, and regarded the child without interest.

'He must have a name.'

It suddenly seemed to matter to Hetta that she should give the child something—some semblance of respect, of dignity, in his uncaring world.

'He needs a name, so that we can talk to him. He should be baptised,' she said.

Sarah looked at Hetta in astonishment, then appeared to decide that she had, after all, only been joking.

'I'll call 'im Little Daffy,' she said, with a giggle, "acos that's what I give 'im. A little daffy!'

Before Hetta had realised what she meant to do, while she was still registering surprise that Sarah should have cared enough to purchase Daffy's Elixir for the child, Sarah moved over and tipped her bottle up to the baby's lips.

'Everyone knows a bit of daffy does a baby good,' she said. 'You call 'im Daffy!'

Hetta pulled the choking child back in horror. She had heard that nurses might add a little gin to their charges' medicine, but she had not witnessed a baby fed neat spirits before.

'Sarah, that cannot do him good,' she said angrily, 'or you either. See how he chokes, poor child.'

She held the spluttering child against her shoulder, and reflected that the unfortunate Reverend Daffy would doubtless turn in his grave could he see what was done in his name.

'I am serious, though,' she tried again. 'Let us go and arrange a christening for the child. I will speak to the clergyman. I would like to do that for him. Think: what names would you give him? What of your father's name, perhaps?'

Sarah perceived that her odd new friend was, improbably, serious. 'Well, my father was Richard,' she said dubiously. 'Richard Battey.'

'That would do very well,' Hetta said. 'Richard Battey sounds admirable.'

'But I would like to name 'im for you too,' Sarah went on, suddenly enjoying this novelty. "Enry, like you're 'Enrietta. An' if I named 'im for your Jonathan, maybe 'e'd show an interest in 'im, like, you know?'

Hetta knew exactly what sort of interest Sarah meant, and where the pecuniary offering would end up if given, but knew better than to comment.

'So, Richard Henry Jonathan,' she said. 'It's a great deal of name for such a tiny thing.'

But she smiled down at him, where he continued to cough with a weak persistence, his tiny head lolling against her shoulder.

'I think,' she said with sudden anxiety, 'that we should book his christening immediately. He is not well.'

Once determined, Hetta would not sit waiting. Meggie, who had been sitting throughout in silent disapproval stitching a torn flounce, was persuaded to take baby Richard, and Sarah was persuaded to leave her bottle behind and tie on her best bonnet, and the two girls sallied forth in search of a church.

Their walk was enlivened by the offers and suggestions of Sarah's friends and customers, and their ribald comments on receiving her toss of the head, and airy assurance that she could not possibly stop, having an urgent appointment with a vicar. Hetta giggled, half amused, half horrified, and wondered fleetingly what her brother Robert, or even Jonathan, would think if they could see her now. She pushed the thoughts away, and pressed on, picking her way distastefully through the filth on the road.

The church Sarah led her to was tiny, and very old. It looked as if it might once have been happily nestled in the midst of some country hamlet, a few rustic cottages about it with a road that might wind away to the main village over the hill. Now it squatted forgotten in the sprawling tangle of alleys and leaning houses that pressed up on every side, threatening to overrun it altogether. Its stub of spire barely seemed to top the two yew trees that filled the churchyard, the ancient stone was blackened and crumbling with soot, and an old newspaper blew disconsolately in the porch. Chilled but determined, Hetta approached the door, though it seemed improbable the church would be occupied, and there was no clue as to where the incumbent might be found.

The door scraped reluctantly ajar, and the sheets of newspaper rustled eagerly through the gap and into the dank darkness within. Hetta and Sarah squeezed in after them.

The church was very dark, the tiny windows obscured by years of filth and the encroaching yew trees, but a single tiny lamp was burning by the altar. As her eyes accustomed themselves to the gloom Henrietta could just distinguish a man rising from his knees and turning towards them.

'Coo, this is a rum do, innit!' Sarah muttered, moving closer to Henrietta.

The man, small and thin with a tight pinched face, stood in his clerical black, hands clasped behind his back, and, after a studied perusal, regarded them with chilly disapproval.

'Is it possible I can help you?' he asked, repressively.

Incensed at this welcome, Hetta felt no surprise that his church was unfrequented. She held out a hand firmly towards him, and the hint of Alnstrop arrogance was oddly at variance with her garb.

'How do you do,' she said, coolly. 'I am Henrietta Cairshaw, and this is my friend, Miss Sarah Battey. We wish to arrange for a christening for Miss Battey's baby son. Today or tomorrow if possible, for the child is sickly.'

The curate, for such he was, had automatically taken her outstretched hand and admitted to being Mr Smith, but now he stepped back in horror.

'A son of *Miss* Battey's! A child of sin! I am surprised you even consider he has a place in the church.' His voice was stiff with distaste.

Sarah recoiled, and twitched at Henrietta's arm to pull her away. But Henrietta was glaring round the dank, decaying church, the stench of its chill, damp ages filling her nostrils.

'Really, Mr Smith?' she said, dangerously quiet. 'Is that so? Then tell me, sir, who *does* have a place in your church? Who comes to fill your pews, besides the worms who devour them? Who is familiar with your prayer books but the moth and the beetle? To whom'—she flung her arm towards the creaking door—'in all those God-forsaken buildings full of damned souls that crowd up to your doorstep, have you brought a glimpse of salvation?'

She was shaking with rage, but she could not stop. Her voice was low and quivering with the intensity of her furious upsurge of caring for all the Lauras and Sarahs and baby Richards who lived permanently in the defiant misery of their half-world, unrecognised or condemned by the respectable fortunates, in a world of which, until a few weeks previously, she had remained virtually unaware.

'What is the Christianity that *you* follow, Mr Smith? Where do you find it, this Christianity that leads you to despise the people who are your neighbours? Is it the Christianity of Our Lord who befriended publicans and sinners? Who befriended Mary Magdalene? Who loved children? Is it? Or does Mr Smith have some new way of judging his fellow men that deems them all unfit to enter his church?'

She drew breath, quivering. She knew she had been unforgivably rude, but she was unrepentant. She could not bear that so tiny a child should be denied even a name. She steadied her breathing. Poor Sarah had edged over to a pew, which she clutched as if for support, and was staring aghast, wanting only to retreat as her Blue Ruin bravado evaporated.

Mr Smith continued to stare at Henrietta, his thin face shadowed in the gloom.

'Well,' Henrietta managed, stiffly, 'I have been extremely rude. Please accept my apology. We won't trouble you any longer.' She turned to leave.

The thin man shook his head, his face creased with puzzlement. 'Possibly I misjudged you, Miss Cairshaw,' he said slowly, reluctantly. 'I dare say I could see you tomorrow morning for the christening? At ten?'

She swallowed her anger. 'Thank you, Mr Smith. That will do very well.' Hetta regarded him for a moment, but could think of nothing more to say, and, with a nod of her head, turned to go. With an alarmed bob, Sarah followed.

'Lor', 'Etta! You didn't 'alf tell 'im. I didn't know where to put meself.' They were hurrying back through the narrow streets as if to quickly distance themselves from the church and Mr Smith.

'I never thought this foul air of London would smell good to me, but it does after that church,' Hetta muttered.

''Ow did you know all that stuff to say to 'im? You sounded different, like. Quite the nob!' Sarah persisted.

Hetta shrugged irritably. She was aware that her outburst had been foolishly out of character, but she could not care. It had achieved what she wanted.

'Oh,' she said carelessly. 'I learned all that stuff as a child in Tunbridge Wells. I was sweet on the vicar, you see,' she added naughtily, and was relieved when Sarah giggled.

'Oo, you! I might 'ave known!' she said appreciatively, and Hetta could hear her muttering 'sweet on the vicar, indeed', and chuckling all the way back to Lockchain Terrace.

Henrietta was belatedly remembering Jonathan's advice not to become involved with Sarah's baby. She felt a twinge of guilt, anticipating his disapproval, and scowled defiantly, then tossed her head. Who was he to tell her how to dispose of her affections? Her affections had nothing whatever to do with him. Nothing at all. She would care for whomever she wished. Become involved wherever she wanted. He was keeping his own affections for Miss Esther Wanhope. And much joy might she have of them.

As it happened, Miss Wanhope *was* enjoying Mr Dane's affections that day. He had been nagged by a feeling of guilt at his irritability with his beloved, and had determined to make amends. With the memory of the Kashmir shawls he had given to Henrietta in the back of his mind, he had taken Esther shopping in the morning, and had purchased for her a shawl of her choice, and had not made a single quibble at the exorbitant price. He had taken luncheon at the Wanhopes' house, and made every effort to please Mr Wanhope as well as his daughter. In the afternoon he had driven Esther out to Hampton Court, and although there was a chilly breeze they had spent a pleasant hour walking in the gardens and exploring the maze.

Esther had ventured out undecided. She felt she was now gaining a little town bronze, and she had heard whispers about the Dane family that had made her wonder if she should continue her acquaintance with Jonathan. It was not that people did not receive them, of course, the Danes of Thwayle were welcomed everywhere, but there was something not quite 'the thing', so she gathered, about the family as a whole. And she certainly did not want an association that was not quite 'the thing'.

She had determined to behave with greater coolness towards Mr Dane, despite his reputed wealth, and encourage young Lord Glenby. Now she was not so sure. Jonathan was being everything that was most charming, obliging and generous. She squeezed his arm a little to attract his attention before pointing out the elegance of the statue they were approaching, and she smiled that demure smile, with a look from under her lashes, that she knew men found irresistible.

She had quite decided, as they approached a secluded corner of the yew walk, that she would toy with his proposal almost seriously when he renewed it now. She was certain he would do so. She would toy with it and let him really think she would accept this time before very sweetly putting him off for just a little longer while she thought about it some more.

She was therefore very surprised, and more than a little piqued, when his offer was not renewed, and even more surprised when he informed her that he would be busy on the morrow, and could not therefore accompany her to drive in the park.

She immediately determined that she would contrive to meet Lord Glenby, and be seen driving with him by a great many talkative people who would all, hopefully, make it their business to mention the fact to Mr 'Too Busy' Dane.

She set herself to talk with honeyed sweetness throughout the drive home.

CHAPTER ELEVEN

SAMUEL PERKINS erupted out of his aunt's coffee shop before the chaise had pulled to a halt, cramming his large checked cap over an unruly tangle of mouse-brown hair. He leapt to the horses' heads and stood panting and grinning as Dane jumped down. Dane laughed and flicked him a coin, which he caught and secreted into an inner pocket in one swift, practised movement. Samuel approved of Mr Dane, and of Mr Dane's generosity. He had found that his constant employment by him had bestowed an edge upon Samuel over the other lads in the street that he found most gratifying. He stood to attention.

'Message for you, sir.'

Dane, who had been about to hurry in to Mrs Crabbe's, impatient to collect Henrietta and proceed with the Dane and Cairshaw investigations of number twelve, Eleanor Street, paused and frowned.

'What sort of message?'

'From your Miss 'Etta, sir. They've not long been and gorn, you only just missed 'em. They're down at some church. That old one, the other end o' William Street. It's for the baby. They're 'avin' a baptism!'

'A baptism! Are you certain?'

Samuel nodded importantly. 'That Miss Meggie told me so when she came for the bread this morning.'

'I would never have thought...' Dane was muttering. 'Oh, Lord, this must be some start of Henrietta's. Wretched girl. I told her not to become involved... Where is this church, Sam?'

'Down there, sir. Far end o' William Street, which is beyond Turk's Alley. Not far, sir. Will you be takin' the 'orses, sir? Or shall I take 'em into Pa's yard?'

With a sigh, half amused, half exasperated, Dane turned away from Mrs Crabbe's.

'Take them in for me, Sam. I'll walk to find Miss Henrietta.'

'Yes, sir!' And he grinned knowingly at Dane's retreating figure. 'They'll be wanting you to stand godfather, sir!'

Dane swung round, a startled frown under his immaculate beaver hat, but the boy was already leading the horses away into old Perkins' yard.

He made better speed over the rubbish in the roadways than Hetta and her little entourage had done, for he strode out, his irritation at Hetta's obvious folly in becoming more deeply involved with these people overcoming any concern he might have felt for the well-being of his Hessian boots.

What a fool the girl was. Could she *never* learn to leave well alone? Could she *never* do what she was told? As for standing godparent to that poor brat, for he had no doubts at all as to who would be the godmother, how could they make a long-term commitment to such a child? How could they honour it in the future when this charade they were playing out in order to find Laura was over? It was absolutely essential for the safety of Henrietta's reputation that the Hetta from Tunbridge Wells should be able to vanish without trace, leaving only Lady Henrietta Cairshaw, who had no connection at all with Lockchain Terrace, who had merely been rusticating with friends for the good of her health. Now she was trying to jeopardise all that.

His mind conjured up hideous visions of a resentful Sarah with a greedy, calculating gentleman friend, arriving at Alnstrop House to blackmail Lord Alnstrop with threats to expose the folly of his sister; or worse, arriving at St Dunstan's Street to threaten Henrietta herself with exposure. She could be bullied and blackmailed. She could be ruined socially forever.

By the time Dane had arrived in view of the grimly huddled little church, and had seen Henrietta, Meggie and Sarah just reaching the porch ahead of him, his anger was out of all proportion.

'Henrietta!'

His voice rang loud across the road as he lengthened his stride towards them. They turned, and he saw Henrietta hand the tiny bundle that was the baby to Sarah, before running over to meet him. He stopped where he was, breathing hard.

'Jonathan! I am *so* glad you are here in time. I wanted you to be here. Did Sam explain? I was determined that poor child should have something to start life with, even if it was no more than the proper gift of a name. But you will stand godfather, won't you? He will be partially named for you, after all, and Sarah is very hopeful!'

Her cheeks were flushed and her eyes bright with pleasure beneath the ridiculous chestnut wig. She was wearing the bonnet with the red cherries, and they made little clacking sounds as they bounced together when she moved. She laid a hand coaxingly on his arm.

'Henrietta, you are being wickedly irresponsible in this.' For some reason he could not explain his anger was further inflamed as he looked down at her. 'Did I not tell you not to get involved? Can you not see how you lay yourself open to discovery if you do this? Has it not occurred to you that you cannot continue to sponsor this child without risking Sarah's discovery of who you really are? And do you seriously think she will not talk of that discovery? That it might not lay you or your brother open to threats of blackmail? And if your signature is recorded as a godparent of this child in this church, have you thought that that will give incontrovertible proof to any mischief-maker who wishes to exploit your folly? Have *any* of these truths occurred to you for your consideration before you started out on this crack-brained scheme?' He paused, still breathing hard, glaring at her.

Henrietta, her pleasure at seeing him instantly erased, glared back, pursing her mouth shut and defiantly tilting her chin a little higher. As it happened, none of those things had occurred to her at all. She had thought of nothing but the baby's welfare; her concern was all for that. Strangely, she seemed almost to have forgotten that her life in Lockchain Terrace was a charade to be undertaken with the greatest of discretion. The unwelcome truths put before her by Dane gave her a chill of horror. Her glare at him was icy.

'Naturally I have considered all of these things,' she said, coldly furious. 'And naturally I discounted them before the greater need of the child. Must I value some remote possibility of damage to my position of privilege as of greater moment than giving this benefit in life to a child who has so little? What a despicable thought!

'But how like a *Dane* to think that the needs of the poor are of no consequence beside the maintenance of our privilege and comfort! And how like a Dane, too, to think you can order me about as you please, just disposing of women as you see fit, as it suits your convenience! I tell you, Mr Dane, if I choose to give my affection and support to this child, it is certainly no business of yours to stop me, as it is no business of yours what I do in *any* part of my life!'

She was breathing as hard as he now, both gripped by rage. Her eyes sparkled dangerously, and there was a hint of angry tears in them.

'If you have truly considered all that I have pointed out to you, and indeed discarded it as of no importance, then you have far less sense than I credited you with, my girl——'

'I am *not* your girl,' she interjected furiously.

'And as for the rest, don't be a damned fool, Henrietta. You are talking nonsense, and you know it.' He wanted to pick her up and shake some sense into her silly head.

She stared rigidly away from him towards the jumbled, leaning houses of William Street, her mouth tight with barely controlled fury. She could not immediately trust herself to speak. He glanced away from her across the street. A thin man dressed in black had joined the little group in the porch, and was unlocking the door and ushering them in. Sarah was waving to them to come. Henrietta, catching his look, turned and saw them.

'I have nothing more to say to you, sir,' she said, head still high, with a further attempt at icy cool. But her lip quivered. 'I will join my friends now.'

He heard one small, defiant sniff as she turned away.

'Henrietta!'

She ignored him, but she had to wait before crossing the street while a vast brewer's dray rumbled and creaked past the church.

'Henrietta!' He caught her arm.

'Let me go, sir!'

'Henrietta...'

She glared at him and he dropped his hand.

'Are you truly so set on this? Please, Henrietta. Only think. Could not Meggie stand godmother in your stead? The child would be christened, and I could escort you home to await their return. You could assist the child as much as you wish through Meggie, without exposing yourself.'

She looked up at him. His rage had evaporated, but there was no mistaking his concern, the intense concern in those slate-dark eyes. She gave a little shiver, and drew a deep breath. She thought of Sarah, the baby, and the words she had used to the curate yesterday. She laid a hand lightly on his arm.

'I am sorry, Jonathan, but I have to go. I have promised Sarah. She is frightened of the curate, and needs my support. It was I who arranged it with the curate. He is not an easy man and I wish to be there to see all is done well. But mostly, I promised to the child that I would be there. This is my small gesture to him. I won't break that. You wait back at Mrs Crabbe's. We will not be very long.'

'You are quite set upon this.'

'Yes, I am.'

He stared at her for a long moment, his dark eyes unfathomable. 'Oh, drat you, Henrietta,' he said unchivalrously. 'Come along, then. We'll be late.' Taking her arm, he escorted her firmly over the road.

'You do not have to do this,' she said.

'I know that,' he replied. With a small, ironic bow he stood aside to allow her to pass by him and into the gloomy entrance of the church.

Mr Smith was waiting impatiently by the font, listening to the plaintive mewlings from the wrapped bundle of baby with his nose pinched with distaste. He took out his watch and studied it pointedly as Dane and Henrietta entered. Her words yesterday, Hetta reflected, might have stirred something within that shrivelled soul, but they had not changed the nature of the man.

'Good morning, sir,' said Dane, coolly. 'I apologise if we have delayed you. No doubt you are busy. Do, please, proceed. We are all assembled.'

Mr Smith regarded this newcomer with dark suspicion, but, as no explanation was offered for Dane's presence, he proceeded, drawing his own dark conclusions.

Jonathan stood a little back from the group, watching. He could see, now that his eyes were becoming accustomed to the dusky interior, that this must once have been a charming little church. The plain round arches and squat pillars were ornamented only with zig-zag patterns cut into the rough stones, patterns which showed in the dimness as bars of alternating shadow and candle-glow. Looking up, he thought that the vast roof-beams were carved in strange designs, but the candle-light was too dim to distinguish wood from shadow. The smell of centuries of damp and chill hung all about them, twined in candle-smoke, and conjured for him twisted anxious memories of his childhood at Thwayle. He frowned, pushing those old unwanted thoughts back into the recesses of memory.

The candles by the font caught the little group there in a soft circle of gold. The baby, he could see, was dressed in a long white robe, pleated and laced around the bottom, which trailed down over Sarah's arm. It looked more like a lawn shift than a christening gown...and it probably was, he suddenly realised, hastily adapted, by Meggie, no doubt. Over it the child had been wrapped warmly in one of the Kashmir shawls he had given to Henrietta. He gave a small, wry smile.

He watched Henrietta's face. She was following earnestly the words of the priest, looking from his face to that of the baby. The words being spoken surfaced into his thoughts '...steadfast in faith, joyful through hope, rooted in charity...' That was Henrietta, he thought. 'Rooted in charity'. All those foolhardy impulsive acts into which she flung herself wholeheartedly, with no thought for her own well-being, all were rooted in charity. All came from that immense capacity for caring, and caring especially for those less fortunate than herself. She might drive him to regularly contemplate with pleasure the prospect of wringing her neck, but... He looked at that intent little face, and the warmth of his response startled him. He found he was smiling. As if she felt his thoughts, she looked across at him and for a long moment their eyes held—across the font, the candles and the tiny whimpering child.

They were all glad to leave the church when the little service was over, for the clammy chill had crept steadily up through their feet from the stone-slabbed floor. Some way through the service two old women had sidled in through a small side door. They had crept close to see the pouring of the water, and had muttered together in complaint at the small protesting wail set up by the baby Richard on receiving his name. It was not a loud enough shout to let out the devils in him; there would be trouble with that one, for sure, they said. Their gloomy muttered prognostications formed a background chorus throughout the remainder of the service, until they sidled, complaining now about the cold, back through their little door.

Mr Smith seemed only too pleased to usher them all firmly off the premises. He had not enjoyed the pointed look the opinionated female in the cherry bonnet had given him as he read the words from the tenth chapter of St Mark, and no one had given him an adequate explanation of who she, or the arrogant-looking man, might be. He could think of only one way in which such a man might be involved with such a baby, and he was outraged at the entire procedure. No amount of standing godfather and making fine-sounding promises could alter that. He had been a fool to allow himself to be persuaded.

Only Henrietta and Sarah looked entirely happy as they emerged into the thin sunlight outside. Meggie strode off ahead to make up the fire in readiness for them, and Dane's own face was thoughtful, but Hetta's glowed with a great contentment as she tucked the Kashmir shawl close about her tiny new godson, and held him close inside her pelisse.

It was Sarah's delight that most surprised Dane. Released from the overawing church and priest, she could not stop talking and laughing.

'Gor lumme, but we done 'im proper, eh, 'Etta? We done 'im good an' proper! I jist wish my pa could've seen it, 'im 'avin' 'is name, an' all. We really done 'im proper, didn't we, 'Etta? Little mite. 'Ooever woulda thought it!'

She could hardly contain her delight, and it seemed to Jonathan most unexpected, until he reflected that this was probably her first tentative foray into the accepted world, the recognised world, the world of regulation and authority, in which she had never before gained even a toehold. She had never lived within society, always without it. He was suddenly very proud of Henrietta, that she had seen how to give this morsel of self-respect to the girl.

Sarah was certainly looking much better than when he had first seen her. Her hair was glossier, her face fuller, she stood more upright. He knew of her addiction to Blue Ruin, knew she would probably never change her way of life, and held out little real hope for her future, but he knew also that her friendship with Hetta had much improved her life at present, and he was glad that they could thus repay in kind the help that she had once given Laura. Dane strongly suspected that much of the coal and food that he paid to be supplied for Henrietta and Meggie found its way across the landing to Sarah and the baby. In fact, knowing Henrietta he was certain of it.

Back at Lockchain Terrace they toasted the baby with champagne.

'He deserves the best,' Henrietta announced, looking defiantly at Dane, but he merely raised his glass, whether to her or the baby she was uncertain.

They drank a few more toasts, then ate a splendid cold luncheon sent across in honour of the occasion by Miss Perkins, who had conceived an admiration for Dane every bit as intense as her nephew's.

Afterwards Jonathan did his godparental duty, while telling himself wryly what a fool he was, and placed a gold coin carefully into each of his godson's clenching fists. Sarah was most impressed, and thanked him profusely, then hastily rescued the coins from her small son. 'Just in case,' she said, 'the little toad should take it into 'is 'ead to swaller 'em, like!'

Thus it was mid-afternoon before the hopeful rivals to the Bow Street Runners left Lockchain Terrace in the search for Eleanor Street. In fact, although the streets were busy, it took not twenty minutes to find Eleanor Street, and pull up outside number twelve. The street was narrow, lined with tall thin houses which gave the appearance of gathering in their skirts about them, clinging primly to their last vestiges of respectability against the encroaching waves of vulgar poverty.

The woman at number twelve was suspicious, but not willingly unhelpful. She just had no help to give. She had lived in the house for four years, and that was the longest stay of any of the present occupants. No, she had never heard of anyone called Laura, it wasn't a name you came across that often, was it? Lotte, who had rooms upstairs, was the sort of girl, she sniffed, who might know of this Laura.

Lotte, when applied to, had come lolling down the stairs looking sultry, inviting, and, as Henrietta remarked tartly, chronically unwashed; but although she had ogled Jonathan shamelessly, she had had no information about anyone named Laura. Jonathan left his card with the woman, and Lotte pouted and promised to apply her mind constantly to any problem that might please him, but although it was just possible that someone in the street might remember her, it was not likely, and the Dane and Cairshaw investigating team returned to Lockchain Terrace despondent.

Later, sitting opposite each other at the mahogany table, the two candles between them casting long moving shadows over the red velvet of the armchairs, the jewelled elephant, and the demurely flowered chintz bed-hangings, they talked across heaped platefuls of another of Miss Perkins' triumphs. It was a ragout, steaming hot—and made especially to please that nice Mr Dane, 'because he could do with a bit more flesh on him when all's said and done!'—and they began to think determinedly once again.

'It is absurd for us to sound so defeated,' Dane was saying earnestly to Henrietta, leaning towards her, and making little gestures with his forkful of ragout to emphasise his points 'just because we've met with one blank. We know so much more of Laura's life after she arrived in London now, and we can make far more intelligent guesses about new places to start searching again. For example, we know she chose to go to the Haymarket to work, that that was where she met Blanding. So that is an obvious place to begin asking...'

Hetta let him talk, content to listen, nod, eat her ragout, and watch him. She watched his hands, always moving as he spoke, holding their own little conversation in gesture. They were lean and sinewy—long-fingered, strong, still tanned from the Indian sun, with the nails cut short and workmanlike. They were hands that would not shirk hard work, she thought, and doubtless had not shirked it in the past.

A vision of Justin's hand came into her mind, long-fingered also, and strong—that she knew and she shuddered a little—but white, and lightly scented, the nails always over-long, for he liked to trail his hands elegantly over the arm of his chair. She pushed the image of those hands away, suddenly repulsed at ever having thought she loved such a man. Flushing a little, she brought her thoughts back to Jonathan.

His lashes, thick and dark, shadowed his eyes in the candle-light until he looked up and she could see the points of flame reflected in the grey. Shadows moved in the hollows of his cheeks as he talked, and around his narrow, fine-boned nose. She watched his mouth, and the little quirk at the corners when something secretly amused him. He was watching her watching him.

'I preferred it a little longer,' she said, evasively, almost randomly.

He looked his query.

'Your hair.' He had had his hair cut short, and the paler sun-bleached brown had gone. 'I preferred it as it was, a little longer.'

He smiled. 'I had not thought you would have noticed. But I too prefer hair longer. I prefer your hair as it was when I first met you. A mad riot of black curls spangled over with raindrops.'

For a long moment they looked at each other, then Henrietta dropped her eyes. Her memories of that night still troubled her.

'I am sorry for what I said to you this morning,' she said, anxious to change the direction of her thoughts. 'To be truthful, I had not once considered any of those possibilities you put before me, and you have frightened me a little. I cannot think that Sarah would ever knowingly wish to harm me, but I can understand your concern. Certainly I would not wish to do anything that might bother my brother, for I love him dearly and would hate to cause him distress. I will *try* in future to be more discreet! As for the rest that I said, well, I *am* sorry. I do not *really* believe it to be true, or we would not be searching for Laura together. At least,' she amended, and chuckled at him, 'I don't believe it much!'

He regarded her from under his lashes, but did not respond.

'I owe you an apology also,' he said, after a few moments, 'for I should not have berated you as I did, out there in the street. I'm not surprised you were angry. But I'm afraid you will continue to find me an interfering Dane, disposing of his women as he sees fit. For while you are involved with me in the search for my cousin, and living here where you require my protection, I shall continue to take every interest in your safety and welfare, whether you wish it or not.' He looked at her, a hint of severity in his eyes. 'And *nothing* will shake me from that, Lady Henrietta Cairshaw.'

'Well, thank you, Mr Jonathan Dane,' she said. '*If* you insist, I shall *endeavour* to accept your interest uncomplainingly! Though I must say,' she went on, 'that I cannot be sorry we held the baptism service, whatever your misgivings, for I was so pleased both for Sarah and for the child. And I have not yet thanked you for standing as godfather. Knowing how you felt, it was noble of you!'

He shrugged. 'If any awkward questions are ever asked, it is possible that my presence can be used to offer some explanation for yours,' he said, somewhat obscurely. 'It was the two ghastly old crones who amused me, muttering gloom and doom from the murky shadows like a Greek chorus——'

'No,' Hetta interrupted, laughing, 'they were perfectly cast for Macbeth's witches, and I swear their cauldron was bubbling away behind that little side door with the third of their number stirring busily. I was glad to get poor baby Richard safely away from their clutches. Who knows what new ingredients they were after! They certainly did not look like the traditional fairy godmothers bringing blessings to the feast!'

'If you are right,' said Dane, amused, 'I can only wish they had had the forethought to bring their bubbling cauldron a little closer to the font. Perhaps it would have taken some of the chill from the air!'

'Yes, indeed! Oh dear, *wouldn't* Mr Smith be distressed to hear us talk so? *Such* a proper little man, so miserably narrow and prim. I am ashamed to say I was extremely rude to him yesterday when he was on the point of refusing Sarah's baby, as being an unsuitable candidate for his church.'

Dane chuckled. 'My turning up today certainly did not improve his view of the situation. His looks made it quite plain that he considered my involvement with this brat to be far more than just godparental, and his opinion of the entire situation, and the future of my soul in particular, appeared gloomy!'

'No! Truly? I had not realised! How funny!'

'I am *so* pleased it affords you some amusement! While he is no doubt calling down imprecations upon the heads of all sinners, and me in particular!'

'Well, it is amusing, you have to admit! When I think of how fiercely you endeavoured to persuade me to dissociate myself from the whole business. Then for you to come to protect my good name and then become cast as the villain of the piece... And consider!' Hetta's face was brimming with laughter. 'If he thinks that you stood godfather because you had in fact fathered the child, whatever do you think he thought of me, who fought to have the service take place, and then stood as godmother? Perhaps he considers that we are jointly the parents of the poor little scrap, and are wickedly abandoning him to a feckless foster mother for our own pleasure-loving convenience?'

She laughed; then, looking at him, thought at first that she had shocked him with her speculations. But he smiled a long, slow smile.

'Had we in fact done so,' he said, sipping his wine and regarding her over the top of the glass, 'it would indeed have been a wondrous begetting. A year ago, at the requisite time, we were half a world apart. I do not think that even *I*, descendant of all those lusty Dane grandfathers, have the prowess to beget sons over the span of continents!'

She had not shocked him. Despite his insistent concern over *her* reputation and the proprieties, he was not a man with a narrow, conventional soul. She could talk to him as freely as she could to Robert or John. In many ways he had taken the place of her brothers in her life.

'Oh, sir, I would not mention these little imperfections in your prowess if I were you,' she said demurely. 'They might become talked of, and a Dane of Thwayle has a certain reputation to keep up!'

He gave a laugh. 'You are an outrageous minx, Henrietta,' said Jonathan.

CHAPTER TWELVE

IT WAS almost a week before Jonathan visited Lockchain Terrace again. He had business in town that he had been neglecting and that had now become pressing.

He also had an increasing number of invitations to the Wanhope household, to dine and to make up a party when they went out to the theatre or opera. Mr Wanhope, in particular, seemed to be regarding his suit with favour. Suddenly alarmed at being seen so frequently escorting Esther, Jonathan endeavoured to excuse himself, though he found he could not give himself a satisfactory reason why this should be. Only a few weeks previously, to be with her constantly had been all his desire. Now he hung back, resenting the feeling that he was being pushed into a relationship for which he was perhaps not ready, despite his previous proposals. However, his protestations that he was too busy, was trespassing too much on their time, had other engagements, were swept genially aside by Mr Wanhope, who patted his shoulder in a paternal way, and insisted Dane be with them. He could only take comfort from the fact that Lord Glenby was of the party almost as often as he was himself.

Jonathan, in addition, had been visiting the haunts of the London prostitutes, especially around the Haymarket, but his enquiries had so far brought him only suspicion, abuse, raucous jests and exhaustion from lack of sleep. He had hoped to go back to Hetta with some news he had discovered for himself, something to surprise and please her, so they could continue to follow the trail, two detectives working together. But he found nothing, so each day he waited, hoping that that night's search, walking the streets after he had seen Esther safely home with her father, would bring him some news of his cousin.

Furthermore, he was, though this was not a fact that he examined closely, somewhat disturbed at his feelings for Henrietta. He had never met a woman like her, one with whom he could be so free, so relaxed, could feel so at home. His keenness to see her bothered him. He had felt initially that this masquerade would help her, that he was assisting her through a time of intense misery and depression. Now that was changed. He turned to her as a friend. Yes, just as a friend, he assured himself, for it was certain that, even though she might be recovering from her entanglement with his cousin, Justin—and the thought of that relationship gave him an unexpected pain—she still detested all the family of the Danes of Thwayle. That knowledge made him wary of this new joy he surprised in himself at the prospect of seeing her. That, and his own uncertainty, made him stay away.

Hetta was disappointed at his non-appearance, despite receiving a note explaining he had pressing business and would call as soon as he was free to do so. She spent much of the time caring for baby Richard—Dickon, as she affectionately called him—worrying over his thin body, lack-lustre eyes and persistent nagging cough. She kept him wrapped warmly in a drawer by the fire, and fed him milk through the clay pipe.

'You are a fool to waste your time on him, Miss Hetta,' Meggie said disapprovingly. 'He'll not survive, and then you'll break your heart over him. You shouldn't get involved so. That Sarah, she's only using you for her own convenience.'

But Meggie was always ready enough to wash his clothes and warm his milk, and, when Hetta teased her over this, would sniff and grunt, 'Well if you will insist on having the child here, the least we can do is care for him properly. It's more than the poor mite gets from that feckless mother of his.'

Sarah was certainly out a good deal. She had tried her best to get Hetta to accompany her to the White Cocks, or even to the King's Head just down the road, but Hetta was adamant. She would not again risk exposing herself as she had on that dreadful night at the White Cocks when she'd met Em'ly. She still shuddered at the thought of that man. Sarah could not understand her refusals at all.

'Your Jonathan ain't 'ere, so come on out and enjoy yerself. Meggie can watch the child. Go on, jist fer a couple o' glasses, jist fer a mouthful o' Blue Ruin. Or a jug o' that shrub you said you was so took with.'

But Hetta reiterated her story, that Jonathan would kill her if he ever heard she had ventured out to such a place without him. When she mentioned his generosity, and how she couldn't risk offending him, Sarah gave in, reluctantly—a respect for hard cash she understood—and went off to enjoy herself with more convivial souls at the tavern.

Hetta also met the other occupants of the house, always hopeful that someone else might remember Laura, but she had no success. The two girls who occupied the floor below, Dora and Collette, both worked in the milliner's across the road, and only supplemented their income on the streets when driven by necessity. But they were both too young to be of any help to Hetta; they seemed hardly more than children. And as for the young man with rooms on the ground floor—a clerk in a solicitor's office—he deemed all the females in the house quite beneath his notice, spoke frequently to Mrs Crabbe of moving on to somewhere better as soon as he was able, and refused to speak to Hetta at all. Mrs Crabbe, by contrast, was happy to gossip for as long as she could keep Hetta by her, but she had nothing to say to the purpose, and Hetta found her chatter tedious in the extreme.

In fact, Hetta was realising, a little ashamed, she found all these people dull. The novelty of the company of people so different from herself was fast evaporating. She pitied them, and cared unexpectedly deeply about what became of them, but they could not interest and amuse her, and she found she longed for lively, intelligent conversation.

She thought wistfully of Alnstrop and of the company of her two brothers, who could always make her laugh, and her sister-in-law, Louisa, with whom she could happily chatter for hours. She even caught herself thinking of Jonathan, who could also be so lively and amusing. Though he *was* merely a Dane, and if he was too busy to call she had no intention of wasting her time thinking of him. Except, of course, that she would like to continue in the search for Laura, to find that elusive lady, and to restore her to her cousin, to the notice of her family, and to her share of the fortune. Then perhaps she, Henrietta, Lady Cairshaw, could move back into more amusing society.

Meggie, to whom these sentiments were voiced, smiled dourly to herself and reflected that at least this whole ridiculous escapade had distracted her mistress entirely from that wastrel Justin, and a good thing too.

Eventually, Jonathan, exhausted and disheartened after almost a week of wasted late nights, was beginning to think that perhaps he should abandon the search for Laura. Sitting gloomily in his club, where such a short time ago he had been so excited to discover from Justin the name and address of Sir Jeremy Blanding, he swirled the brandy morosely around in his glass and contemplated failure. Despite his determined talk to Henrietta when they had last met, it did seem that they had exhausted all the possibilities. Laura had vanished, and there was no way to trace her. He irritably brushed aside the newspaper that had been considerately placed at his elbow, and it fell to the floor.

It was absurd for Henrietta to remain at Lockchain Terrace when no further good could come of it. He would have to go round there and persuade her of that fact. Remembering her previous demonstrations of self-willed obstinacy, however, he found he did not relish the prospect. She had made such an absurdly personal quest of this search for Laura, he knew she would not give up easily. He sighed.

'Dane! Good to see you again, my lad. Why, I've not laid eyes on you since that time in Madras . . . That meal with the poor young lad fresh from England...what was his name...? And the hot peppers... Do you remember?'

It was Buffy Twiley. He was an acquaintance from Dane's childhood years in Thwayle, for the Twiley lands marched with those of the Danes, and he had also sought his fortune in India, and while there had become a friend. After an hour's talk with Buffy, several more brandies, a story concerning his cousin Justin that made him laugh heartily, and more news about his own family than they themselves had given him in years, Jonathan was considerably cheered. He wanted urgently to talk to Henrietta. He had an idea of where to extend their search. It might not bring results, but there was always a chance, and at least he would be doing something. He also wanted to tell her the story about Justin.

Jonathan bade a cheery but hasty farewell to Buffy Twiley, and hurried home to wash and change. The letter he found waiting for him at his lodgings made him laugh, give a cheer that startled Mrs Stockwell, who almost dropped the tray of cold meats she had hurriedly prepared for his luncheon, and gave an added impetus to his new enthusiasm to reach Lockchain Terrace as soon as possible. Ignoring his housekeeper's cry of protest, he waved aside the proffered tray, insisted he would be eating out, and was back on the road the instant he was changed.

Hetta had heard the sound of carriage wheels on the road outside, but she had just been settling Dickon back to sleep in his mahogany drawer, and had not looked out. She was not certain that it was Dane until she heard his footsteps bounding up the stairs. He beat a rapid tattoo on the wood of the door with his knuckles.

'Meggie, see who is at the door, would you?' Hetta called, coolly, and continued to tuck blankets around the tiny sleeping child. She ignored him as he entered, and ignored his cheerful greetings as he handed his hat, coat and cane to Meggie. She took time ensuring the baby was settled just to her liking, then went over to the fire and shifted the kettle into the heat.

'We were about to take a light luncheon and a cup of tea, Mr Dane,' Henrietta said, her tones chilly. 'Would you care to join us? Or are you still too busy to make a long stay?'

Jonathan laughed, and laid a hand lightly on her shoulder. 'I know. I know. I deserve all your strictures. I have neglected you far too long, and I am sorry. But I truly have been busy. I now have a great deal of news to give you, and, yes, I am famished. I could demolish any number of light luncheons, or heavy ones, come to that. Threaten me with any food you have in the house! Oh, come, Henrietta, *don't* scowl at me so! Have I offended you so direly?' He flung himself extravagantly on to one knee before her. 'There, I make my apologies *abjectly*. Do forgive me, feed me and listen to what I have to tell you!'

He sounded so happy and looked so absurd that Hetta could not continue her chilly hauteur. She laughed. 'Do get up, you fool! You look ridiculous!' she said. 'How can I be affronted and keep you at a chilly distance when you behave so absurdly. It really is not fair. Sit down, do, and Meggie shall feed us, won't you, Meggie dear, while you tell us all this news you are so big with, Mr Jonathan Dane.'

He settled back into the armchair opposite her, his face alight with amusement. 'To tell the truth, I have had a wretched week, doing a great many things I had rather not be doing, with a great many people I had rather not be with, and, despite walking the streets around the Haymarket every night until dawn, achieving nothing but exhaustion. I got no news of Laura at all. To tell you the truth...'

He smiled at Hetta, who, as usual, had curled up in the chair with her feet tucked under her, the chestnut wig flung aside when she sat down, and was running idle fingers through her black curls. The dress she was wearing, a hideous bright red taffeta with large patterns of exotic birds in shades of green, was low-necked and tight, pushing up the white curves of her breasts. She looked every bit as seductive as her role demanded.

'I would trust that you always do, sir!' she said, laughing at him.

'Do what?' He found he had completely lost the thread of what he had been saying.

'Tell me the truth, of course. Come on, Jonathan, do give me this news you are so excited about. I shall die waiting.'

'I am sorry. Yes. To tell truth, I had concluded that the entire search was fruitless. I was steeling myself to face your undoubted wrath'—she laughed quietly at him, and he grinned back wryly—'and tell you that I wished you to return to your home. I was going to waste my time no longer, and was going to persuade you not to waste yours. You should know that I was sitting thinking these gloomy thoughts at White's, over a comforting brandy or two. Then, amazingly, a friend, Buffy Twiley, whose lands run with ours up at Thwayle, so he is well versed in the sagas of our disreputable family, appeared before me. He told me a story about Justin that made me laugh a great deal, and reminded me of someone who might help in our search. I rushed home to change before coming to visit you——'

'Why, *truly* I am honoured, sir!' Hetta remarked demurely, but he ignored her, intent on the climax of his tale.

'And waiting at my lodgings I found this letter! The very one we have been waiting for! So which do you want first, the story, the idea, or the letter?'

He was enjoying himself. It was a long time since he had felt so cheerful. Perhaps it was the mellowing effect of all those brandies with Buffy!

'Oh, the letter!' cried Henrietta. 'It must be the letter. What is it we have been waiting for? Oh, is it from Sir Jeremy? Has he remembered? Do tell!'

She was bouncing on the chair with impatience, reaching out her hand. She looked so desirable, leaning over to him, her face alive with laughing impatience, her breasts catching the pink of the firelight. He was suddenly acutely aware of the demurely curtained bed in the corner behind him. He knew how soft it was; he had chosen it himself.

'A kiss will get you the letter,' he said with a laugh, though his voice was husky. 'You must not get out of practice in your role as my doxy!'

'The impudence of the man!' Henrietta said. But she had jumped up, planted a peck of a kiss on his cheek and tweaked the letter from his hand before he had time to respond. For Meggie, just then, brought in plates of bread, cheese, meats and fruit from the back room where she had been preparing them, and called them to the table. Henrietta was crying out, 'Listen, Meggie, Sir Jeremy has remembered! Laura's friend from Eleanor Street was called, of all things, Magnificent Millie!' And Dane reflected ruefully that chance had saved him from what would undoubtedly have been a brandy-induced folly. He went over to eat.

'Magnificent Millie!' Hetta was laughing again as they ate. 'No wonder poor Sir Jeremy so obviously remembered her as of statuesque proportions! She must have been special to achieve such a name! Do you think we can possibly trace her?'

'We can certainly try. She is the person who knew Laura the most recently of all those we have discovered. She may still be working in that area. She may even be known to Sarah. We can certainly try.'

'The Dane and Cairshaw investigators are once more on the trail!' Hetta remarked with satisfaction.

'Indeed they are.' He smiled.

'So now,' said Hetta. 'Tell me this story about the despicable Justin. Will I laugh? If so, it will be the first time anything about that man has amused me for a very long time.'

'Ah, well, I think you might.' Jonathan disposed cheerfully of a large forkful of beef. 'This is what Buffy told me. Firstly, do you remember this precious fortune of Great-Grandfather's, that all "The grandfathers", uncles and cousins had hung around Thwayle waiting to inherit?'

Hetta nodded.

'Well, by the time he reached ninety-six and finally died—it didn't exist! Every penny of it had gone in paying off the debts that worthless lot had accumulated! But Great-Grandfather never said a word. He kept them all sitting up there in Thwayle, forced by the terms of the will to be civil to each other, and all the time it was for nothing! How it must have amused him, it was just the sort of thing that would appeal to the cantankerous old curmudgeon. I had to laugh. Buffy said all of Yorkshire was laughing.

'No wonder they never sent word of it out to me in India, and by then Buffy was already back in Britain, and he never wrote a letter in his life, so I had no way of finding out. No wonder, too, that the remaining grandfathers and half the uncles followed the old man to the grave in a matter of months. There was nothing left to live for! Apparently, when my dear cousin Bentley came into the title, he had to sell part of the estates in order to make the remainder viable.' Dane chuckled, and reapplied himself to his food.

'That is all very good,' said Hetta, 'and it is just what your worthless family deserved, so naturally I share your unfamilial delight at their disappointment. But where does that leave Justin?'

'Poor!' Dane said, and laughed. 'It leaves him with not a feather to fly with, not a bean in his pocket, not a groat to call his own. Thus...' he gave a generous shrug, a slice of bread in one hand, and his knife, a lump of butter stuck precariously on the end, in the other '...thus the imperative search for an heiress.'

'But I knew nothing of this,' Hetta said.

'Naturally not. Justin would be the last to mention it, and Bentley would keep mum to save the family face. The Danes had kept so much to the north recently that they and their doings have not been of much interest to the tattlemongers here in town. Which is why Justin could pass himself off as he did.'

'Certainly I never suspected his affairs were so bad. He always appeared beforehand with the world, and indeed made quite a show. He was never rigged out in anything but the best.'

'He wouldn't be. Justin always liked to look the fine gentleman. But it was all on tick, creditors dunning him all the time, I dare say. So, of course,' Jonathan said, 'he found your fortune as well as your face extremely appealing.'

'Until he discovered that my fortune was only a respectable competence,' Hetta continued for him, bitterly, 'then the face of his gullible little heiress from Lincolnshire was suddenly much more desirable.'

'Now listen to the funny part of Buffy's story,' Dane said. 'She *isn't* an heiress at all! Justin has been taken at his own game!'

'What *do* you mean?'

'Just that! She, by all accounts, has indeed come from Lincolnshire, but she has no more fortune than Sarah here. She and her mother were determined to catch one though! They rigged themselves out as fine as they could, and put it about that the girl had been left a hundred thousand by some rich uncle. Justin, rigged out as fine as fivepence, and implying in every sentence that he had a tidy fortune of his own and was about to step into the title any day, fell for the girl's story and snapped her up! She thought she was next best thing to being rich Lady Grimsett of Thwayle. He thought he was made for life. I suppose they were both desperate, or they would have found out more before tying the knot. But it was done, as you know, and they are both busily regretting it! From what Buffy has heard, the girl is a shrew, and the mother a perfect harpy! No wonder Justin spends all his time lurking behind a newspaper at his club! I can almost find it in me to be sorry for him!'

Dane did not look sorry at the fate of his cousin. He looked very amused. Henrietta began to laugh. She put down her fork and laughed until tears ran on to her cheeks.

'Oh, poor Justin!' she gasped eventually. 'Poor, poor, very poor Justin!' And she giggled again. 'But do you know, I almost feel sorry for him too, and that is some sort of miracle! I never imagined I would feel a tender thought for that man ever again! But, however will he manage with a young wife to support? Poor girl, I dare say she got her just deserts, but I can find it in me to pity her. Justin is a devilishly attractive man, but he has the devil's own temper too when he is crossed.' She paused, and thought for a moment. Then, 'Perhaps you could do something to help them both?'

Jonathan looked at Hetta in astonishment. 'Do you truly mean that?'

She nodded, and looked down, embarrassed. 'I don't seem to need my hatred for Justin any longer. It has gone. I despise what he did to me, and I despise your family for what they did to you, and most especially, to Laura, but I would not wish a new cycle of misery on Justin's young wife. Not if you could help them.'

'Lady Henrietta Cairshaw, you are an amazing woman. You continue to astound me! To please you, I will certainly consider offering assistance to Justin, for I am well able to do so, but what he would say to an offer of help from one whom he has always referred to as "little snivelling Johnny-boy" I cannot imagine.'

'I can,' said Hetta drily. 'He'd say, "Thank you, and how much can you spare?"!' She took an apple and began to quarter it neatly. 'And now tell me,' she continued, 'what was your idea?'

'Oh, that. Perhaps it will not be necessary now that we have Magnificent Millie to hunt for. It is just that when Buffy was talking he happened to mention our old nanny. I hadn't thought of her as being of any importance, for I early outgrew her attentions. But I suddenly remembered that she and Laura had always been very close. Bentley mentioned to me when I saw him that Great-Grandfather had pensioned her off and she had moved back south and taken a cottage somewhere in Sussex, in the village she had come from as a child. If Laura had needed someone to run to, it is just possible she might have run to Nanny Hedges. I thought I would ride down into Sussex and find out.'

'Not ride,' Henrietta said, 'drive!'

'Why, I thought——?'

'Dear Jonathan, I have to come with you! This is *our* search, after all. You cannot follow up such a promising clue alone, it is too unfair. Why, Laura might be peacefully living there keeping chickens, and then you would discover her without me. It would be too bad! Take the carriage, and I shall come with you. You would enjoy the company, now, wouldn't you? And if I am left to moulder between these four walls much longer I swear I shall be making my way back to the bridge. I can be ready whenever you wish. What do you say?'

He looked at her eager face. 'It would not do, Henrietta. I shall have to spend at least one night away from home. I could not have you with me.'

'Oh, don't be such a prude, Jonathan. I am a respectable widow, remember, not a green girl, and anyway I shall have Meggie as my chaperon and you as my escort. What could be more proper? And our purpose to pay a visit to an ageing retainer! Even Robert could not object. When shall we go?'

He looked at her again. She was laughing at him, knowing he would give in. He shrugged, stifling his misgivings. 'Friday?' he queried, resignedly.

'Friday it shall be,' she said.

CHAPTER THIRTEEN

FRIDAY morning dawned cold but bright, the thin autumn sunshine sliding long fingers of pale gold over the tiled roof-tops, through the smoke belching or wisping from the red-brick chimney-stacks, and into the shivering shadowy recesses of Lockchain Terrace. Meggie flung back the red velvet curtains on the top floor of number three, and the sunlight slid on to the bed where Henrietta lay, propping herself up on the mound of white pillows, her black curls springing disorderly about her head, while she lazily rubbed her eyes.

'Oh, how I hate early mornings!' she exclaimed, yawning. 'This expedition had better be worth waking for at such an ungodly hour!'

Jonathan had insisted on the early start. He wanted to ensure that it was only necessary to spend one night away from home. His desire to be fair to Henrietta's wish to accompany him had warred with his sense of propriety, instilled all those years ago by Grandmama Alathea, and had produced this compromise: that they make the trip as brief as possible, and stay at a quiet inn, well off the busier roads.

'That will only make our business seem the more furtive!' Hetta had teased him. 'We should do whatever we wish with a flourish, and consign all our critics to the devil!'

'Along with your reputation,' he had retorted, 'Will you never learn a little sense and caution? Anyone would think you were hell-bent on ruining your name at the earliest opportunity.'

He remained adamant that she would conduct herself as he wished. She smiled into her cup of chocolate, and nibbled at her toast. He had also insisted on demure propriety of dress. She was to travel as nobody's doxy, but as Lady Henrietta Cairshaw, with adequate baggage, the closed carriage, and every proper attention.

'Yes, Mr Dane,' she had submitted primly, 'though it is a role I have almost forgotten how to play, accustomed as I am to acting as your fancy-piece from the *demi-monde*!'

She selected a travelling dress of fine blue woollen cloth, and a rather severe cut, that she thought would suit his notions of propriety, and packed a simple sprigged muslin for the evening, with one of his Kashmir shawls against the draughts that would doubtless pervade this obscure inn where they were to spend the night. Meggie, ever practical, heated bricks by the fire to wrap at their feet in the carriage. She had no faith in a man to remember such a detail, nor in the English weather to make their journey comfortable.

By eight o'clock they were packed and ready, pelissed, bonneted and elegantly charming. Dane, impressed, was able to escort them straight down to the carriage and, paying off the disappointed Samuel, who had hoped to have charge of the horses for the morning, they set out directly, heading for Westminster Bridge, and the Brighton road.

'Now only see, Meggie,' remarked Hetta, settling herself back comfortably on the maroon velvet squabs and arranging the rug Jonathan offered her gratefully over her knees. 'There *are* hot bricks provided! How could you possibly doubt that a man who could think to provide coal in our yard and preserves in our cupboard would overlook a necessity like hot bricks for our feet! What little faith you have!' She snuggled her feet on to the welcome warmth, for despite the sun the air was still sharply chill.

Meggie sniffed an unwilling approval. 'No harm to have extra, they'll keep their heat longer. I dare say it was your housekeeper thought to put them in?'

'You wrong me, Meggie,' Jonathan smiled. 'I ordered them myself.'

'Well, there's a deal more sense in your head than in that of that cousin of yours, that I can say,' she grudgingly admitted, and, tucking her own rug about herself, concentrated her attention on the passing houses, and the fashions of those few people of ton already abroad.

Henrietta smiled at Jonathan. 'I dare say it is really Mr Joshua Priestley I have to thank for my hot brick!'

He looked momentarily puzzled, then laughed. 'I dare say. It is all his "careful attention to the fine details", isn't it? What an excellent memory you have. I had forgotten I had told you of him.'

He settled back to amuse her with more stories of Joshua Priestley, and his life in India, tactfully distracting her and making her laugh as they crossed the bridge and made their way down to the Kennington turnpike.

'It seems an age since we came down this way to visit Sir Jeremy,' Hetta remarked, poking her head out of the window to discover the delay at the turnpike gate. A red-faced man was arguing the cost of a ticket for his cart-load of vegetables, but, subdued by the combined verbal assaults of the gatekeeper and Hudgell, Dane's coachman, he finally paid up as requested and they were able to purchase their own ticket and pass on through.

She sat back in her seat. 'Imagine him reflecting on his misspent youth and suddenly recollecting the name of the amazingly proportioned Magnificent Millie! Then having to furtively write his letter and smuggle it out without the knowledge of his wife! Poor man! It was brave of him to bother.'

'Oh, come now. I see no reason for him to be furtive in his own private correspondence. A man can write to whomever he wishes, about whatever he wishes, he doesn't need the permission of his wife!'

Hetta chuckled. 'There speaks a Dane! Try telling that to Sir Jeremy! I saw the look he gave that door to check if he was safe to speak! It was easy to see who rules that household, no matter how far he removed himself from his in-laws! I bet he had the devil's own job to explain who we were, too, when he was cross-examined later! He was a pleasant man, but I doubt he has a ready wit.'

'You paint a gloomy view of marriage, Henrietta.'

'Oh, no.' She smiled. 'Only some marriages.'

Brixton village, and the long pull up Brixton Hill, were past, and it was not long before Streatham, and the turning to Blanding's house, were also behind them. The road was clear over Streatham Common and they were able to make good time down into Croydon. They changed horses at the King's Head in Market Street. Nowhere was as busy as it would be at the height of summer, when a flood of traffic used the road on the way to Brighton, or the quieter Worthing, and the inn yard was quiet, except for themselves and a local farmer with his gig.

'Let's have some refreshment,' Henrietta urged, eager to be out of the coach and smelling the cleaner country air.

'Is it wise, Henrietta, to be seen so near town, when all your friends believe you to be rusticating?'

But Jonathan's doubts went unattended. Henrietta had already flung open the door and, without waiting for Hudgell to lower the steps, had jumped down. She put her head back in through the doorway. 'Dearest Jonathan, do stop worrying and grumping. Come and entertain me royally. There is nobody here but us, nor likely to be. Come, Meggie.'

Like an eager, busy sheepdog she chivvied them inside, and if the entertainment was not royal, at least there was steaming fresh coffee and new-baked cakes set out in the comfortable parlour.

Hetta, whose spirits had risen with every mile between them and her restrictive world of Lockchain Terrace, went over to Jonathan and laid an appeasing hand on his arm. She looked up at him. 'Don't be angry with me,' she said. 'See how comfortable this is, and you cannot deny it is welcome. You are like my brother, Robert. You worry too much!'

'I have every sympathy with your brother Robert!' he said bitterly. 'Any man having dealings with you must worry too much! How old was he when he first had charge of you? Fifteen? I wonder the poor man retains his sanity!'

Henrietta only chuckled and patted his arm lightly. 'But only think how tedious life will be without me! Once we find Laura and you return to your regular haunts and I to mine.'

'Tedious! Blissfully peaceful, I should suspect!' He felt an odd pang, though, at this contemplation of the end of their association. 'I trust we will remain friends, however, when that time comes?' He spoke lightly, and was surprised at the serious look she gave him.

'I don't know,' she said slowly. 'I don't know.'

'Why? Why do you say that? Because I am a Dane? Surely that has not prevented our friendship until now?'

She shrugged, and gave a little smile. 'You will be too busy spending time with your beautiful Esther to miss our friendship,' she said lightly. 'You have neglected her too much over this, she deserves your time when it is over.' She turned away to Meggie. 'Have you finished? Then let us be on our way. Come, Mr Dane,' she said, taking his arm as they crossed the yard to the waiting coach. 'This is our day out. Let's talk only of cheerful things today!'

The road was becoming increasingly beautiful as they left Croydon and pressed on towards Godstone Corner.

Hetta realised for the first time how much of autumn had passed her by while she had remained restricted to the treeless streets around Mrs Crabbe's house. The woods here were every shade of russet, gold and brown, only the clumps of hollies and yews standing out starkly dark green, looking almost black among the garish livery of their brethren. Crisp dry leaves scuffed and flew under hoofs and wheels as they passed, sometimes drifting so deep they whirled up and into the open carriage window, scattering over the three occupants. Hetta laughed, and refused to shut the window. The sun was strong now, the sky a high arc of bird's egg blue, all the countryside bright and tempting.

'It is intolerable to be cooped up in the coach on such a day, Jonathan. Let's ride. Surely we can hire horses? What do you say?' She watched him, her eyes bright with amusement, waiting to argue him out of his doubts, convince him she could ride quite adequately in her travelling dress, that she would do nothing to alarm him! To her surprise, after regarding her lazily for some moments, his head resting back on the squabs, he gave her a slow smile, that particular smile that so reminded her of Justin at his most attractively seductive, except that Jonathan's held more genuine amusement.

'I should enjoy that very much,' he said, instantly deflating all her arguments. 'I believe we could get some good gallops over Earlswood Common. I shall enquire about horses at Red Hill.'

'Thank you,' was all the reply she could manage, and his smile widened to a grin. 'Detestable man! You knew I had all my arguments marshalled to shoot you down!'

He laughed. 'Then you cannot expect me to stand forever in the firing line!'

'You don't think it wildly unsuitable?'

'I think it will be excellent exercise for you! I am well able to see that your travelling dress will suffice as a habit, that Meggie can undoubtedly clean it for you if it becomes muddied, and that over the common we can ride discreetly away from the main highway.'

'I had not thought of that,' Hetta confessed.

'So I suspected. But *I* had, and with you, a man must learn nimble wits and the art of compromise!'

Hetta was not at all sure that she liked to be so competently managed, and by a man who could look at her in just that way, but she merely smiled, and enquired how far he thought it might be to Red Hill.

They stopped at a small inn near the bottom of the hill, and the landlord, his custom slack, was happy to hire them two hacks, one, a placid-looking grey, guaranteed suitable for a lady, the other a more showy bay.

'Leave them at Horley, if you please, at the Chequers. I've a man going over there tomorrow. He can bring them back.' With the cheering clink of coin in his pocket the man retired back into the tap.

They walked the horses companionably up the steep hill behind the coach, the tired coach horses doubtless glad to lose their weight from the carriage before the long haul. Once on to the common they left the main road and trotted briskly along the grass tracks, picking a course roughly parallel with that of the coach. The views were magnificent, clear towards the South Downs the hills and valleys rolled gently ahead of them, the scattered villages each with their own spiralling haze of smoke in the bright air. All over the common the bracken was turning rust-brown, but the clumps of gorse, as always, sported their bright yellow flowers.

'On a day like today,' Hetta called, and waved an extravagant arm at it all, 'it is *so* good to be alive!' She pointed ahead, down a wide, open track to a distant pine. 'First to the tree!' she shouted, and kicked up her docile grey hopefully.

Startled, but game, the animal responded valiantly, breaking into an unaccustomed gallop and thundering down the track. Hetta could hear the bay behind her, steadily closing the gap between them, and glancing back saw Jonathan laughing as he urged it on. She thought she would just keep her lead as they plunged up the last slight incline to the solitary pine, but her mare was slackening her efforts, and the bay nosed up beside them as they breasted the rise and Jonathan rounded the tree just ahead of her.

Hetta laughed, breathless and exhilarated. 'Wretched man! I thought I had the edge on you there! She's out of condition.' She slapped the grey's neck affectionately. 'Like me, she lacks exercise.'

They rested a moment, gazing at the view, and watching the coach pulling along the road behind them.

'Look,' Jonathan pointed. 'We can take that track out into the common, and it looks as if there is a road that cuts back to meet our own before we enter Horley. I have asked Hudgell to meet us and take you back into the coach before we reach the village. The Chequers is usually busy, and I think it preferable therefore for you to arrive in the carriage, don't you?'

'Oh, very well, Jonathan. Yes, you are quite right, as you always are, for I will look a windswept hoyden by the time we arrive. Come on, let's make the most of the time we have.'

They trotted briskly round the winding paths, and managed another gallop from the reluctant grey before they took the small road back to the highway. They could hear the carriage distantly coming to join them, hidden from view by a bend in the road, and high hawthorn hedges.

Jonathan dismounted and walked round to jump Hetta down. She rested her hands on his shoulders as he grasped her waist firmly and lifted her from the saddle. He did not immediately release her, but remained holding her, looking down at her face, flushed and bright from the exercise.

'Thank you, Jonathan,' Hetta said. 'I enjoyed myself.' Her hands still rested on his shoulders as she smiled up at him, and she was suddenly aware of their breathing, rapid after their gallop, of how her chest rose and fell so close to his, and the warmth of his breath on her face. She felt acutely aware of every part of her body, and every inch of her fingers, where they touched the broad strength of his shoulders, suddenly very still, beneath them. She looked up into his face. He was looking down at her with an odd intensity. His grip about her waist tightened, and his hands slid round to her back, his fingers hard against her as he pulled her towards him. She drew in a long, shuddering sigh, and she could not look away from his parted lips. She was unsteady, startled, when he abruptly released her.

She had been unaware of the carriage, pulling up beside them, and their horses shifting restlessly.

'It was a pleasure, Lady Cairshaw,' Jonathan said, his voice sounding grim, and he handed her into the coach.

Hetta sat subdued, her feelings in a turmoil at her reaction to his touch. Angry at herself, confused as to his intentions, she testily informed Meggie that she was weary now and would not talk. She waited tensely for Jonathan to rejoin them in the carriage at Horley, determined to ignore him and gaze out at the countryside, hating the idea that he might have seen how much she had wanted him then, fool that she was, when she knew his affections were engaged elsewhere. Certainly, she wanted no more entanglements with men of his family.

She was unreasonably cross, therefore, when, having handed over their hacks, supervised the change of horses and brought out a tray of lemonade and cakes when she announced she was unwilling to leave the coach, Jonathan told her that he would sit up with Hudgell for the remainder of the journey. They would soon be taking to the by-roads, and the hamlet they sought, rejoicing in the name of Blackbird-under-the-Wood, might be difficult to trace.

By the time they had traversed numerous narrow stony lanes, sunk deep between banks and hedges, with the sunlight glowing on the yellow leaves and burdens of red hawthorn berries, the bright beads of briony, and the fluffing mounds of old man's beard, Hetta was convincing herself she had been foolish.

After splashing through several fords, fat white ducks flapping indignantly away from their wheels, and enquiring of any number of keen but uncertain yokels as to their direction, she was certain of it.

When at last they met a small boy with an odoriferous goat, whose grandmother lived over at Blackbird and who could thus direct them with some accuracy, she was telling herself that he had, after all, done no more than lift her down from her horse. The rest was her own hysterical imagination, brought on by the excitement of the ride. She mentally chastised herself, and vowed she would forget it, and be briskly cheerful when they eventually arrived.

CHAPTER FOURTEEN

THEY found the hamlet in the late afternoon, by which time they were all tired and hungry. It was no more than a straggling group of cottages and smallholdings, which seemed to cling tenuously about the one building of any size, the inn. Named the Blackbird, it was a long, white-washed timbered building, with a deep thatched roof, and an unexpected air of prosperity.

Hetta, surveying the place as she climbed down from the carriage and stretched her legs, could only hazard the guess that perhaps its very isolation, hidden and surrounded by thick woods that stretched on all sides, and up the steep hill slope behind the inn, gave it a peculiar attraction to the 'Gentlemen' coming up from the sea with their packhorse trains of forbidden goods. She could think of no other reason for its look of well-being in such an unpromising situation.

They were made instantly welcome, although their arrival necessitated a bustle of activity. A small, cosy parlour with a vast inglenook fireplace and a tiny leaded window was put immediately at their disposal. A boy scurried in with kindling and tinderbox to hastily re-arrange the fire dogs, select logs from the stack within the fireplace, and speedily produce a snapping, crackling blaze. Through the open door Hetta could see girls with hot bricks and clean sheets being shooed up the creaking oak staircase by the landlord's wife, who retired abruptly back into her kitchen stronghold.

Dane, who had been out to overlook the stowing of his carriage and horses, came in looking well satisfied.

He strode over, flinging his coat on to the settle, and went to warm his hands at the blaze.

'It all seems remarkably orderly and efficient for such an out-of-the-way spot,' he remarked. 'I believe we will be more comfortable than I had anticipated.'

'I was thinking,' Hetta responded, 'that the only possible source of wealth in such a spot must be the trade from the "Gentlemen". I know something of their need for quiet locations after we belatedly discovered they were availing themselves of our old ice house at Alnstrop as a halfway store. This, I would guess, would be an ideal distribution point for this area and beyond, and heaven knows how many secret cellars might be hidden under such a rambling old building.'

'If you are right,' Dane said, amused, 'I shall certainly order brandy after the meal tonight. They may have something rather special. I have, incidentally, ordered a light snack of cold meats and bread for us to take immediately, and a hot meal for later this evening. I gathered that a main meal would take a little time to prepare, and I, at least, have far too great an appetite to wait without taking something before. I hope that pleases you?'

With relief Hetta realised that his behaviour was cheerfully normal, quite as it had always been. That moment on the road—it had been all her imagination.

'That will be perfect,' she smiled, taking off her pelisse, and moving to join him by the fire. 'And did you discover anything of the whereabouts of Nurse Hedges? Does she have a mysterious guest living with her and keeping hens? Is the Dane and Cairshaw detecting duo on the trail at last?'

He laughed, but shook his head. 'The news is not as good as that. Certainly Nanny Hedges is here. She has a small cottage some half a mile down the road, at a place I am reliably informed is known as Birch's Bottom. But my informants, the landlord and his stable-lad, are both adamant she lives alone, and has done ever since she moved back down here. They don't even recollect her ever having a visitor before, or at least, not one from "foreign parts" like us! So don't hold your hopes too high.'

'Oh, but how frustrating! I had such great hopes of Nanny Hedges, with a chicken-keeping Laura to accompany her! I thought we had the whole mystery solved. It is too bad!'

'No matter. We can still call to see her. She may have had a letter with some clue to Laura's whereabouts, or know of someone else Laura may have turned to.'

'But you don't really believe so?'

He shrugged. 'It is not so very probable, I suppose, but worth asking—certainly worth asking.'

'And remember,' Hetta chuckled, 'there is always Magnificent Millie to fall back on!'

Dane gave a snort of laughter. 'And what an experience that would be!'

Hetta shot him a look, but fortunately for her composure at this point Mrs Wickenden, the landlord's wife, entered the room at the head of the same two girls Hetta had watched running upstairs with sheets earlier. Now they were laden with trays and plates and a tablecloth, and a vast spread rapidly appeared on the table. Mrs Wickenden herself set the chairs and, having satisfied herself there was nothing more they required, hustled her helpers out, and shut the door.

'Please,' said Dane, 'come and eat.'

They ate and talked companionably, doing full justice to the excellent cold meats and home-made cheeses. When they had done, Dane wrote a note to Nurse Hedges, letting her know they would be calling on her the following morning.

'For it will soon be dusk,' he said, 'and she won't want to open her doors to unexpected visitors after dark. We can walk down after we have breakfasted. It should make a pleasant stroll, and then perhaps you won't be so desperate for exercise on the way back!'

'Perhaps,' Hetta retorted, 'but I have never been short of energy, you know.'

'That I had noticed,' Dane said drily. 'Never content to sit by and look on, are you?'

'No, indeed! How dull life would be if I were. Now I intend to walk about the village and find some vantage point from which to view the sunset, which I guess will be spectacular tonight. Will you come?'

'Just let me find a boy to take this note, then yes, thank you.'

It was spectacular. They had walked up a steep path behind the inn, and found a small clearing which gave views between the remaining trees way out to the south and west, over miles of undulating woodland, all catching the bright red-gold of the sun into their already rich autumnal colours. Henrietta, clutching her pelisse about herself, for as the sun sank there was a promise of frost in the air, stood at Jonathan's side as she watched. She held her breath at the beauty of it, as the sun, a huge red disc, slid with increasing speed behind the thin bars of grey cloud, reappeared with a last triumphant glare of virulent brightness, and slipped gently away into the far distant woods. They watched it go in silence, and stood on after it had gone, looking at the stark black silhouettes of the trees against the pink and turquoise sky. At last, Jonathan took her hand.

'We should go down,' he said, 'you will get cold.'

The drift of woodsmoke came up to them from the houses below. Hetta shivered. 'You are right. I am chilled through. But I would not have missed that.'

He kept a firm hold of her hand as he led her down, the tree roots they had stepped over so easily on their ascent now lurking as unseen traps for the unwary in the dark beneath the trees. She stumbled once hard against him, and drew back abruptly, self-conscious, but he merely steadied her gently by her elbow, and led her on. Ashamed of this sudden new awareness of his presence, this consciousness of his nearness, when doubtless his own thoughts were miles away, with Esther, she excused herself as soon as they regained the warmth and light of the inn, and retired to her room to change for dinner.

The bedroom was tucked in the fold of the roof, snug under its sloping ceiling, the window a tiny low eye to peer out through the bushy eyebrow of thatch. Hetta knelt to look out into the darkness. Dim lights showed at the windows of a couple of cottages, and at one a shaft of gold streamed across the garden as a door opened, a dark shape moved through the brightness, then abruptly it was black again as the door closed. She watched a dim light bobbing down the road towards the inn. As it drew nearer she could distinguish the shape of the lantern, and in its faint glow the outline of face, beard, smock and gaiters, and the head of the dog that trotted wearily beside the gaiters. The unknown man passed by, to become no more than a vague silhouette against the glow of his lamp. Hetta pulled the curtains closed against the darkness and went back to the glow of the little fire.

'Hold the candle closer, would you, Meggie? How do I look?'

There was a small gilt mirror above the dressing-table. Yellowed and peeling with age, it hid more than it revealed.

'Very nice, Miss Hetta. Master Robert, his lordship, I should say, would approve of you, which is more than we can say for most of the gowns you've been wearing lately.'

Hetta paid her scant attention as she peered at her reflection hopefully. The muslin was a warm creamy yellow, very plain, with low neck, high waist and tiny puffed sleeves, its only decoration a frill above the hem.

Her hair was brushed so the curls clustered all about her head; Meggie had done no more than thread a thin cream ribbon through them. It would have to do.

Hetta pulled the shawl around her and, taking a candle, stepped out into the icy draughts of the corridor. She creaked her way along the complaining floorboards, down the polished oak staircase and into their private parlour.

The table was ready laid. Beyond it Jonathan was sitting on the high-backed wooden settle, reclining against the end board, his feet up along the seat towards the blaze. The hand holding his glass was resting idly on his thigh. He seemed unaware of Hetta's entrance. She walked quietly over, and sat on the seat at the other side of the fire.

His eyes were closed. He had changed for dinner, and looked immaculate, Hetta thought approvingly, especially considering he had brought no man to assist him. Like making tea, feeding babies, rescuing distressed ladies and remembering jam, coals and hot bricks, dressing himself perfectly was obviously yet another skill acquired by Mr Dane. Henrietta wondered if there were anything he could not turn his ingenuity and his hands to. Probably not. In his quiet way Jonathan Dane was a remarkably competent and self-sufficient man. A man to turn to in any distress. Even if, dozing before the fire with his face smoothed by sleep, he looked barely more than a boy. The dark lashes lay long on his cheeks, and his lips were just parted. His fingers loosened their grip as he sighed in his sleep, and the glass they held tilted alarmingly.

'Jonathan,' Hetta said softly. 'Jonathan.'

His eyes opened slowly, and, as he saw her there, his face lit with a brilliant smile. 'Henrietta,' he said, with deep content.

Then he woke more fully, gripped his glass, noticed his legs were sprawled up along the settle, and leapt apologetically to his feet. 'Henrietta, I am so sorry. I must have dozed off. You should have woken me immediately. How long have you been sitting there?'

'I have hardly more than arrived,' she said, still disconcerted by that smile.

'Will you take a drink? I took the liberty of ordering some of Mr Wickenden's best brandy, to drive out the cold of the evening, and I can recommend it. It really is excellent. I am happy to believe any suspicions you may harbour as to its origins; they must all be delightfully true.'

'Perhaps a small glass,' she said, 'to keep out the cold.' He poured the brandy and handed it to her. 'Thank you. Incidentally, did I tell you that I asked Sarah about Magnificent Millie?' He shook his head. 'While I was telling her that I would be away with you, and could not have the baby for her. She was so envious, poor girl. She is restless and desperate to move away from Lockchain Terrace, but I think the convenience of my being there to take the baby at need keeps her staying on.' She frowned. 'He looks worse, poor mite, despite all that I do. I do so wish she would not give him gin all the time. I have tried to remonstrate, but I can tell she thinks me merely foolish. It is my belief she would be thankful if the child were to die.' She sipped at her brandy morosely.

'You cannot greatly blame her for that,' Jonathan said gently. 'To a girl in her position a child is an enormous encumbrance, and a sickly child still more so.'

'But, Jonathan,' Hetta's voice was impassioned, 'think of the child. He is no mere whim to suit her convenience, or,' she continued angrily, 'he should not be.'

'No, he should not be, and in an ideal world he would not be. But born as he is, to such a mother in such a place, I cannot think he has much to cling to life for. What will it hold for him?'

Too late Jonathan saw the inevitable drift of Henrietta's thoughts. He should have predicted, he thought ruefully, that this would be her next step.

'When this is over,' she was saying, 'and I am free to do so, I could take Dickon with me. I do believe Sarah would be glad to part with him if she knew he would be well cared for. I could find a suitable family, perhaps on the Alnstrop estates—surely Robert would not object—and see the child brought up in fresh country air and taught a suitable trade. What do you think? I don't know why it did not occur to me before.'

'Henrietta——'

She looked up suspiciously at his dubious tones, and immediately interrupted him. '*Don't* start asking what people will think for I do not care. Even should they all go so ludicrously far as to...' she paused '...as to consider him to be a son of mine, let them. Their small-mindedness is their problem, not mine. Anyway, how *could* they think such a thing? It is outrageous!'

'I actually suggested no such thing, if you recall, though I am glad that you are looking at all possible outcomes of your plan. As to how they could think such a thing—reflect. After your known association with Justin; his leaving you; your sudden mysterious rustication; and then a strange baby to be disposed of on the Alnstrop estates! I think tongues could be forgiven for wagging, don't you?'

Henrietta considered this scenario, outraged and furious at the probabilities it conjured up. 'Oh, why are you always so dampingly proper?' she burst out. 'I suppose you would just abandon poor Dickon to his fate rather than face gossip?'

'Rather than have such gossip about you, indeed I would.'

'Well, I would not, and I do not care what people will say,' Hetta responded crossly. '*I* am not the sort of monster who could ignore the needs of a child for such a reason.' She took a large gulp of her brandy, with scant regard for its excellence. 'Even if you are!'

When she looked up Jonathan was regarding her with great fondness, and a rueful smile. She scowled.

'I dare say *I* could find a family who could take the child, if his mother wishes to part with him,' Dane said, sighing inwardly. 'And you need not be in any way connected with the transaction. Then there would be no food for the gossip-mongers.'

Her face lit up, scowls forgotten. 'Would you do that? Truly? Dear, dear Jonathan, thank you! I am sorry I called you a monster—you are not one at all, but the dearest and most long-suffering friend anyone could have.' She impetuously ran and kissed his cheek, seating herself beside him on the settle. 'That will be wonderful, and it will not involve Robert in any talk or scandal. How good you are, I malign you dreadfully!'

Jonathan shrugged his shoulders faintly, his cheeks tinged red, and changed the subject. 'You never said. Did Sarah know of Magnificent Millie? Do we have a lead there?'

'Yes, of course, *that* is what I was telling you! Yes, and no! She has heard the name, and heard some talk of the girl, but she can't remember what, where, who, or anything else to the purpose. However, in return for my attentions to her poor baby, she is to enquire, and hopes to bring us news of Millie soon. So perhaps we will get back to find another piece of our puzzle waiting for us.'

'I will certainly drink to the hopes of that,' Jonathan said, and they raised their glasses together, smiling. 'As long as she does not prove to be another dead end.'

The food arrived just then, brought by Mrs Wickenden and her entourage. There were plump little pheasants, a vast bowl of mushrooms, a spicy dish of chicken, little rabbit pies, and more dishes Mrs Wickenden had yet to uncover.

'It looks wonderful,' Henrietta said.
'And smells even better!' Jonathan concluded, as Mrs Wickenden beamed. 'If you could just leave it, we will be happy to serve ourselves. Thank you.'
'Thank you, sir. Mr Wickenden will be along shortly, he is in the cellar selecting your wine. Ah, here he is now.'
The wine approved, the Wickendens withdrew. Jonathan held back a chair with a flourish.
'Please, be seated, Lady Cairshaw.'
'Thank you, sir, I shall.'
The food was excellent. Despite the generous cold snack they had eaten on their arrival, Henrietta found she felt famished again, and fell to willingly. She caught Dane watching her with amusement.
'You don't like to pick at your food in a genteelly ladylike manner,' he explained, when she raised her eyebrows in query, her mouth full. 'You enjoy it as good food should be enjoyed.'
She swallowed and grinned. 'I have never been good at the ladylike virtues. I enjoy the pleasures of the flesh too much! I can't pick and pretend, I like to savour things to the full. In fact, I think the life of a high-class doxy would suit me very well!'
He frowned, but answered lightly. 'Hardly! I have yet to meet a high-class doxy with your crusading spirit on behalf of all the world's waifs and strays!'
'Oh?' Hetta chuckled. 'And with how many high-class doxies are you acquainted, dear sir?'
'That,' he said, laughing, 'is not at all a ladylike question!'
'Which just proves my point!'
'No, no! What you need,' he said, 'is not the life of a high-class doxy, but marriage to a not-entirely-gentlemanlike gentleman!'
'A not-entirely-gentlemanlike gentleman?'

'Oh, yes. You would shock a conventional gentleman to the bottom of his top boots; it would not do at all. And if he was not in *any* way a gentleman he would merely break your generous heart. So you require a compromise. That is the problem of being an unladylike lady!'

He was not looking at her, but concentrating on the pheasant meat. She watched him, and suddenly, unaccountably, felt a hot blush creep up her cheeks. Abruptly she looked down and directed her thoughts to her food. It was just too warm, she told herself, with the heat of the fire, and the glow of the candles on her face. She slipped off her shawl on to the back of the chair, and hoped she would cool down.

'Tell me,' she said firmly, 'more about your life in India.'

'Are you certain you wish to change the subject to India?' he responded, a teasing glint in his eye that reminded her strongly of her brothers.

'Quite certain,' she replied with extra emphasis. 'I find your tales of exotic life most fascinating. Do, please, entertain me with some more.'

'Very ladylike!' he murmured, and she bit her lip, but he grinned and obliged her, and she was able to finish her meal without losing her composure.

They sat, side by side on the high-backed settle, by the dying glow of the fire, when they had eaten. The meal had been cleared away, and they were sipping more of Mr Wickenden's best brandy. The exhaustions of the day, the good meal, warm fire and brandy all combined to lull Hetta into a lethargy of weary content. They sat in a companionable silence, gazing into the glowing coals. The shift of a log and a rush of sparks up the chimney roused her from her reverie, and she looked at Jonathan.

'I must go to my bed,' she said, 'or I shall be asleep on your shoulder.'

He nodded, 'Or I on yours.' He stood up, and held out his hand to her. 'Come.'

It seemed natural to stand up into his arms, to feel him reach round to steady and enclose her in a gentle embrace. He was smiling down at her.

'My unladylike lady!' he murmured, tilting up her chin to study her face. 'With such shorn curls!'

He ran his fingers lightly through the remaining clusters of black. The curls sprang and twirled about his fingers, and he laughed softly, running his hand down to the nape of her neck then bringing caressing fingers back under her chin. He held her closer against him, and although his move was infinitely gentle, yet she could feel the pressure of every finger through the thin muslin of her dress. As his fingers ran down her spine she moved involuntarily, pressing closer to him, and a tiny moan escaped her lips. Her eyes closed.

His lips were very gentle, light on her forehead, her cheeks and eyelids. 'Henrietta,' she heard him whisper. 'My sweet Henrietta!' His lips were more urgent now, his hand pushing up her chin, but her need for him rose and her lips were already seeking his. Her hand crept up to caress his face, and at last his lips met hers, tentatively, then with a sudden violence of passion, crushing her to him with bruising yearning, with all the force of needs long suppressed, and Henrietta was swept into a dizzying acknowledgement of her need for him. She responded with a desire she had never known before, and its strength carried her into an oblivion of loving.

She did not know how long they kissed, lost as she was in the delight of his caresses, the joy of touching him, until, devastatingly, a sudden thought doused her like iced water. She broke free.

'Esther!' she breathed, and pulled back in horror. 'Esther! Oh! What have I done?' She broke away from his embrace, shaking away his arm as he reached to hold her again.

'Listen, Henrietta——' he began, but she would not let him speak.

'No!' she said, anguished. 'You love Esther and soon you will marry her. Nothing must spoil that for you or for her! You must forget this ever happened. How *could* I have done such a thing, knowing you feel as you do? Please! Forget it! It was nothing, I was playing the part of doxy, no more. It was just more of my unladylike behaviour. It is not important. Please believe that. Dear God, that I, who know what it is to be jilted by one of your wretched family, should risk the happiness of another girl in such a way. But no harm is done. Please, please, Jonathan, forget this happened, and marry the girl you love!'

She was shaking and shivering, tears running on to her cheeks.

'Henrietta, listen to me...' Dane began, reaching his hand towards her, his face twisted in distress. 'Listen...'

But she would not.

'No! There is nothing to listen to. We have been a little foolish, and now we will forget it. I am going to my bed.' She turned, and looked about, bewildered, for a candle; those on the table had long since guttered and died. Jonathan angrily snatched a new one from the mantelpiece and lit it for her.

'Henrietta... Esther and I... We are not...'

'Don't! Please!' she said. 'Isn't it Esther you are always with? Esther you turn to at every moment? Esther who fills your days when you are not seeking Laura? Esther whose consent you have dreamed of for so long? I *know* it is!'

'Yes, but——'

'You see? There can be no "buts"! Please, give me my candle. None of this happened. Go to her tomorrow and tell her you love her. I *will* not ruin her love or yours. I want you to be happy. And, Jonathan, go alone to see Nanny Hedges tomorrow. I am tired, I shall sleep late and take breakfast in my room. No! Don't follow me! Goodnight.'

And she fled the room, the tears running unheeded down her cheeks, leaving Jonathan cursing himself for acting like a precipitate fool; cursing Esther for hanging on to him for her game of suitors. But unable to curse Henrietta—foolish, impetuous, generous, loving Henrietta—for he had seen in her face what that brave denial had cost her, and he wanted only to kiss her pain away. Fool, utter fool that he was! A typical Dane, he castigated himself, causing her heartache just as Justin had done. He savagely reached for the brandy bottle.

Henrietta lay in her bed in the darkness, listening only to the odd restless rustles of small creatures in the thatch above her head. She clutched her damp handkerchief and stared into the blackness when she eventually heard his footsteps on the creaking boards of the corridor, then the quiet shutting of the door of the bedroom adjoining. She listened to the small movements as he prepared for bed, then all was quiet but for the rustlings in the thatch. Tears slid silently down Henrietta's cheeks and on to the pillow.

CHAPTER FIFTEEN

THE journey back to London was strained. Nurse Hedges, delighted though she had been to see her former charge, had had no news to give him. Her departure from Thwayle had occurred not long after that of Jonathan, and she had had little contact with there since, and had heard nothing at all from Laura. Thus, after a brief account of his visit, Henrietta and Dane found little to say to each other.

She sat close to Meggie and confined her conversation to brief comments on the passing landscape, all uttered with repressive politeness. She refused his invitations to step down for refreshment when they stopped over to change horses, and merely picked at the offerings he brought out to the coach. His every effort to speak with her privately was thus foiled, and he was forced to echo her own chilly reserve.

Matters were not improved when, after Dane had hopefully pointed out one or two landmarks, Henrietta enquired of him how he was so familiar with this road when he had been out of England for so long.

He frowned, then gave a slight shrug and replied, 'Miss Wanhope and her father took a house in Brighton over the summer. I travelled down frequently to see them.'

Hetta forced a small smile.

'Of course. I should have guessed that, shouldn't I?' she said, and relapsed into silence.

Dane frowned across at her small, set face. She looked pale, her eyes dark ringed, as if she had not slept well. His emotions swinging between a fierce possessiveness and desire to protect her, and an irrational fury at her, himself, Esther, and the entire situation, Jonathan's journey was tense. He scowled out of the window, and his replies to any comments became monosyllabic. They finished the journey in silence.

Neither of them noticed, as they traversed the busy streets of the capital, a girl with pale blonde ringlets and a face of pouting, doll-like prettiness, who, stepping from a shop doorway to view a bale of cloth in the daylight, smiled in recognition of the coach and Hudgell. They did not notice her run over the pavement and wave, before distinguishing an unmistakably female face at the near carriage window, with Jonathan's head dimly to be viewed behind. Nor did they see how she dropped her arm abruptly, and, turning on her heel, stalked back into the shop.

Back at Lockchain Terrace Dane assisted Meggie out of the carriage and handed her a bag to take in, then turned urgently to Hetta before handing her down.

'I need to speak to you, Henrietta. This is absurd.'

'There is nothing to say, Mr Dane. Please let me go in. I have such a headache.'

'But, Henrietta——'

'Please, Mr Dane. Excuse me. I wish to go and lie down.'

He had no option but to let her go, though he handed her down with a poor grace.

'You will understand if I do not invite you in,' Hetta said at the top of the stairs, after he had carried up her bags. Her eyes looked tense and strained in her white face, and he thought it probable she did indeed have a bad headache.

'Of course,' he said with a stiff little bow. 'I hope your headache is soon improved,' and he strode away down the stairs, angry and frustrated.

Henrietta, with a sigh of relief at his departure, wiped a couple of errant tears off her cheeks, and climbed thankfully into her chintz-curtained bed, calling to Meggie to bring a cup of tea as soon as she was able.

It was later in the evening, after Hetta, still propped up against the pillows in her bed, had partaken of a light supper on a tray, that she lay idly turning the pages of the newspaper. She found it difficult to interest herself in anything mentioned, but was desperate for a distraction from her own meditations. She had thought herself over that blackness of depression that had engulfed her at the time Justin had left her, had thought herself to be quite recovered. Perhaps she had been wrong. She shivered and stared with renewed intensity at the pages, desperate to keep her mind occupied, away from her own thoughts.

It was then that the announcements of the next day's church services caught her eye, or, more particularly, the name of Wanhope. She jerked the paper up to scrutinise this more closely. He was to be the guest preacher at Saint Bartholemew's Church, Lower Marle Street at the eleven o'clock service, this Reverend Mr Wanhope. He was to speak about his missionary work in India, and a special collection would be held. Henrietta stared at the words. Dane had told her that Esther always accompanied her father when he preached. She was suddenly filled with an overwhelming desire to see this girl, the girl who held the heart and affections of Jonathan Dane. Lower Marle Street was not too far. They could walk the distance in half an hour.

'Meggie! Tomorrow we are going to church,' she announced.

'Yes, Miss Hetta,' Meggie said gloomily, 'I dare say we need to!'

St Bartholemew's church was new, or sufficiently new for the stone of its construction still to retain its whiteness, as yet unaffected by the soot and filth in the air of London. The last of the congregation were still assembling when Meggie and Hetta arrived, slightly breathless, and they were able to slip in with another group of people and find seats near the back. It had occurred to Henrietta that Jonathan would very probably be accompanying his love, and she was most anxious he should not see her. She edged along the pew until she was behind a lady with a vast bonnet, before she began to cautiously peer forward to where Esther might be.

It was Jonathan she saw first. Looking through the worshippers to the front pew on the other side, she suddenly had a clear view of his back, and she realised with a jolt that she would have known it anywhere—the cut of his hair, the way his head tilted as he leant to speak quietly to his companion, the breadth of his shoulders under the dark cloth of his coat. Knowing her presence to be totally unsuspected, she gazed at him with a guilty fascination.

Then his companion turned towards him. Henrietta only had a glimpse, for an elegant silk bonnet hid much of the lady's features and she turned back so abruptly that it seemed her answer to him was terse, but Henrietta was able to distinguish thick ringlets of a beautiful pale gold, a clear pink and white complexion, wide eyes and full red lips. She was young, much younger than Henrietta, she was very pretty, and she was dressed in the first stare of fashion.

Henrietta thought of all the dresses she had worn for Jonathan, and the wig he so much disliked, and she felt suddenly very small and foolish, every bit the unwanted widow.

Hetta followed through the service automatically, unable to give her attention to the words. She saw Jonathan frequently perform little services for Miss Wanhope—holding her book, picking up her glove—but he seemed to get scant appreciation for his politenesses. Every inch of Miss Wanhope's back appeared stiff and aloof.

Henrietta was unimpressed by Mr Wanhope's address, though she admitted to herself that perhaps her judgement lacked impartiality. She thought him a pompous bore addicted to the sound of his own oratory, and fretted for him to finish so that she could escape from the church. It had been a mistake, she concluded, to come.

At last it was over. She watched Dane rise, and offer his arm to Miss Wanhope, and she watched Miss Wanhope affect not to see it, and turn away from Dane to an elderly gentleman on her other side. They began to move out into the press of people, down the aisle, Esther on the arm of the elderly gentleman, all smiles and charm; Jonathan, grim-faced, walking alone behind. In a sudden panic Henrietta shot out of her pew, pulling Meggie after her, and made good her escape before Jonathan came any closer. She hurried down the wide white steps and away down the pavement, concerned only to put as much distance as possible between herself and Jonathan Dane.

Jonathan also had found the church service to be a difficult time. He had called round at the Wanhopes' house directly after leaving Lockchain Terrace on the previous day, determined to sort out once and for all what his relationship, or preferably his lack of relationship, with Esther was. He wanted to make it clear that he would be happy to agree an end to their understanding if she wished to do so, aware as he was of her increased interest in Lord Glenby, and her apparent lack of commitment to himself. He fretted at his own ambiguous relationship with her, which gave him no privileges of affection, or franker speech and understanding with her, but which would not allow him, as a gentleman, to be the one to withdraw from their agreement.

He was frustrated to discover that she was out, and would be out for the rest of the day. After her shopping expedition she was to make one of a party, at Lord

Glenby's request, to attend the opera. Mr Wanhope, however, assured Jonathan that, as he was so like one of the family, he felt quite happy at inviting him, on Esther's behalf, to attend church with them on the following day. Jonathan gritted his teeth at the paternal tone, and rather curtly agreed that he would do so.

His desire for private speech with Miss Wanhope was utterly frustrated, however. She treated him, when he called at the house, with the chilliest disapproval, made several barbed comments about how well he seemed able to fill his time when he was not with her, but refused him any time, now that he *was* with her, for conversation. Her reserve was icy on the way to the church, her only speech being directed to her father, and she snubbed him throughout the service.

Jonathan, thoroughly irritated, would have welcomed this behaviour had it seemed likely to lead to his release from any commitment to her, but she dismissed him abruptly after the service, with only the condescending information that he might possibly find her at home if he were to call later in the week.

Striding angrily away to find a hackney, he reflected that her behaviour seemed not so much designed to terminate their relationship as to bring him to heel for some misdemeanour. He would have to make a way to speak to her, and hopefully bring matters to a head. In the meantime, he wanted very much to speak to Henrietta, and when he eventually found a hackney he directed it, instead of to his own house, to number three, Lockchain Terrace.

Henrietta strode home at a great pace, her agitated thoughts increasing the briskness of her gait. Meggie, panting and red-faced in her over-tight Sunday-best outfit, kept gasping pleas for a slower pace, and Hetta would slow momentarily, but in no time she would be off again, quite forgetting Meggie's harassed presence.

It was obvious, she thought, that Dane was not treating this Esther as he should, nor she treating him as he would wish. Every inch of her had depicted anger and indignation, outrage at some neglect. And she *had* been neglected, of course. Neglected for Henrietta and for the search for Laura. No wonder, Hetta reflected, as her feet tapped steadily along the pavement with a rapid, angry beat, no wonder the poor girl was indignant. Dane was committed to her, and yet he spent half his time away from her. Naturally she would be angry.

It was the typical behaviour of a Dane, of course. That cool, self-centred assumption that a woman was merely there to serve his convenience. At least Esther was making her disapproval plain. But it need not be so. He need not neglect her. It was not necessary for Dane to spend all his time searching for Laura now. Their only lead was one best followed by Sarah, and the best person to encourage and cajole Sarah into finding out was Hetta herself. There was nothing for Jonathan to do. He should devote all his time to Miss Wanhope, in future, therefore, and rescue his romance before it was too late. He was a fool to risk his own happiness and jeopardise that of such a lovely young girl on a wild-goose chase that Hetta could handle quite well on her own. And so she would tell him if he appeared at Lockchain Terrace again.

She marched up the stairs to her room, an exhausted Meggie trailing behind her, clutching her side and gasping like a landed fish.

They had not been back in the house ten minutes before Jonathan's knock sounded at the door. Meggie, opening it, admitted him dubiously, having received no instructions to the contrary, then retired to her own room, gloomily hoping they would overcome their differences. She had approved of Jonathan Dane, and she disliked the drawn look about her mistress's eyes. It reminded her too strongly of the bad days after Justin had left.

'Henrietta.'

She was standing over by the window, having only just put off her pelisse. She did not turn to look at him, and he walked over to stand beside her. When she still did not respond he put a hand on her shoulder and turned her towards him. She jumped at his touch as if scalded, and drew back. His brows snapped together and he stood stiffly, regarding her intently.

'Henrietta,' he began again. 'We must talk. It is absurd to go on like this. What we did——'

'Was nothing! I said it at the time, and now I repeat it. Just as when you kissed me at the White Cocks that evening. That meant nothing and nor did this. It would appear that we kiss each other in public houses. We are obviously keen on keeping to our roles. No more. It was all play-acting.'

'Don't be ridiculous. That is not true, Henrietta, and you know it as well as I do.'

She flinched a little at the harsh anger of his tones.

'I am sorry you should have misinterpreted the situation, sir. It was true for me.'

She had been glaring at him, but she had never been a clever liar. Her brothers had always teased her that she betrayed everything in her face. Remembering that, she turned and stared out of the window so she need not meet his eye. She felt herself begin to shake, and gripped the window-sill.

'You love a beautiful young girl,' she said, her voice tight in a vain attempt to prevent its quivering. 'And you have neglected her because of the time you have spent with me over your search for Laura. Had I not insisted in joining your search you would doubtless have spent far less time on it, and consequently had far more time to devote to Miss Wanhope. No wonder she is annoyed at your neglect. But that is something you can easily remedy, and as I feel partly responsible for your neglect

I would like to help ensure you have time to be with her now, to make amends for your deserting her in the past.'

'This is nonsense, Henrietta,' Dane began. 'Esther is not...she does not...' He floundered, not knowing how to describe his thoughts on Esther.

'You have not broken your understanding together, have you? Your proposal?'

'Well, no——'

'And it is true she is annoyed with you, isn't it?'

'Yes, but——'

'And it is also true you have not spent all the time with her you could have done?'

'She has had a great deal of my time.'

'But so have I, and so has this search for Laura, and like a typical Dane you have expected Esther to wait quietly on your convenience. She is angry, and I don't blame her. She should be angry. If you are any sort of man, stop wasting your time here with me, and go and woo your Esther, and just hope you have not broken *her* heart in that inimitable way Dane men seem to have.'

'Henrietta, I am *quite* capable of dealing with my relationship with Miss Wanhope for myself, as I am also quite capable of searching for my cousin, and capable of managing my relationship with you, all without committing my every move to Miss Wanhope's scrutiny...'

'Typical arrogant Dane!' Hetta muttered, then, rounding on him, 'And you don't *have* a relationship with me!'

'I most certainly do! At the very least I am responsible for your safety while you take part in this harebrained scheme, and, in addition, you *will* admit that we have enjoyed a working relationship, if nothing more.'

'Well, that need not continue. Sarah is the best person to pursue our search for Magnificent Millie, and I am the person to care for her child while she does so. There is nothing for you to do, we do not need you, you are redundant. Sarah and I can do the searching for you, and you can devote your time to Miss Wanhope.'

'Henrietta, Henrietta, can't you understand that I don't *want* to devote all my time to Miss Wanhope!'

'Well, you should! Think of her feelings!'

'And as for abandoning you here to pursue the search with Sarah, without the benefit of the protection my visits must give you, I would not for a moment consider such irresponsibility. What happens to you is entirely my concern.'

'You speak as if I am a child, not a twenty-seven-year-old widow! I have no need for your over-officious protection. Take it to someone who wants it!'

'No need of protection? You, who leap from one disastrous impulse to the next, with no thought for prudence, decency or propriety? Absurd. You have no more sense than a child! Under no circumstances would I leave you without masculine protection.'

'Well, you don't have to!' She swung round at him furiously, and burst into speech, too angry to care whether her lies showed or not. 'You don't have to. Because there is another man who will be only too happy to protect me; who has done so in fact when you were away those days! He will be here to care for me, and you will *not* be needed!'

He flinched as if struck, and his face went quite white.

'I don't believe you,' he said, very quietly, his voice shaking in his effort to keep it steady. 'I don't believe a word of this.'

'Why not? What role do you think I have been playing here all these weeks? That of a nun? I have been a whore, a harlot, a strumpet! And very convincing I can be. Haven't *you* appreciated my performance? Other people have. So much so that I have found me a charming gentleman who is only too pleased to be with me, and you have become entirely surplus to my requirements!'

She turned abruptly back to stare out of the window, unable to meet his horrified stare. She had seen the shock in his face, and knew that she must have utterly disgusted him. Surely now he would feel free to go back to his wretched Esther and leave her in peace? She angrily rubbed her sleeve across her cheeks, for the tears would not be held back, and fumbled in her pockets for a handkerchief. Silently, Jonathan offered her his own large, white, immaculately pressed square of finest linen, but she ungraciously shook her head, and produced a damp and crumpled morsel of cloth of her own. She blew her nose into it defiantly.

Watching her, Jonathan's expression softened.

'Henrietta,' he said gently, 'I don't know why you are saying this to me, but I refuse to believe it of you. I will not believe it until you can look me in the eye and swear to me that it is true, and I don't think that you can do that.'

Hetta knew that she could not.

'What do I care if you believe me or not?' She turned on him angrily. 'What do I care? *I* know what is true. You! You despicable Dane. You can believe anything you like; it is nothing to me. But get out of my room, and out of my life, and go and believe it somewhere else! Go! Go away and leave me in peace!'

His expression set hard once again as he stared at her rigid back, then, swinging round, he strode to the door.

'Goodbye, then, Miss Hetta from Tunbridge Wells!' he said bitterly, and he was gone. She heard his footsteps down the stairs, and the bang of the outer door. She watched him from where she stood as he strode rapidly away down the street, but he did not look back.

'What have I done?' she muttered, her face a mask of pain. 'Oh, whatever have I done?'

She curled up in the bed, and pulled the covers over her head, cutting out the day. Meggie, peering dubiously in, sighed heavily, and put the kettle on.

CHAPTER SIXTEEN

DANE had not felt so utterly miserable since those days at Thwayle, when he was no more than a child, when all his cousins had combined to torment him. His feelings of rage, hurt, futility, exasperation, and frustration conjured sudden vivid memories of the boy who had hidden under the benches in the potting sheds, beating his clenched fists raw on the brick floor and nursing just such emotions. A small, detached part of his mind stood back and jeered at him that he had handled this situation now no better than he had done those others as a child. He sat, his face buried in his hands, oblivious of the trays of food brought in by a disapproving Mrs Stockwell.

He could not believe that what Henrietta had said was true. Oh, he had half believed it, and had stormed out in the heat of the moment, but—and he took comfort from the recollection—she had evaded his challenge to claim it to his face. She had not said it. No. It was just some foolish, impetuous quirk of hers, determined to reunite him to Esther. He frowned. But until he had spoken with Esther he was unable to put things right with Henrietta. So—and he stood up decisively—so, Esther must speak with him. Now.

Leaving a despairing Mrs Stockwell to remove the untouched food, he summoned his carriage, and made his way to the Wanhopes' residence.

He was shown through to Mr Wanhope, alone in his study.

'Good evening, my boy, good evening,' he beamed. 'You know you are welcome here at any time. What can we do for you?'

'I would like permission to speak to your daughter. Alone, if I may,' Jonathan replied, aware that his voice sounded stern.

Mr Wanhope regarded him gently for a few moments.

'Oh, dear,' he said. 'I suspected as much, for she has seen so much of him. But there, she has always known her own mind, even from a child. I shan't interfere. Of course you may see her, dear boy. She is in the small parlour, upstairs, I believe. I will have you shown up.'

'Thank you sir,' said Dane, 'but don't trouble. I will find my own way.'

She was sitting by a bright fire, poking half-heartedly at a piece of embroidery. As the door opened she thrust it guiltily away and snatched up the Bible which lay open on her lap. On seeing that it was only Dane she giggled and laid the book down again, before she remembered that she angry with Dane, and not in the least pleased to see him.

'I don't know why you have come,' she exclaimed pettishly, 'or why Papa let you come up. I'm sure I made it plain I had no wish to see you just now.'

He closed the door and stood looking down at her. He was amazed, looking at her coldly, that he had ever believed he loved her.

'I am not certain, Esther, that you ever have a wish to see me, other than as a convenient and biddable escort. It has seemed to me that we take increasingly less pleasure in our relationship together, and indeed, you do seem to find Lord Glenby's company a most acceptable substitute. I think it is time we reassessed quite what our relationship is supposed to be.'

'Well!' she said indignantly, her colour rising. 'What if I do find pleasure in Lord Glenby's company? You are so frequently off on mysterious business of your own, is it surprising I turn elsewhere? Lord Glenby is always ready to entertain me.'

'Indeed,' Dane said coolly. 'I believe he is a most amiable young man.'

'Well, yes, he is. *And* he comes from a family without any slur on its name. *He* does not have strange cousins in disgraceful circumstances to be chased after, or others making marriages that become the joke of the town. Everyone approves of him, and envies me the attachment.'

She spoke defiantly, a little toss of her head making the fat ringlets bounce.

'I am sorry my family connections have embarrassed you, Esther. But there is no necessity for us to keep up our relationship, you know. It has always been for you to say.'

Well aware of this, Esther paused, sulkily. She had discovered from encouraging friends, at her first acquaintance with Jonathan Dane, the vast size of the fortune he had amassed while in India. This knowledge had remained in the forefront of her relationship with him; in fact his only drawback had been his lack of a title. Had he had a title she would have accepted his offer in Madras. But she had remained convinced that in England she could snare a fortune *and* a title. So she had waited, but not letting Jonathan quite off her string, just in case.

Lord Glenby had a title and a reasonable fortune. Not vast, but more than adequate. Unfortunately, he had not yet proposed marriage. But surely, Esther cogitated, he very soon would, and then she would have no need of Jonathan Dane with his dubious family and his disapproving stare.

'And now I *do* say,' she replied, making up her mind crossly as she suddenly recollected the carriage she had seen outside Welling's, the draper's. 'You are quite right that *I* take less pleasure in our relationship. And I am certain *you* do, for when you tell me you are off on business, how is it that I see you skulking through the streets in a closed carriage with some unknown lady? What sort of *business* is that?'

Dane recognised that this must be the misdeed for which Esther had been punishing him throughout the morning's church service.

'Oh, you saw us returning yesterday, did you? That business, Miss Wanhope, was part of my search for my cousin,' he said coldly. 'And you have made it abundantly clear to me, on several occasions, that you wish to have nothing to do with my search. Otherwise it could have been you accompanying me in that carriage.'

'You insult me, Mr Dane, by the suggestion.' She drew herself up, her chest quivering with indignation. 'No *lady* would involve herself in such a search, and I have no doubt your *companion* was just another woman of the streets. Well, I wish you joy of her, for you will repel any honest lady while you keep such company, just as you have repelled me. From now on we have *no* understanding, and I am relieved to be free of such an undesirable connection.'

He gave a short bow.

'I am happy to accept your dictate,' he said, truthfully, 'and I wish you every joy in your relationship with Lord Glenby. Goodbye, Miss Wanhope.'

'Goodbye, Mr Dane,' she said, pettish at losing an admirer. 'I wish you joy of your relationship with your...' she paused, then blurted defiantly '...your strumpet!'

Unexpectedly, Dane smiled.

'Thank you, Esther,' he said. 'I do have hopes that my strumpet will bring me great joy!'

He quietly shut the door on her gasp of shock and outrage, and made his way out of the house.

His sense of relief lasted throughout the drive home, and while he, to Mrs Stockwell's gratification, finally ate a meal. It was not until he sat alone by the fire and stared moodily at the spot where his bejewelled elephant used to stand that the doubts began to worry him again. Had Henrietta meant it? Was it true? It *was* possible... she had spent so much time alone in that dreary place... he could hardly blame her for wishing for company... But the thought of Henrietta with some man she had casually met caused him so much pain that he groaned aloud and forced his thoughts away.

Should he go back to Lockchain Terrace and demand to speak to her? He remembered the way she had flinched away from his touch and demanded that he leave, and shook his head. He sat morosely, watching the fire die.

The bottle of port left at his side by Mrs Stockwell had mysteriously emptied itself as he sat. He glowered at the empty glass in his hand, and shook the unrewarding bottle irritably. Banging both back down on to the table, he grabbed up his coat and left the house.

After his months of searching for Laura, the night-time streets of London were familiar territory for Dane, and he walked absorbed in his thoughts, unaware of filth underfoot, the snap of a stray dog, rowdy bands of revellers, or of figures huddled into doorways or flaunting themselves hopefully on street corners.

He walked without direction, led on only by a need to escape the very thoughts he carried inexorably with him. Eventually it was collision with a drunk reeling out of the doorway of a public house that penetrated his abstraction. Brushing himself off as the man stumbled away, Dane looked about him in surprise. The road was unfamiliar to him, but the open door looked welcoming, streaming bright light into the dark and cold of the street. He looked up. The pub was of no great age, built solidly of red brick, and christened the Admiral Nelson. He shrugged, indifferent, and went inside.

He ordered brandy, and stood regarding the other customers with unenthusiastic detachment. In one corner a group of eight or ten young bucks sat round a table covered in bottles of Blue Ruin. One of them was trying unsuccessfully to build a tower of the empty ones, egged on by the shrieked encouragement of the inevitable gaggle of women who hung about them or sprawled in their laps, clothes in disarray.

Closer to him two old crones sat hunched over their glasses, chins and noses nearly touching as they muttered to each other. A mother sat beyond them, a baby suckling at her breast and a toddler sitting in the filth of the floor at her feet, his eyes closed, his thumb in his mouth, and his face streaked with dirt and tears. The mother clutched a glass of the ubiquitous gin, and called occasionally to one of a group of men playing dice at a further table, but if she expected a response she was disappointed, for all the men remained engrossed in the clatter and rattle of the dice as they landed on the wooden table-top. Another baby, left alone in a ragged bundle of shawl on a bench against the far wall, wailed with a weary plaintiveness.

Dane sighed, and turned to contemplate the rows of glasses and tankards on the shelves behind the bar. Behind him, the efforts of the young buck to construct a tower of gin bottles had ended in a predictable melee of noise and broken glass, shrieks, cut fingers and blood, but his companion had swept the table-top clear with one brush of his arm through the debris, and had now slung a girl up on to the surface with raucous commands to dance, while his friends grabbed at her skirts and peered lewdly underneath them. Dane, who had turned at the noise, turned back in disgust.

Just then he felt a tug at his sleeve. It was a girl, though he had not noticed her approach. She edged up close to him, and rested her hands on his chest.

'You're lonely, sir,' she said. 'An' mis'rable. I could keep you comp'ny. She slid a hand inside his coat and gently caressed him, reaching up to squeeze his nipple through the soft cloth of his shirt. She gave him a naughty little smile. 'A mis'rable man alone needs comp'ny,' she said.

She was very small, her curls barely level with his heart. He reached a hand and ran his fingers through them, a rich chestnut-brown, and she turned her head and nibbled at the base of his thumb, peeking up at him under her lashes. His sudden aggressive surge of desire surprised him, and he pulled her head roughly back, kissing her little red, pert, smiling lips with a kind of fury.

'Come on,' she said, taking his hand and pulling him towards a door at the side of the bar. 'There's rooms upstairs.'

In the corridor beyond the door he stopped her again and pulled her to him. The noises from the taproom were muted now; they were alone in a stone-flagged passage, lit only by a branch of flickering candles on a rough table. She stretched up to put her arms around his neck, stroking his hair and wriggling her body against him, but as he bent his head to kiss her again his gaze seemed to clear. He paused, staring down at her, frowning.

She was not only small, she was young. Very young. Her body felt fragile as a sparrow's beneath the grip of his hands, her little ribs heaving beneath his fingers as she giggled up at him, waiting for his kisses. Her tiny breasts, plain to be seen down the front of her ill-fitting dress, had no more than budded, just a swelling of her soft pink nipples. Her hair curled like Henrietta's, but her eyes were dark; they could have been Laura's.

A wave of total self-disgust swept over him, leaving him cold and nauseous. She was no more than a child. Another Laura, lost and abused. She could have been that Laura of years ago.

But he. What of himself? Was he truly no better than those despised men Laura had been forced to solicit? Men the very thought of whom had made him feel ill with impotent fury? The thought sickened him with shame. Gently he set the child away from him.

'No,' he said.

'You were keen enough jist a moment ago,' she said coyly, reaching out to touch him again, not really believing he no longer desired her. 'That kiss...you were keen enough then!'

'I am sorry,' he said, still gentle. Filled with disgust at himself, yet he felt pity for the child. 'I have changed my mind. But I will pay you for your inconvenience.'

Mutely, she held out her hand, and he fumbled for coins.

'Why do you do this?' he asked, futilely, for he already knew the answer. But her reply surprised him.

'Fer food,' she said, grinning at what he had given her. 'I buys sausages with this, 'ot sausages and buns. Then I eats 'em.'

'Have you no family to feed you?'

She shrugged.

'Pa works here, round the cellars and stables, odd jobs. That's why landlord lets me use the rooms. Good for custom, see, though I 'as to give 'im a bit o' what I makes. But Pa's money, why, 'e drinks it all, see. So I earns me own.'

She grinned at him chirpily. He had been generous and he had not hurt her. The evening looked good to her.

Dane shrugged, impulsively pressing another couple of shillings into her hand. 'Eat a few more sausages for me,' he said, and strode rapidly out. Out through the bar where several girls were now prancing on the tables and several bucks snored under the tables, both in various stages of undress, and out into the welcome cold air of the street.

Aghast at what he had almost done, angry at himself, angry at Esther, angry at Henrietta, he walked rapidly through the streets, nursing a gathering headache. Brushing aside a hopeful prostitute with a brusqueness that made her stagger and shout an oath at his retreating back, he strode on, until at last he found a street he recognised, and he was able to make his way back to his house, and to his bed, and at last, thankfully, to the oblivion of sleep.

CHAPTER SEVENTEEN

HENRIETTA had no energy to get out of bed. She felt miserably apathetic, she had no idea of how to spend her day, and there was a steady drizzle falling outside. She pushed aside her breakfast tray and, wriggling down under the covers, buried her face back into the pillows.

'Nothing to be gained by staying there, Miss Hetta,' Meggie said, regarding her mistress with fond disapproval. 'Need to get up and occupy yourself with something useful.'

Hetta raised her head fractionally.

'What would you suggest, Meggie?' she asked bitterly, her voice still muffled in pillows. 'Stitching a sampler?'

'No need to take that tone, Miss Hetta. There's letters you could write. What of His Lordship down there at Alnstrop not knowing where you are? It would be a kindness to let him know what you are doing.'

'A kindness, Meggie? To send him a quick note to say I am living the life of a deserted prostitute in Lockchain Terrace? Much he would thank me for that! It would give the poor man an early apoplexy.'

'You, Miss Hetta, are helping Mr Dane in his search from no more than true Christian charity, and living as decent and blameless a life as any saint. As I can testify.' She shook out the shift she was holding irritably. 'And more's the pity!' she ended on a mutter, but Hetta heard her.

'Oh, Meggie, Meggie, what have I done?'

'Acted like a blame fool, Miss Hetta, that's what you've done. You and your high principles. He's a good man, that Mr Dane. Worth a whole parcel of his cousins. Why you should want him to go back to that female, who's kept him dangling like a marionette, I do not know. If a woman can't take what's good for her when it's offered, well, that's her fault, I say. No worry of yours.'

'But Meggie, he loves her. Can't I want him to be happy? I did it for the best. For him. And so *she* would not be hurt as *I* was...'

'Huh,' Meggie grunted disparagingly. 'If he loves that one he doesn't know what's good for him, that's for sure.'

'Oh, Meggie, what shall I do?'

'Stop wallowing in those pillows and get up and dressed, for a start, Miss Hetta,' Meggie said briskly. 'I've warm water here for you to wash. Come on, do.'

Hetta gave Meggie a weak, reluctant smile, and edged her toes out of the side of the bed.

It was early afternoon when there was a knock on the door. Hetta was sitting huddled by the fire, dutifully mending her petticoat where she had torn the hem, catching her heel in it while she was riding on Earlswood Common. Her heart froze when she heard the knock, and her hand seemed poised for an eternity, unable to push the needle into the cloth, until Meggie opened the door, and Sarah came in, clutching baby Dickon. Time began again, and Hetta pulled the stitch through.

''Ow are yer, then, eh? 'Ad a good time away, did yer?' Sarah sauntered over, cheerfully at home, pulled another chair up to the fire, and shifted the kettle into the heat. 'Cuppa tea, eh?'

Hetta smiled. 'Of course. When do we not? How is Dickon?'

Sarah shrugged.

'Not so good, I reckon. 'E's quiet, like. 'Ere, 'ave a look fer yerself.'

Hetta hastily pushed aside her sewing as the baby was dumped into her lap. She studied the child while Sarah rummaged in the cupboard for the tea caddy and pot. He was sleeping, with one thin fist held to his mouth. He sucked at it as she watched, then sighed and turned his head aside. The flesh of his face had fallen away even since she last saw him. There was no plumpness at all in his cheeks now; the bones stood out against the shadowed hollows below. His skin was a yellowish grey, almost translucent, the veins showing as blue threads beneath. His lips were thin and colourless, and his fingers were as skinny as young twigs on a winter tree. There was a crusting of dirt around his nose, and little dry coughs shook him as he slept.

In a wave of pity, Hetta held him against her.

'Has he been fed this morning?' she asked.

Sarah was busy with the teapot.

''E's not got much of an interest in food, to tell yer the truth. If 'e's asleep I jist leaves 'im be.'

Hetta frowned.

'Put some milk on to warm, would you, Meggie?' she asked, keeping her other thoughts to herself. 'Leave him here with me,' she said, 'if you want to go out today. I'll gladly take care of him.'

Sarah grinned.

'I was 'opin' you might say jist that, 'Etta. I'll tell yer fer why. Acoss I jist met a new man. 'E's no great looker, mind, but 'e's a kindly soul, 'e's generous, and 'e's meetin' me this afternoon at the King's 'Ead! I've bin 'opin' fer somethin' a bit steady, and this might jist be the one, so I don't want little 'un around to put 'im off, do I?'

'No,' said Hetta. 'I don't suppose you do.' She took the cup of tea Sarah handed her, and watched while Meggie poured the milk. They had acquired a glass feeding bottle for the baby. It was not ideal, but easier to manipulate than the clay pipe! 'You can leave him here for as long as you like at the moment,' she continued. 'I would enjoy having Dickon here; he will be a distraction for me while I am on my own. Jonathan will probably not be coming around for a few days.'

She paused, not wanting Sarah to catch the bitterness in her voice. But Sarah had her nose in her teacup, and was not listening closely.

'I'll leave 'im with yer, then, and be on me way,' she said cheerfully, clattering her cup down and getting to her feet. 'By the way, I've kept askin' abaht that Millie. There's a lot o' people remember 'er, but I've not found one 'oo knows where she is now. But don't worry. I'll keep on askin', an' I've got friends as are doin' the same. Should find aht before long.'

With a grin, a wave and a bang of the door, she was gone, and a few minutes later they heard her clattering down the stairs and out into the street.

Hetta held the glass side of the baby's bottle against her cheek to check the warmth of the milk, before edging its spout gently between Dickon's lips. He spluttered as the liquid trickled into his mouth, but he swallowed feebly, and Hetta gained hope. She settled herself to the long task of coaxing the nourishment into the apathetic child.

She held him all day, rocking him and crooning, stroking his head and nestling him against her, her need for comfort as great as his. For hours together she sat with the bottle of milk, cajoling him, stroking at his cheek to make him suck, kissing him and pleading with the tiny scrap to make some effort to feed himself.

Meggie watched her with very mixed emotions. She was pleased to see Hetta distracted away from herself, and her own gloomy thoughts, but looking at the child she could not believe that he would survive. She judged it might be only a matter of days, even less, and what would happen to Miss Hetta then she did not like to think. Her thoughts were interrupted.

'Meggie, there is a little shop we passed, on the way back from church. It looked like a chemist's store. It seemed to sell drugs and such like, do you remember? It certainly had those great coloured glass bottles in the window. I dare say it is no better than a mediaeval apothecary's, but we must try something to help. Do you know where I mean?'

'Yes, I saw it, Miss Hetta.'

'Run round there for me, Meggie, and see what he can offer for a baby; a baby who is very thin, lacks appetite and coughs continually. Anything at all that he has that might help. Oh, and Meggie, ask if he can recommend a doctor who might come round and see Dickon. Urgently.'

Meggie nodded, stifling her doubts. 'I'll be off right away,' she said, and fetched her long cloak to wrap about her against the persistent misty rain. 'I'll be as quick as I can, miss.'

The chemist's shop was in an old, beamed building, the tiny leaded panes and low front door set back beneath the overhang of the upper storey. The door scraped along the step as Meggie pushed it open, and just as well, she thought, otherwise she might have tumbled headlong down the couple of steps into the shop, obscured as they were in the gloom. The lowering greyness of the day, and the tiny windows, combined to leave the interior of the chemist's in almost total darkness.

Over on a counter a single candle burned, framing in a circle of golden glow the head and shoulders of a hunched old man, who was grinding away with a pestle and mortar. His hooked nose showed harsh contrasts of light and shadow, the spectacles perched on it winked and glinted, his jutting eyebrows shot up his forehead as he studied Meggie, and his wide-brimmed hat threw crazy shadows on to the shelves of bottles, jars, boxes and bundles of drying herbs that were ranged behind him. With a sudden terrifying apprehension that she was entering a witches' den, Meggie advanced to the counter.

'Well, my dear, and how can I help you?'

He set aside his pestle and mortar, a waft of spicy aniseed reaching Meggie as he did so, and smiled, taking off his spectacles and rubbing his eyes. He looked instantly twice as human, and approachable, and with a sigh of relief Meggie poured out the story of little Dickon and all his symptoms.

'Truly, sir,' she concluded, 'I don't think he can last more than a few days, but the mistress will rest the easier when he's gone if she knows she's done all she could. Have you anything that might help?'

'Hmm.' The old man raised his wide-brimmed hat, scratched his head, and walked along the back of the shop, studying the laden shelves and muttering to himself.

'If you are right, there is not much to be done,' he said eventually, returning to the counter with bottles and jars, 'but these may be of some help. Emetic Tartar,' he carefully shook a few grains of powder into a bottle, and filled it up with water from a kettle that had been quietly hissing on a small fire at the end of the room. 'Shake that bottle for me, will you?' he continued, pushing in the cork. 'This'—producing another bottle—'is Balsam of Life, and this'—a larger bottle—'is for the cough. You will also need camomile tea.'

At last, laden with remedies, advice, instructions and the address of a doctor, and having parted with an unexpectedly small number of coins, Meggie staggered back through the rain to Lockchain Terrace.

'Thank heavens you are back,' Hetta greeted her. 'Take off your wet cloak quickly. What did he say, what have you brought?'

'Emetic Tartar.' Meggie put the bottle on the table and rattled off the instructions while they were fresh in her mind. 'Two teaspoons every quarter of an hour will make him vomit and clear the poisons from his system. A small drink of camomile tea should follow each vomit, to settle the stomach. He swore this was better than James's Fever Powder. The Balsam of Life,' she held out the bottle, 'will work against any manner of undetected diseases within, and provide an excellent strengthener for the whole body—one teaspoon three times a day—and this,' she produced the last bottle, 'is the cough medicine. It contains opium and aniseed and liquorice and wine and honey, and... oh, I forget what else, but you can give it whenever it is required, two teaspoons at a time.

'Oh, yes, and he said the only doctor he knew who would call round here is Dr Warner, but he is a crusty old character with the devil's own temper. He lives in Mountain Street. Do you want me to fetch him?'

'No, no,' Hetta said, her attention on the medicines. 'Sit down and dry out. If this man is so bad-tempered he can at least wait till we have tried what your chemist can do.' She reached for the bottle of emetic.

Whether because of the medicines, or because of the regular feeding, warmth and loving he was receiving, Dickon looked a little better by evening. He had some colour in his wasted cheeks, and showed an interest in his food. Hetta had decided to use the emetic just before each bottle of milk, to clear his system to accept the feed, and she gave a little camomile tea after the milk, to encourage digestion. As evening drew on and his cough bothered him more she increased the amount of cough medicine, and at last he slept peacefully, tucked up in his drawer by the fire. Hetta was exhausted, barely able to swallow her own supper for the yawns that engulfed her. Later, when they were all in bed, she heard Sarah return, obviously with male company. Predictably, no one called to collect the child.

In fact, Hetta was surprised the next morning, approaching midday, when she heard the door across the landing slam, and a sharp rat-tat on her own. Sarah came in, somewhat bashfully leading a man. 'Mr Tupp, Mr William Tupp.'

He was a pink, plump man, with a round, cherubic face, wispy fair hair, and chubby little hands, one of which constantly clasped one of Sarah's own. He beamed at Hetta with the air of a man amazed at the goodness of life, and professed himself all agog to see the baby of his dearest Sarah, to meet the friend of his dearest Sarah, and to spread a little of his joy at having met his dearest Sarah to her friends. Upon which words he flourished two large bottles of champagne and insisted they all toast his new-found happiness.

Sarah grinned sheepishly, half apologetic, for it could not be said that Mr Tupp cut a romantic dash, and half delighted at the little man's devoted attentions. Hetta thought him comically charming. He exuded good humour and affection, admiring the room and its furnishings, admiring the baby, and pressing a gold sovereign into his hand, and praising Hetta for her care of the child. Every comment from either of the ladies brought on a burst of cheery laughter, every intimacy of Sarah's a throaty chuckle, wink and squeeze. Throughout, he lavished attentions on Sarah, and Hetta had to smile to see how the girl blossomed under the blandishments of her unlikely swain.

It emerged that he was a farmer from Wiltshire, a widower, and had come up to town on business, to be settled with his brother-in-law who lived in Covent Garden. He hoped to remain in town for at least another eight weeks, and expected to enjoy every one of them now he had the company in which to do so. He laughed again, with comfortable satisfaction, and he gave the giggling Sarah a smacking kiss on her cheek.

They stayed for over an hour, sharing a meal of cold meats sent over from Miss Perkins, before setting out for a shopping spree, leaving baby Dickon, to her relief, with Hetta. She settled to feed him again in the peace that followed their departure.

Jonathan Dane had woken, the morning after his visit to the Admiral Nelson, to a thundering headache and astonished self-disgust. He sat long and gloomily over the coffee at his solitary breakfast, brooding over Henrietta's words, his break with Esther, and his own behaviour. None of his thoughts lightened his countenance. He spent the day morosely in his house, pacing the floor of the small living-room, ignoring his food, and driving Mrs Stockwell to complain to cook that he must be liverish, and it was playing havoc with his temper.

It was not until the following morning that at last he decided that he *must* see Henrietta. He must tell her of the finality of his break from Esther, attempt to convince her of his feelings for her, and discover if there was any truth in what she had said about another man. He still refused to believe it, but if there was—he found his fists were clenched at the thought—he would oust the fellow permanently from her affections and show her where her future lay. With him.

He spent some time choosing his clothes, even longer arranging his cravat to his satisfaction, and then spent time hunting for flowers to purchase, to make his peace. It was nearing midday by the time he had managed to purchase an extravagant bunch of the unusual autumn chrysanthemums, and had made his way to Lockchain Terrace.

He felt absurdly nervous, mounting the stairs to her room, acknowledging to himself finally what he should have recognised weeks ago, that he was coming to court her. He had no idea what her reaction would be on seeing him. He clutched the bunch of flowers determinedly, touched his cravat to ensure its folds were unsullied, and paused before knocking on the door to clear his throat and compose his mind.

As he stood there a burst of laughter came from within the room. It was masculine laughter, and as he listened, the flush of embarrassment draining from his cheeks to leave his face pale and set, he heard the voice of a man, unmistakably chaffing, familiar and affectionate; and he heard a woman's voice softly, lovingly he thought, reply. There was a further chuckle of laughter. It sounded very intimate.

It seemed hours that he stood there, motionless, even breathing suspended, unable to cease hearing those sounds of affection from within the room. In fact, he realised later, it was probably only seconds before he began to withdraw down the steps, hurt and anger filling him with acute pain.

By God, but she had wasted no time. Not she. And it had been true. All damnably true. He realised, with a certainty, that in his heart he had never believed it of her until now, now that he had heard the proof. It had offended every conception he had of Henrietta, to think that she should so casually find some other man from the streets. But it had been true. He shook his head in a vain gesture to rid it of such impossible revelations, then, striding over the road to retrieve his carriage from young Sam, he flung the chrysanthemums into the gutter.

CHAPTER EIGHTEEN

IT WAS two days before Jonathan Dane returned to Lockchain Terrace. Two days of despair for Mrs Stockwell and outrage for his cook, two days of hard wear on his much-paced carpets, two days when he could not bear to think about Henrietta, but could not keep his thoughts away from her.

The treadmill cogitations took him nowhere. Reason said he should forget her, abandon his fruitless search for Laura, leave this small, unfashionable, understaffed house that he had hired merely for convenience while he conducted his search, and seek some imposing residence in the country where he could live as became his status and wealth. He should, sensibly, settle to marry one of the biddable new offerings of the next London season. Dane was well aware that, whatever Esther might think of his family, once the extent of his fortune became known in polite circles, he would be viewed as a very desirable catch indeed. He would be left with no time to mourn the loss of Henrietta.

Such were the dictates of reason. Emotion spoke otherwise.

The desire to inflict barbaric physical injuries upon this unknown man Henrietta had chosen for her favours was at times so strong that Dane was certain that, had the man appeared in his sitting-room—and could the longings of vengeance have procured that end then he must have done so—then he would instantly have killed him. If not instantly, then lingeringly. The physical acts he wished to perpetrate with Henrietta were no less primitive, and just as compelling. He knew that no biddable miss fresh from the schoolroom would ever compete with his infuriating, impulsive, intrepid, adorable, unpredictable, irreplaceable Henrietta, and when he purchased his home in the country he wanted no other mistress of it than her. No one at all could take her place. That was a conviction that no amount of reason could overset.

It was not in a mood of doubt and uncertainty that he arrived back at Mrs Crabbe's, at a time when breakfast would be barely finished. He gave not a thought to his appearance, he bought no flowers. His heavy caped great-coat flapped open in the stiff autumn wind as he jumped down from the carriage, his dark green superfine beneath was carelessly unbuttoned, his cravat crumpled. A hard frown knit his brows. His mouth was grim as he handed the horses over to young Sam, and he strode up the stairs with a ferocious determination that bode ill for anyone who stood in his way. Reason had not brought him here, only emotion.

He was intent on claiming Henrietta, and he would fight any obstacle to get her. He hoped the other man *was* there. He would throw him bodily down the stairs with the greatest of satisfaction. Tense, his breathing quickened, and his rap on the door with the head of his cane was sharp, demanding. Suddenly his anticipation of her was keen.

The tableau that greeted him as the door was pulled back froze him as he stood, all the fight and fury draining from him. Meggie, her face white and strained, a smudge of rubbed tears on her cheeks, was just before him. Beyond her, on the chair by the fire, was Henrietta, her eyes huge hollows in the grey of her face, staring blindly at him, a glass feeding bottle on the chair beside her, a small, pathetic bundle limp in her arms. The child was dead.

It seemed to Jonathan, after the aggressive vitality that had carried him to her door, that time now moved very slowly, with the quality of a nightmare, every fraction of a moment etched on his mind as he moved into the room. Meggie shut the door behind him and took his hat and great-coat and cane, her movements slow and mechanical like a puppeteer's doll, though a hint of hope now broke the tense misery of her face. Hardly seeing her as she moved on the edge of his nightmare, he went on towards Henrietta.

She was gently laying the child in the drawer that had been his bed, staring at him with grief-blind eyes as, with trembling fingers, she closed the paper thinness of his lids. The lashes lay, stark and dark as moth's wings on the death-paled cheekbones. She stood up and turned that wide, shocked stare upon Dane's face. After a moment in which she seemed, agonisingly, not to know him, a quiver of acknowledgement broke the blankness of her gaze.

'Jonathan,' she said. 'Oh, Jonathan, you are here.' As she spoke, a shuddering sigh shook her slight shoulders, and tears, hitherto unshed, welled into her eyes. 'Thank God. You came.'

She stepped forward into the comfort of his arms as naturally as she would have turned to her brothers, and the hugeness of her unleashed grief shook her in great gasping sobs. She leant her head blindly against his chest, and wept.

He stood for an eternity holding her, his face harsh with pain, staring sightlessly at the window-frame, stroking her hair and feeling the shudders of her sobs against him. There was nothing to say, nothing that could yet be said. He waited, while the racking gasps quietened.

Time did not begin again for him until a series of wet sniffs recalled him to Henrietta's lack of handkerchief, and the dampness of his green superfine, and his buff kerseymere waistcoat. He produced the previously spurned handkerchief from his waistcoat pocket and silently pushed it into the damp little hand that clutched at the plated buttons of his coat. She took it and blew her nose vigorously, retaining the damp square of linen clutched in a tight fist. Slowly she raised her blotched, tear-stained face to his.

Her eyes were ringed by exhaustion and swollen by tears. Her nose was red and damp, her cheeks streaked, her hair unkempt but, he knew with a surge of warmth, she had no thought whatever for herself. Her lips trembled as she fought to steady them to speak. So fierce was his possessive, protective love as he gazed down at her in all her misery that he could not help but tighten his grip about her, pulling her hard against him as if he could thus absorb the pain and grief that racked her and take it to himself. He fought down an urge to kiss away the blotches, the tears and the exhaustion, and bent his head to listen as she began to whisper.

'He's dead, Jonathan. Dickon is dead.'

She broke off as she began to tremble violently, her teeth chattering so she could not speak. Jonathan turned his head abruptly aside to where Meggie was standing, wringing her hands together and staring at them, as if the events of the day had frozen her wits.

'Make the fire up, Meggie, pile it high. We shall want hot bricks; and make tea, hot and strong, and something to eat, toast or some such. And a small draught of laudanum if you have it. Hurry, now.'

Given a task to do, Meggie came to life and began to busy herself by the fire. Dane, his arms still about Henrietta, swept her easily up and carried her to the bed, pulling aside the screening curtains and sitting her on the covers.

'Bed for you, my girl,' he said firmly, 'and no arguments.'

She sat unresisting, numb, as if unaware of any need for arguments, while his fingers deftly undid the row of tiny buttons at the front of her dress, and the cross-over tie under her breasts. He thought briefly, wryly, of his determined desires as he had run up the stairs to her door such a short time before. Now her only response to his gently touching fingers was the automatic shuddering of shock. He slipped the dress off her, but though she raised her arms with the compliance of a child, she seemed hardly aware as he lifted her again and tucked her under the blankets, plumping the pillows and laying her gently back.

'Bring that hot brick, Meggie, or two if you have them.'

'Yes, Mr Dane, sir.'

As the bricks were tucked in beside her Henrietta began again to speak, raising her eyes anxiously to his, the tears rolling once more on to her cheeks, but Dane commanded she lie quietly until he allowed. He would not let her talk until she had drunk two cups of tea, and been reluctantly bullied into swallowing a piece of toasted bread, coaxed down her mouthful by mouthful as if she had been a child. He washed her face and hands himself, as she lay, soothing her tear-swollen eyes with firm, cooling strokes of the flannel, softly towelling her dry, gently brushing the disordered curls. All this in silence. No one spoke, except for Dane's brief requests to Meggie, as if by putting nothing of what they did into words they could turn the extraordinary familiarity of what he did for her so competently into mere commonplace attentions.

When he had finished, and Meggie had taken away the ewer of water, he took Henrietta's hand in his own, smiled down at her for a moment, then bent and kissed her forehead. She looked so vulnerable and defenceless, so much in need of his care . . . and so very desirable. He was suddenly acutely aware of his own suppressed desire, the quickening of his pulse as, still holding her hand, he gazed down at her. His eyes drifted to her lips, still swollen, bruised almost, trembling.

'Jonathan,' Her voice came out as a broken whisper, and she coughed, and repeated more strongly, 'Jonathan, please—move him to where I can see him.'

Knowing himself to have been thinking like a fool, Jonathan collected his scattered wits, gently released Hetta's hand, and brought the little makeshift cot over, standing it on a chair near the bed. He saw the tears well up in her eyes again as she looked at the child, and quietly fetched more handkerchieves from Meggie.

'Now,' he said, 'tell me what happened.'

It was a damp and sorry tale. A tale of Sarah persuading some man to take her on a trip to Brighton, the baby, of course, to be left with Henrietta. Of medicines from a chemist that seemed to work, then did not, with a sudden dreadful weakening of the child. Of a panic-stricken dash by Meggie to fetch a doctor, while Hetta sat, alone and terrified, listening to the laboured breathing of the dying boy. Of the hours before the irate doctor would leave a difficult labour and come to them, then the relief of his arrival followed abruptly by his rudeness, his assumption of a gross neglect of the baby by a woman such as she appeared to be. Then his callous assurance that the child would die, there was nothing to be done at this stage; it had been too late for many a long day for little Dickon, and he doubted if any would mourn his passing; a child was inconvenient in their trade, was he not?

Refusing payment before any was offered as if to take anything from them would defile him, the doctor had hurried away to another labour that was as unwanted as it promised to be troublesome. Hetta had sat up all night, holding the child, trying to ease his passing. She had not dared send Meggie out alone in such a district at night to search for the priest, and she had no faith, after the reactions of the doctor, that he would have come had Meggie been able to find him.

Dickon had died not long after dawn, while Hetta held him, dry-eyed, and Meggie dozed restlessly in the other chair. She had sat holding him, unmoving, until Dane's arrival. Sarah was still in Brighton, but they expected her back today. She would have to be told. The violent trembling, which had calmed as Hetta talked, began once again.

'Enough,' Jonathan said. 'No more talking. Drink your laudanum now, you are going to sleep.'

'Jonathan, I *cannot*. I must see Sarah as soon as she returns. I have to explain. I am responsible.'

She began anxiously to push herself up off the pillows.

'Nonsense. You are responsible because she abandons her child to you? What absurdity.'

'Don't you understand? She left Dickon in my care.'

'She did. And you did everything a living soul could do for that child, and far more than Sarah herself would have done had she been here. Admit it, Henrietta. Sarah will not be heartbroken at Dickon's death. She cared for him far less than you did. You have done everything you could. Now you are going to sleep.' His voice was stern, authoritative. He handed her the glass he held.

'I will stay here, with Meggie, and we will watch over Dickon. I will tell Sarah, when she returns, all that has occurred, and I will make all the necessary arrangements for his funeral, at the little church where his christening was held. You must sleep so that you are strong enough to attend. So, no arguments. Drink.'

He stood up peremptorily from the edge of the bed, where he had been sitting as she talked. After watching as she opened her mouth to protest, looked at his face for a moment, then paused, gave a tiny shrug, and instead obediently drained the draught; he took the empty glass from her, and reached to draw the curtains of the bed.

She stretched out a hand to him.

'Thank you, Jonathan,' she said.

She lightly touched his hand, turned away, and closed her eyes. He pulled the curtain across and went to stand by the fire, waiting for Sarah's return.

He wondered, as he stood there, about the identity of the other man. He studied the room now with a spurt of angry, jealous curiosity. There was no sign of a masculine presence in the room. Did that mean he did not exist, or that Jonathan had been unaware of his existence for weeks, because he had never left any sign of his visits? Dane frowned. He knew the man existed. Henrietta had said he did. He himself had heard him. The frown deepened, his brows a hard line across his forehead, his stare fixed broodingly on the closed curtains of the bed.

Sarah arrived back sometime after midday. As she did not immediately come over to fetch Dickon, Dane crossed the landing and knocked at her door. She answered it, holding her gown across her chest, and giggling over her shoulder at a chubby, pink-faced man, whose air of solid yeoman respectability struck Dane as oddly incongruous in the squalor of Sarah's room.

He told the news of Dickon's death briefly. He knew he was not mistaken in the flicker of relief that crossed Sarah's face, before the plump gentleman took her in his arms and began to comfort her supposed grief with surprising tenderness. They agreed with alacrity to Dane's offer to arrange the funeral, and he withdrew, assuring them he would let them know as soon as arrangements were made. Sarah had not, he noticed, asked to see the pathetic scrap that had been her child.

Henrietta was still sleeping, so, leaving her under Meggie's watchful eye, Dane set off down Turk's Alley and William Street to the tiny church.

It took him some time to track down the Reverend Mr Smith, but by means of persistent questioning of the seemingly witless local population he eventually discovered the cleric sipping tea in the best parlour of an elderly parishioner. With hasty apologies for his intrusion he managed to coax and bully the startled Mr Smith into agreeing to a burial the following afternoon. No, he said in response to Dane's pressure, nothing could be done sooner; the haste would be unseemly—here the old woman nodded severely—and besides, the sexton could not have the ground dug any sooner.

Dane was forced to be content. He wanted the whole business finished as soon as possible, and Henrietta able to put it all behind her.

The funeral, the following day, was very quiet. They stood, a motley little group in their unaccustomed black garb, at the graveside, in steady rain, their feet slipping in the mud.

Sarah, important with a sense of occasion, leaned heavily on the arm of Mr Tupp, dabbing at the raindrops on her cheeks with a handkerchief, while he patted her hand comfortingly. Henrietta stood alone, stiff-backed and white-faced, having moved away from Jonathan's proffered arm with a mute shake of her head. He stood a little behind her, watching her thoughtfully. Meggie sniffed, with doleful, easy tears, and beyond her Miss Perkins and young Sam stood solemnly. Under the shelter of the yew trees the two crones from the christening—Dane was certain they were the same—stood gazing and whispering together, their cloaks pulled tight about them against the wet.

Mr Smith's words intoned drearily through the raindrops, half drowned by the spattering of water from the mouth of the grotesque stone gargoyle in the guttering of the church roof behind them landing on the gravelled path below.

When all was done, Mr Smith, still regarding them with suspicious distaste, vanished back into the church; the two witches disappeared without trace from beneath the yew trees, and Dane shepherded his little flock back into his carriages. They returned to Lockchain Terrace, to do justice to the spread of food provided by Miss Perkins. There was wine too, and he ensured that Henrietta was warm by the fire with a glass of wine before he tended to the others, easily assuming the role of host in those cramped quarters with a quiet courtesy that made them all welcome, and excused Henrietta's numbed silence.

This strange dulling of her feelings had stayed with Henrietta since that one outburst of her grief, distancing her from events and people. She heard none of the talk in the room around her, and watched Jonathan with an incurious detachment, aware of that quiet competence upon which she had come to rely so heavily, aware of the reassurance of his presence, but without any response. Her emotions remained deadened, numb.

She watched without interest when Miss Perkins took her leave, shepherding out a green-tinged Sam who had been discovered, hidden on the far side of the bed, quietly swallowing the last drops from a wine bottle he had acquired.

It seemed an age before Sarah and Mr Tupp took their leave. They appeared to feel it obligatory to finish all the offered refreshment, especially the liquid refreshment, and their eventual departure was in a haze of good cheer, the reason for their excesses quite forgotten.

At last they were alone again. Jonathan looked at Henrietta. She was staring into her wine-glass, the wine hardly touched.

Once again he stifled all thought of the things he so urgently wanted to say to her, to ask her. He sighed, with a wry little smile. At least the other man had not appeared at the funeral. Dane had had an unreasonable fear that he would, and that circumstance would force a polite greeting. He was thankful, at least, to have been spared that. He rested a hand lightly on her shoulder.

'Bed once more for you, my girl,' he said.

'Yes, indeed, Miss Hetta,' Meggie joined in. 'You look like a death's head yourself. But sir,' she turned to Dane, 'we have no laudanum left, and I do think . . . not that I like her to take it often . . . but just for tonight . . .'

'I will go out and endeavour to procure some. Get your mistress into bed. Don't forget the hot bricks!'

'As if I would, Mr Dane, sir!'

He eventually purchased some in the same odd little chemist Meggie had used, still open despite the lateness of the hour, and took it back. Henrietta was propped up on the pillows, sipping at a hot posset under the eagle glare of Meggie, who was standing, arms akimbo, daring her Miss Hetta to show one ounce of defiance in draining every drop. Jonathan smiled, and handed her the laudanum.

'I will stay with Henrietta for a moment, Meggie, and I promise to see that she drinks it all,' he said, 'then I shall be returning home. I will call you when I go.'

Meggie scowled at him, not liking this plain dismissal from her post, but something she saw in Dane's face must have reassured her, for she gave a curt nod, and retired into her own room.

Jonathan sat down on the edge of the bed. Henrietta looked absurdly young, both hands clutching her beaker, regarding him solemnly over its brim, the bright blue of her eyes dark with the buffetings of exhaustion and grief. The red of the firelight flickered over the white of the pillows, and the creamy, soft folds of her nightdress, tied demurely at her neck, and the little lace nightcap perched on the black curls. He looked at her; but he made no move to touch her.

'Finish your posset, or I shall be in trouble with Meggie.' His voice was gruff, and he coughed, and cleared his throat. 'I want to tell you something,' he said, watching her. 'No questions, no arguments—just tell you a fact for your consideration. Then I shall go home and leave you to Meggie's ministrations.'

She nodded, and he thought her eyes looked apprehensive.

He drew a deep breath.

'My connection with Miss Esther Wanhope is entirely at an end,' he said abruptly. He saw her eyes widen but she did not speak, and he continued. 'We agreed to acknowledge something that has become increasingly plain to us both over the past few weeks: that we were taking less and less pleasure in each other's company. Esther offered to terminate our so-called "understanding". She admitted that her affections are now engaged elsewhere, and I believe we will be hearing shortly of her engagement to Lord Glenby. With this I am more than content. *We* would not have dealt well together, but it pleases me that she has found what she wishes with somebody else.'

Henrietta was obediently draining the posset, her eyes still fixed on his face, but now she paused.

'Drink it,' he said, before she could speak, and waited while she did so. He had not meant to say more. Just to let her know that he was free of Esther. Nothing else. But he looked at her, stricken as she was by the events of the last few days, and he was filled with a cold fury at this other man who, whatever she had claimed about having another protector, had done nothing for her in her grief, leaving her alone and vulnerable. He deliberately spoke on.

'I also had to tell her,' he continued, taking the empty beaker and setting it aside, 'that my own affections were now engaged elsewhere, a fact she had suspected. She...er...' he grinned twistedly '...she wished me joy of my new relationship.'

'Jonathan——' Henrietta began anxiously, her voice little more than a whisper.

Unable to bear the thought of what she might be about to say to him, he raised a finger and laid it gently on her lips, shaking his head.

'No,' he said, 'no discussion. Not tonight, for you are in no fit state. But you must have suspected how I feel about you——'

'About me?' She still sounded dazed.

'Of course about you, Henrietta. Has *nothing* I have done given you to suspect? And I mean to claim you, no matter how many other men you have involved in your life.' He could not quite keep the bitterness from his voice, but took her hand and gently raised it to his lips.

'But Jonathan——'

'No. I could not talk calmly about any other relationship of yours tonight, and nor, I believe, could you. But in view of what I have told you...now you know my feelings...may I come back tomorrow morning?'

He had stood up, regarding her gravely, waiting on her verdict, uncertain whether he had been wise, or a precipitate fool, or profoundly selfish, to risk all in such a way at such a time. He was ridiculously aware of the heavy pounding of his heart.

'May I?' he repeated.

'Yes...' uncertainly, then, 'Yes, please Jonathan,' she said.

In a huge surge of relief he bent and kissed her briefly on her lips.

'Till tomorrow, then,' he said abruptly, and, calling to Meggie, he took his leave.

CHAPTER NINETEEN

SARAH and Mr Tupp, arms linked, faces beaming, were emerging from the door of Mrs Crabbe's house when Jonathan returned next morning, on their way to breakfast at the coffee shop. Miss Perkins, seeing them all, waved and called a cheery good morning as she briskly swept rubbish from the doorway of the shop across into the gutter, then called to Sam to take Mr Dane's horses double quick, and not keep the gentleman waiting.

It was another golden day, totally unexpected after the dismal rains of yesterday, the sky a bowl of thrush-egg blue above the smutted rooftops. Already, wherever the rays of the sun had reached, the buildings were steaming, drying in its warmth. One of Mr Perkins' bony nags, waiting patiently between the shafts of a cart loaded with timber, dozed in the grateful glow, while a huge marmalade cat washed itself luxuriously in the golden light, on the top of the yard wall.

'Wonderful day, innit, Mr Dane? Jist wonderful.'

Sarah looked as radiant as the morning, while her improbable swain beamed like a child's first drawing of the sun itself.

'An' we'd like you to be the first ter know, wouldn't we now, Willy?' she continued, glancing affectionately at her chubby-faced escort.

'Yes, indeed,' beamed and nodded Mr Tupp emphatically. 'Quite right. Very fitting, especially after all he did for the poor babby. You tell him, my dear.'

Sam, who had scurried up still hauling on a vast leather belt to buckle up his trousers, waited, holding Dane's horses, to hear this revelation, peering inquisitively from beneath his cap.

'We're to be wed!' Sarah burst out, her face alight with such a mixture of joy and amazement that it seemed she could hardly believe what she herself had said. 'Wed! An' I shall go ter Wiltshire and 'ave a farm! I shall learn ter keep the 'ens and ducks and geese all meself, and everythin' I make in the keepin' of 'em shall be me own profit! An' maybe we shall 'ave a fam'ly to make up for poor Dickon, and all Mr Tupp's babies from 'is fust wife, that lie with 'er in the churchyard in Wiltshire. There'll be puppies, an' kittens, an' a gig I can take in to the market, if Mr Tupp'll teach me to drive it!'

She giggled, and clung tight to the arm of her fiancé, who patted her hand and nodded approval, evidently deeply satisfied at the picture she evoked.

Dane, who had listened to this ingenuous outburst with an astonishment that mellowed rapidly into a sincere, if surprised delight, remembered his manners and hastily offered heartfelt congratulations, reflecting as he did so that the change begun by Henrietta in the life of the dreary, hopeless drab they had first met on arriving at Lockchain Terrace seemed to have borne such fruit as none of them could have imagined.

Food and warmth given freely by Henrietta had certainly played their part, but it seemed to Jonathan that it was the confidence and self-respect she had given, along with her friendship, that had helped to produce this glowing girl who had captured the long-term affections of a Wiltshire farmer, and had given her the courage to leave the life she had known for so long and start anew in what would be, hopefully, prosperity and respectability.

He raised Sarah's hand to his lips in an elegant gesture. 'To the bride-to-be,' he said, and she blushed with pleasure, while Sam grinned like a monkey and muttered, 'Coo-er!'.

Dane shook Mr Tupp firmly by the hand, and congratulated him on his good fortune.

'Aye,' that man said, looking momentarily solemn, 'and well you might. She's a lovely girl, and she makes me very happy. Oh, I know how her life has been, and I know what some people might say, but I've wed and buried a pious woman, and not a morsel of mirth did she bring me, not a moment of joy. But Sarah now, she brings me delight in every way, every moment we're together, and I believe I can fairly say I do the same for her. I know they do say there's no fool like an old fool, but you have only one life, after all, and no point in wasting it! No, we'll deal very well together.'

'As would you and your 'Etta,' Sarah suddenly put in, laying her hand on Dane's arm and leaning towards him earnestly, the sun falling bright on her straw chip bonnet. ''Tis ridiculous for you to be apart 'alf the time when 'tis plain to everyone 'ow much you love each other. Why,' she spoke with an added conviction born of her own new-found happiness, ''tis obvious in yer faces. I've seen the way you look at 'er when she doesn't know it; and I've seen 'er watching for yer carriage, and the look in 'er eyes when it never shows, an' then when at last it appears. Don't you throw it all away, mister. Make an 'onest woman of 'er, and an 'appy man of yerself! You marry 'er.'

Dane was studying her intently, Sam and Mr Tupp forgotten. There was no doubt she spoke what she believed to be the truth.

'I had thought,' he said, diffidently, 'that perhaps her interest had waned.' He gave a small, apologetic smile. 'That maybe she had met somebody else.'

Sarah's look of astonishment was utterly unfeigned.

'Your 'Etta? Some other man? Do yerself a favour! She's 'ad eyes for no one but you ever since I met 'er, and not much 'appens in that 'ouse but I get to 'ear about it! You mark my words. The only "other man" there's been in our 'Etta's life 'as been my little Dickon, and now she's lost even that poor scrap. Nah, nah.' She suddenly looked at him more sharply. 'Whatever made you think that, anyway?'

Dane shrugged, and spoke casually. 'Nothing, really. Just something Henrietta once said. And hearing a man in her room once when I called...' He stopped, feeling both foolish, and elated, as the strength of Sarah's conviction sank into his mind. He hardly listened to her explanation, her assurance that it would only have been Mr Tupp he had heard, and what a terrible thing it was to let a bit of misguided jealousy run away with you.

'She needs you,' Sarah was assuring him earnestly, 'and, what's more, she needs a baby of 'er own. And'—she gave him a leering nudge and a wink—'I dare say you could do something about that for the poor girl, wouldn't you say, Mr Tupp?'

Jonathan grinned at her. He knew she was absolutely right, and suddenly he was impatient to be gone.

'I cannot possibly argue with a lady; and I must not keep you longer, I am sure you wish to be alone together. Hop it, young Sam, and wipe that grin off your features sharpish if you know what's good for you! Your ears have flapped for long enough. Run away and earn your keep, and don't keep the horses standing!'

With a grin and a wave, he pushed open the door to number three and vanished within. Sarah regarded her espoused with a more than satisfied smile, and allowed herself to be shepherded towards the wafting smells of coffee.

Meggie opened the door to Jonathan's knock, but instead of admitting him she looked disconcerted.

'There, sir, I was listening out, but I never heard you arrive, and to tell truth I didn't think you'd be so early. If you could wait, sir, and take a turn up and down the street, for Miss Hetta's still in her bed. I thought it best to let her sleep on after all the doings of yesterday, but just give us half an hour, sir, and she'll be ready to receive you.'

Jonathan's smile was broad as he glanced at where the bed curtains twitched. He moved firmly past the indignant Meggie and into the room.

'Meggie,' he said, 'you are in every way admirable, but at this present instant I believe you are just a trifle *de trop*. Go to Miss Perkins, and procure for yourself a breakfast of sumptuous excellence—to be placed upon my account, naturally—before, in a most leisurely manner, returning here with a like repast for your mistress and myself——'

'Meggie! Don't you dare go out and leave me!'

The squawk came from behind the curtains. Dane continued as if there had been no interruption.

'You will find Sarah and Mr Tupp over there. They have some splendid news I am sure they would like to tell you themselves.' He was edging the uncertain Meggie nearer to the door all the time he spoke. 'And remember,' he finished, dropping his voice to a note of pleading, giving an irresistible smile and a conspiratorial wink, 'take your time!' He made as if to give her a push, but, with a sudden decision made, she beamed a smile at him and whisked out, turning to throw a cheeky wink back at him before he firmly closed the door.

'Meggie! Meggie...? Meggie, you wouldn't dare!'

With a slow smile Jonathan walked over to the bed. He paused a moment, hand to the curtain, then pulled it back.

'Meggie discovered an urgent need to refuel the inner woman over at the coffee shop!' he said, his voice grave, his eyes abrim with laughter. 'She may be some little while. Can I be of assistance?'

She sat, leaning forward, knees up, her nightcap pulled off and flung on to the covers. Her hair was an untidy tumble of dark curls above wide, startled blue eyes. She held the edge of the sheet, dragged firmly up to her chin, and she rested that small chin defiantly on her clenched fists as she glared at him.

'Jonathan... Mr Dane! This is quite outrageous! How dare you dismiss my maid against my express wishes!'

He ignored her, pulling back the rest of the curtains to let the bright sunlight stream on to the bed, for he loved to see the light of it on her curls; then he calmly took off his caped great-coat and laid it on the chair, before sitting on the bed near her, as he had the previous night.

Hetta edged herself a little further away from him, and retained her grip upon the sheet, aware that he was regarding her with growing amusement. She had thought unexpectedly long upon his words of last night before she had slept, and had been forced to acknowledge a very complete change in her attitude to the name of Dane, or at least to one of those who held that name. She had been forced to admit to herself that she had been fighting futile battles against her true feelings for far longer than she cared to recognise. She had remembered that initial kiss in the back room at the White Cocks, and she blushed in the darkness at her own response to it, just as she felt herself hotly blushing now, as she gripped the sheet to her and glared at his amusement.

'Your being here at all without Meggie is outrageous,' she continued, but her conviction was wilting before his raised eyebrow.

'And *your* being here at all? In Lockchain Terrace? Is not *that* just a *little* outrageous? But I had thought you above such trivial considerations!'

He was laughing at her, and she opened her mouth to protest, but he stopped her with a gesture and a chuckle.

'No, no, don't tell me again of the excellence of your intentions, for I know it all, my dearest love. For many a week now I have followed willy-nilly behind the most excellent of your intentions, and, for my sins, down every contorted path along which they have led us!' He laughed again, 'To think I once led a normal and respectable life!'

'Well, I don't believe it!' Hetta pronounced abruptly.

'Believe what?'

'I don't believe you ever led a normal and respectable life. I believe that, despite your big bullying cousins, you soon learned quiet and cunning ways to go about doing precisely what you like, *and* to avoid being caught, and that you have done so ever since, however outrageous it may be. I dare say that, far from pitying the young boy who was so rudely abandoned to life in India, we should be pitying the merchants of India among whom you arrived! No wonder you acquired such a fortune! I believe you are not at all the proper gentleman you like to appear. If you were, you would certainly not be here now! You are, in fact, a most ungentlemanlike gentleman!'

She suddenly remembered the origin of those words, spoken by Dane that night in Sussex: it was the description of the man he had recommended as her ideal. She stopped in confusion.

'My darling,' he said, 'there is no denying that you are, as ever, quite irresistibly correct. If you cannot bring yourself to care for an ungentlemanlike gentleman such as I, then I much regret it, but...' He paused and looked at her, then laughed outright. 'But how can I consider your rebukes seriously, when you perch there regarding me for all the world like an indignant squirrel caught raiding a picnic hamper?'

'Squirrel?' Despite herself, she was caught into a breathless chuckle.

Jonathan leant down, and very deliberately began to pull off his Hessian boots, casting them aside in a careless manner not likely to endear him to any gentleman's gentleman.

'Jonathan!'

'Yes, my darling?'

He turned to seat himself beside her, stretching his long legs in their beige pantaloons on the covers, and lying back into the pillows, his ruffled brown hair seeming darker against their whiteness. She still sat, tensely upright, beside him.

'Relax, small squirrel!' he said.

'If I were indeed a squirrel,' she replied with a burst of spirit, 'I should either be away over the rooftops with a flick of my tail by now, or, preferably, have bitten you in my attempts to escape!'

She turned her head to look defiantly down at him as she spoke, but that proved to be a mistake. He was smiling up at her, his eyes regarding her lazily from under his lashes, and as she turned to look at him he raised a hand and gently stroked her cheek.

'You are quite mistaken,' he said, his voice low and laughing. 'When I was a boy I secretly tamed a squirrel in the grounds at Thwayle, and eventually it would run up my arm'—he ran his fingers up her arm and on to her neck—'and take cob nuts from my lips.' And with the tip of his finger he touched her mouth. He felt her quiver of response and, sliding his hand down to her shoulder, he pushed her gently back on to the pillows beside him.

Henrietta looked up at him as he propped himself on his elbow. She solemnly studied the lines of his face, the thick dark lashes, the laughing slate-grey eyes. When he reached to trace again a gentle finger down her cheek, his expression all tender delight, she at last relaxed, and with a great sigh of contentment she turned towards him. She stretched her hand up and lightly touched his face, overwhelmed by an inexpressible tenderness as his eyes closed under her caress. She slid her hand around his neck, and pulled him down towards her. He paused for a moment, his face just above hers, gazing down at her, while she grew breathless with desire and her lips ached for the touch of his.

'Oh, my dearest love,' he murmured with a little groan, and then his lips were upon hers and he was kissing her with all the intensity of the weeks of frustrated doubts and uncertainties, bruising her lips with the fury of his need, thrusting aside the restricting covers that prevented him from holding her, caressing her and, in a tangle of sheets, blankets and clothing, possessing her.

Later their loving was gentle. Henrietta knelt, still demure in her nightgown, beside Jonathan, and stripped him of his clothes, stroking his body as she bared it to the sunlight and kissing the whiter marks of old scars, while he stretched, luxuriated, and chuckled under her questing touch, murmuring teasing remarks about bites from man-eating tigers, a swipe of a mad elephant's tusk, a sabre-thrust from an Indian warrior defending the honour of his royal mistress! But when he slowly pulled her nightgown over her head, and gazed at her with the sunlight glowing on the warmth of her skin, and soft shadows about the curves of her breasts and thighs, his gaze was of such yearning that she shyly blushed again before it, as he pulled her down to him once more.

Later again, she lay contented in his arms as he relaxed propped in the pillows, her head resting on his chest, and the blankets snug about them.

'I still maintain your behaviour is outrageous,' she murmured sleepily.

'Which must be why you find it irresistible, my own unladylike lady.'

She chuckled, her eyes closed.

'No...' his hand was moving gently in her hair, twining the curls '...the only truly outrageous thing you did was to try to convince me you had found some other man to take my place.'

'I know,' she said. 'But I did it for you. I thought *then* that you truly loved *her*...'

'Idiot.'

'Yes... I'm sorry.' She crept closer against him. 'Was it so very bad?'

'It doesn't matter now,' he said.

'Jonathan...?'

'Hmm?'

'I have to admit this. Even thought you *are* a Dane. I...well...I love you. I am afraid I have done for weeks.'

She felt rather than heard his answering chuckle as he tightened his hold about her.

'I have a guilty suspicion that I began to love you when I scooped you back to my house that first night we met. Though I did not permit myself to consider the matter for many a long day, so blinded was I by my confusions over Esther.'

'I had determined I could not like you because you were a Dane! So foolish!' She sighed, and ran a caressing hand across his chest.

'It will doubtless scandalise the servants,' Dane said idly, 'but I believe that I might insist upon spending every morning like this after we are married. So much more satisfying than formal breakfast!'

Her eyes were wide, and she was gazing at him, startled.

'But, my darling,' he said, surprised, 'surely you *will* marry me? Won't you? For you will have no peace until you do. I shall pester you ceaselessly, till the walls of your resistance crumble before my merciless assault. Which will all be a tedious waste of time that could be *much* better spent!'

'Are you certain? Truly certain?' she asked.

'Little idiot. Of course I am certain.'

'Then... why... oh, yes, Jonathan, please. I would like nothing better than to marry you immediately!' she said, and he was obliged to find another handkerchief for her as, muttering incoherently how happy she was, she shed tears that trickled and tickled their way down his chest.

When Meggie returned, clattering with a pointed racket up the stairway, and clashing dishes on the landing, Jonathan was dressed again, and Henrietta, charming in a casual mantua thrown over her nightgown, was preparing the table. Her careful nonchalance was no match for Meggie's determined scrutiny, however, and Hetta, blushing sheepishly under the ruthless stare, moved over to stand by Jonathan.

'Congratulate us, Meggie,' she said, 'for we are going to be married!'

Meggie's effusions were gruff, but heartfelt. She had both liking and respect for *this* Mr Dane, and considered that he would suit her Miss Hetta very well. And, she pointed out with satisfaction, the marriage would put a much-needed gloss of respectability over their relationship of the past few weeks, and enable *her* to face Lord Alnstrop with something approaching a clear conscience when next she saw her mistress's brother. 'For heaven knows he must be wondering where you are by now!' she concluded.

'Certainly we shall be informing Robert,' Henrietta replied, then chuckled, 'but as for this worry over respectability...! You must know that Jonathan and I are quite above such trivial considerations!'

Meggie snorted her outrage at such nonsense, and retired to her own room, leaving them to demolish an ample breakfast between them, while Jonathan revealed to an astounded Henrietta that they were not the only happy couple that morning, and sketched for her a lively picture of Sarah's delight, and her improbable but hopeful future on the farm, surrounded by her poultry, sundry young livestock, and her gig!

It was as they were finishing the meal that a rapid knock came at the door, and it opened to reveal Sarah herself. She glowed with pleasure under Hetta's ready kiss of congratulation, and received their news with genuine joy, and another lewd nudge and wink for Jonathan's benefit!

'But I can't stay,' she said, 'for my Will is ter take me up to Oxford Street ter shop fer a ring! 'Ow abaht that, then, eh? An' what I reely came ter say was that I jist now remembered what I should've told yer when I fust came back from Brighton; but what with the poor mite, and the funeral, and Mr Tupp popping the question, like, well it quite slipped my mind.' She paused to give dramatic emphasis. 'I found 'er!'

'Found her? Found who?' Henrietta's mind was a whirl of confusion, not helped by the reminder of yesterday's pathetic little funeral.

'Why, the girl you wanted, of course! That Magnificent Millie, as they call 'er. An' cor blimey, yer can't arf see why! Built like a statue an' a couple o' bolsters! The size of 'er! Quite made my Mr Tupp's eyes pop!'

Dane gave a smothered snort of amusement.

'You make me wish we had traced her ourselves!'

'Nah! Like I told Mr Tupp, yer better off wiv wot you've got. 'Cos I tell you, fer all she talked so lah-di-dah, an' 'ad got 'erself a posh 'ouse by the sea, she's still in the oldest game, jist like the rest of us, an' jist like the poor drab on the promenade what told us where ter find 'er. An' I reckon, from the way she greeted us, that she 'as the devil's own temper, and one clout from 'er; well...even if it was you, Mr Dane, I still reckon she'd knock you clear into next week!'

'But what did she say?' Hetta burst in. 'Did she know anything? Did she remember Laura?'

'Oh, yes! Remembered 'er well. 'Ad seen 'er recently, in fact, wrote down your Laura's direction, once we'd convinced 'er we was friendly, an' I've got it 'ere!'

She paused to fumble hopefully down the bodice of her gown and, after a couple of false attempts, retrieved from the depths a twist of paper which she handed, with justifiable pride, to Henrietta.

'There!' she said. 'An' that fust note's 'er private residence, this Millie said, and underneath is 'er business direction. An' a very classy little lady she sounds, too!'

'Private? Business? What do you mean?' Hetta's ideas of the poor waif to be rescued from despair on the streets tumbled into confusion as she heard Sarah's words and, with Jonathan peering eagerly over her shoulder, she untwisted the scrap of paper and read the address scribed upon it in an unexpectedly cultivated hand. It gave addresses for two houses in one of the most exclusive areas of the west end of Lôndon.

'But . . . I don't understand . . . what do you mean? She owns these houses? Herself?'

'That's what this Millie said!'

'And her business? What is that?'

'Well, you know the answer to that, don't yer, 'Etta, me love? It's the business she's always been in, since she started with that Count. An' by all accounts she's got 'erself right to the top. It seems she 'as this other 'ouse, that backs on ter 'ers in the next street, so's she can walk between 'em without using the road. Very discreet, eh? An' Millie claims it's the best 'ouse, with the best-treated girls, in the 'ole of London, an' she should know, cos she worked there once, didn't she, afore she found a titled gentleman to keep 'er comfortable in the sea air!' Sarah turned to the door. 'But I must be on me way. Mr Tupp'll be wondering where I got to!'

'But Sarah!' Hetta was still bemused. 'You mean that Laura runs some sort of . . . well . . . high-class brothel?'

Sarah gave a guffaw of laughter.

'You may've made 'er 'appy, Mr Dane, but I reckon you addled 'er wits with it! Acourse that's what I mean, 'Etta, love, an' a fine little pleasure 'ouse it must be. She's made 'er fortune at it too, so we 'eard! Good fer 'er, I say! Ta ra!'

With a twirl of her new gown, gift of Mr Tupp, Sarah was gone.

'Good heavens!' Hetta collapsed back into a chair. 'Jonathan, I am astounded! It is something I never even dreamed of!'

She looked up at him. He was still standing by the table, the scrap of paper in his hand. He raised his eyes from studying it to look at her, and a rueful smile spread across his face.

'I know of this house!' he said, 'and I believe it *is* held to be the best in London! No, no! I have never been there. But I have had it recommended to me at White's with paeons of praise, but the warning that it is extremely exclusive, and admission is entirely at the whim of the owner. She will admit the man she likes, and refuse the one she does not, regardless of his rank or fortune.' He paused. '*Could* it be Laura?'

Henrietta gave a sudden chuckle.

'If she is *your* cousin, then yes! This is precisely what she would do! Like you, she was abandoned by her abominable relations, and like you she has turned around the situation and made herself a fortune! After all, there are very few professions where a woman can rise to heights of independence. Laura, forced into one, did just as we should have expected all along from a cousin of yours. She rose to the top! It is extraordinary, Jonathan, but we should have considered it! How poor at detection we were!'

He grinned at her.

'Well, the next step must be to go and visit her. And whatever will Meggie, and worse, your worthy brother, think about that?'

CHAPTER TWENTY

IT WAS just after they had turned into Oxford Street that Hetta, surveying from the carriage window the crowded roadway, the fashionable shoppers and the tempting emporiums as if she had been marooned on Crusoe's island, away from civilisation, for months, suddenly caught sight of Robert, Lord Alnstrop, her eldest brother. He was striding purposefully down the street, acknowledging the greetings of acquaintances with the briefest of nods. His dark brows were pulled together in a frown that seemed much at odds with the bright autumn sunshine of an afternoon that had brought an air of frivolity to the other strollers, out to see and be seen.

His appearance in town was due entirely to the arrival, at Alnstrop House, of an extraordinary letter. In it, Hodgson, that most reliable, discreet and loyal of family retainers, who had been years at Alnstrop before taking the position as Henrietta's butler, had claimed to have utterly mislaid his mistress! According to the anxious and confusing missive over which Robert and his wife, Louisa, had pored, Henrietta had vanished weeks previously. She had left no indication as to her future whereabouts, taken only her maid, and no great supply of funds, and had departed in the company of a gentleman hardly known to the household. He, by all accounts, had only rarely been seen in town since, and then in the company of quite another lady, who was not even an acquaintance of Lady Cairshaw's.

Hodgson had dutifully followed Lady Cairshaw's instructions: to carry on as normal, ignore her absence, and inform anyone interested that she would be staying in the country indefinitely; but she had left no forwarding address, no hint as to her intentions, and no word had come from her since. Hodgson, torn as to what his duty should be, had placed the entire mystery in the lap of his lordship.

His lordship was not best pleased. He had no wish to be in town. Lady Alnstrop was imminently expecting to present him with another addition to their family, and only the knowledge that more harm would come to her from worrying over her much loved sister-in-law Henrietta than would come from parting with him for a few days had persuaded him to come up to town at such a time.

He had hoped to uncover some simple misunderstanding and put all to rights immediately, but things had seemed more perplexing, particularly the sworn assurances of the staff at Hetta's St Dunstan's Street house that the man last seen with Lady Cairshaw was Mr Dane, but not the Mr Justin Dane with whom he had anxiously watched his sister pursue her relationship. No, he was assured that Mr Justin Dane had abruptly married elsewhere, to Lady Cairshaw's distress, but no one knew whom the other Mr Dane might be, or where he had met Henrietta.

Robert, thoroughly bewildered and beginning to worry, began to see that enquiries endeavouring to trace his sister might well produce just the sort of speculation and gossip that both she and he would wish to avoid; but he felt that trace her he should. As he walked back to his own town house, sunk in thought, to suddenly hear his sister calling his name seemed almost unreal. Her cry came loud over the rumble of wheels and clatter of hoofs and, looking up, he saw her, hanging from the window of a plain closed carriage, lively and laughing under her smart silk bonnet, and waving to him, beckoning for him to join her in the coach.

'Robert! Robert! Oh, look, Jonathan! No I will not sit back and be discreet, for no one could possibly guess where we are headed, and it's my brother, there, in the olive coat. See? *Robert!* He's seen us. I am *so* pleased. It seems an age since I saw him last and we have so much to tell him. Oh, Jonathan, we could not have met him on a better day! Robert, it is *so* good to see you. Climb in. You *can* spare the time to join us, can you not?'

Hudgell had stopped the carriage to allow Lord Alnstrop to join them, and he jumped lightly up as the door swung open, his emotions a warring mix of relief at finding Hetta so easily, obviously alive and well, exasperation at all the upset and anxiety she had caused, and wild curiosity. While his sister was greeting him extravagantly, he was frankly studying the man who was with her, a man who, from his general appearance, and particularly his unusual grey eyes, must be related to Justin Dane—must be the mysterious escort.

Despite the instinctive animosity Robert had felt towards Justin, he found he was regarding *this* Mr Dane with approval. He liked the lean, fine-boned face, which struck him as not only open and honest, but intelligent and sensitive too. Most particularly, however, he liked the wry amusement which mingled with deep affection in the looks he was giving Henrietta as she prattled on, her usual carefree, exuberant self. Any man who loved Henrietta would require a sense of humour, he reflected, regarding her with great affection himself.

'Robert, dearest Robert, what a wonderful coincidence that you should be here! I had not looked to see you in town at such a time, for I know that Louisa... But how is my favourite sister-in-law? As blooming as ever, I trust, and as well as ever she was before the arrival of little Henry? And how is that young gentleman? Certainly *you* look wonderfully well... But forgive me...my manners are abominable!

'Robert, I must introduce you to Jonathan. But first I must warn you that he is not only my very dearest friend, and my most chivalrously archaic protector, he is also my companion in detection, my unwilling follower into all my follies and catastrophes, and the man I am engaged to marry! I shall take it in very poor part if you do not make every effort to become friends! Robert, Mr Dane, Mr *Jonathan* Dane. Jonathan, my brother, Robert, Lord Alnstrop.'

As the men shook hands, Jonathan, who had watched the predictable mix of emotions that had crossed Robert's face as he listened to this ingenuous speech, regarded him with a somewhat rueful smile.

'After such an introduction I am hard put to it to know what to say,' he began, and Henrietta chuckled, 'but,' he continued, directing at her a would-be quelling glance which only had her chuckling the more, 'I am certainly glad to meet you, my lord, for Henrietta speaks of you frequently, and clearly holds you in the greatest affection. Furthermore, anyone who has contrived to act in the role of guardian to her throughout her formative years and has managed to survive, with his sanity, clearly must command both admiration and respect!'

Robert smiled, watching her affect outrage. The relationship between his sister and this man was an almost palpable thing, charging the air about them with the exuberance of their joy, and reminding him brightly of his own courtship of Louisa. He took the man's hand in a positive grip.

'Any man who loves and delights my sister will become a friend of mine,' he said, simply, then grinned. 'Any man who survives, that is!'

'Then I believe our friendship is assured!' Jonathan replied, but his long, slow smile was directed at Henrietta, who, looking up into his eyes, very prettily blushed. She turned back to her brother.

'If you have both *quite* finished these extraordinary insinuations...' she said, then continued with a certain airy nonchalance, 'You will no doubt be surprised to find me engaged to *Jonathan*, not *Justin* Dane...'

She paused, and Robert gave a small disclaiming shrug, although his dark eyebrows were quizzically raised.

'I was most *dreadfully* mistaken in that abominable man!' She frowned, and Robert noticed what her previous mirth had disguised: that her face was thinner than when he had seen her last, as if she had been ill, or suffering. 'You were quite right, for you never liked him, did you? And I should have trusted your opinion. But I was stupidly, inexplicably dazzled... However! That horrible man, and his despicable behaviour, are now a matter of complete indifference to me. I care not a jot for him. Those miserable months are as wiped clean from my past, and I dare say that when I am married and *must* acknowledge him as cousin I might even find the strength of mind to greet him with a semblance of civility!'

'*You* might be able to, but I'm more than certain I could not!' Jonathan interposed. 'I say we cut the connection entirely, and the same goes for most of the rest of my relations! They are none of them worth a groat!'

'Of course, sir, we will swathingly cut any number of your relations, if that is your command,' Henrietta replied, suddenly most improbably demure, 'for naturally you will be master in your own home, and I would not dare gainsay you!'

'Very gratifying to hear! I wonder why it is that *nothing* in our previous relationship has led me to expect such an idyllic situation...now control yourself, girl!' He was laughing, catching her hands. 'Whatever will your brother think of your behaviour?' For Henrietta was displaying an alarming tendency to resort to physical violence.

'Speaking, as we were, of your many and varied relations,' she said firmly, sitting back in her seat and retrieving the hands that he had captured and then held hostage between his own, 'I believe we must confess to Robert exactly where it is we are going, and why, or when we arrive shortly in Fitzadam Street he is going to be more than a little surprised!'

'Perhaps,' suggested Jonathan, 'in view of your having just met your brother after so long, it would be sensible to delay our visit to Fitzadam Street.'

Henrietta thought.

'Oh, no,' she said. 'Unless it would distress you to have us both accompany you, let us go now, and end our quest. It seems an optimum day for solutions and conclusions.'

He nodded. He too wanted the search for Laura to be at last over, behind them, and then to celebrate a speedy marriage that would herald the return of them both to the more conventional world of respectable society. Lord Alnstrop would doubtless know the worst eventually, he thought, resigned, so rather sooner than later.

'In that case, I think a turn about Hyde Park is required, if you have no objection, my lord, while you are apprised of all that has been happening over the past few weeks. I only hope that at the end of the tale you do not feel inclined to hurl me, or even both of us, bodily from the coach!'

Robert smiled. He had been content to watch them both with amusement and pleasure; he was becoming steadily more convinced that, whatever had been happening over the past few weeks, this man would suit Henrietta very well, so much better than the abominable Justin, and would make a welcome addition to the family.

'I await the tale with bated breath,' he said, 'and as for hurling you bodily from the coach, you must rest assured that my position as guest in your vehicle will naturally control my otherwise overmastering inclinations for violence!'

Jonathan grinned, Hudgell was redirected, and Robert settled back to listen to Henrietta's story. She told it all herself, merely looking to Jonathan for occasional confirmation of some detail, and although she glossed over many of her own emotions, and concentrated on her passionate desire to help this unfortunate cousin, Laura, much more was plain to her brother than she had perhaps intended.

Although he was profoundly shocked and distressed by her account, Lord Alnstrop found, reflecting as he listened, that it was the contemplation of Henrietta, driven by despair to the dark edge of Westminster Bridge, that shocked him more than any other part of her hair-raising and socially unforgivable escapades. He instantly forgave much, of her and of Jonathan. For he realised that it was by absorbing herself in these very follies that Hetta had been able to draw back from the brink to which she had been driven by Justin and his calculating heartlessness, and achieve the joy she had found today.

It was the culminating revelations, of Laura's present whereabouts and business successes, that goaded him into unguarded comment.

'Good God!' he exclaimed, as he heard the address of her exclusive establishment. 'I've been there!'

Hetta gave a whoop of startled laughter.

'Robert! You haven't! Well, really...! But that means, surely,' she added after brief reflection, 'that you must have met Laura, *and* met with her approval to gain admittance! Won't you tell us what happened? Well, not *all* of what happened, of course...!'

Robert glanced apologetically at Jonathan, regretting his outburst, but Dane shrugged reassuringly, and shook his head slightly. He had had many weeks to imagine worse fates for Laura than this.

'*Do* tell us, Robert,' Hetta persisted, so with a wry grimace Lord Alnstrop confessed.

'It was—naturally, for I am now a staid married man!—many years ago, six or seven, I imagine. The house was newly opened and visiting there was all the go. Every man aspired to the kudos of admission, for it was kept *very* exclusive! A gentleman calling would send in his card. Many were refused at the outset, and for them no one was ever at home! Others were invited in to meet Madame Laura—yes, the name was Laura, I had forgotten after so long—in a very formal drawing-room! If she approved them they were invited to partake of a little refreshment within...!' He paused, and smiled reminiscently.

'Robert, I think I am probably scandalised!' reproved his sister, intrigued in a most unladylike way! 'To think that when I thought you up in town on business... Men! I suppose,' she rounded on her beloved, 'I suppose you behaved just the same in India!'

He grinned at her, and lightly flicked her uptilted chin with his finger.

'Customs are not so *very* different out there, after all,' he said, teasingly, 'though perhaps a little more exotic!'

She glared at him, but only momentarily. She turned back to her brother.

'And if a man was not approved, what then? I can understand why Laura enjoyed keeping her house exclusive and rejecting the men she disliked. How few men she had found to like or respect since she was sent from Thwayle. I dare say she was tempted to reject them all, and I have a lively sympathy!'

'If they were rejected,' Robert said, 'they were offered no refreshment, and Madame Laura politely requested they be brought their coats. As the men who brought the coats were two Negroes of vast stature and strength, there was rarely any objection! Certainly her policy seemed to work. From all I hear, the house is still exclusive and much sought after, and Madame Laura reputed to be fantastically wealthy! I have even heard that several of her girls have made advantageous and highly successful marriages!'

Hetta turned to Jonathan and smiled.

'You see,' she said, softly, 'she is as unconventional and successful as you are yourself. Let us go and call on her immediately. I can't wait any longer to make the acquaintance of my new cousin!'

'You cannot,' said Robert, aghast, 'be intending to visit this house! I may have thought nothing more could shock me, this crazy afternoon, but *that*, Henrietta, is too much!'

'Not the house *you* visited, stupid! Her private residence in Fitzadam Street. Even I,' she chuckled, 'would have balked at persuading Jonathan to introduce me to her business premises. Who knows *who* I might not have encountered there? But the private address, if approached discreetly in a closed carriage, we agreed would be quite acceptable! So don't, dearest Robert, make any problem, or we shall have to abandon you here in the park.'

The house in Fitzadam Street was an elegant town house from the previous century, its brightly polished sash windows looking out with an aristocratic hauteur over the immaculately blacked front railings. A delicate fanlight, its panes of glass spread like a peacock's tail, topped the black-painted front door, and the brass knocker was burnished so that it winked brightly in the afternoon sun. Everything about the home bespoke a caring and wealthy owner.

The door was opened to them by a huge footman. His skin as black as ebony, his demeanour imposingly solemn, he was impeccably clad in coat and breeches of celestial blue, generously trimmed with silver braid. His haughty look expressed faint enquiry.

With an appreciative smile at his cousin's arrangements, Dane stepped forward and held out his card, and a letter he had written before they set forth.

'Be good enough to take these to your mistress, if you would, and perhaps we might wait within for her reply?'

The giant of a man studied the card dubiously, but just then the butler appeared, took the card in chilly silence, read it briefly, then nodded.

'Follow me, if you please.'

They were led into a small drawing-room, furnished with a tasteful elegance that had spared no expense to achieve the best. The room, Henrietta thought, amused, would have been the envy of many a top society matron.

'Please, make yourselves comfortable.' The butler withdrew.

Henrietta and her brother both sat down to wait, but Jonathan paced the room, looking about him with an astonished perplexity, as if after so many weeks of searching, and so many desperate imaginings of his cousin's fate, this elegant and sophisticated room seemed impossible to comprehend. Hetta caught his eye, and gave a quick, reassuring smile, but just then the door opened, and all their attention was riveted on the lady who walked slowly in and stood staring, her eyes fixed on Jonathan.

She was small, her body as delicate as a bird's. Her rustling lavender crêpe dress, its very simplicity speaking much for the exclusive modiste who had designed it, and her matching cap with hanging ribbons, gave an added air of fragility. She would have passed anywhere as a wealthy and demure young widow. Her rich brown hair was looped simply back to frame her face and give a quaint, old-fashioned look, and her enormous, slate-grey eyes, fringed with thick dark lashes, gazed at where they were curiously reflected in Jonathan's own face.

'So it *is* you,' she breathed. 'They told me you were dead.'

She still did not move from the door, and it was Jonathan who went to her and, without a word, took her in his arms. After a minute he held her away to look at her, unashamed of the tears that stood in his eyes.

'I have been searching for you for so long,' he said. 'Ever since I arrived back from India at the start of the year. I can barely believe that I have found you at last. But come,' he placed her hand on his arm and led her forward, 'I would like you to meet my fiancée, Lady Henrietta Cairshaw, and her brother, Lord Alnstrop. Without Henrietta's assistance I doubt if I would ever have found you.'

Laura's greetings were self-possessed and cordial, but understandably restrained, particularly with Henrietta, and it was not until the whole elaborate story of their search had been told again, largely by Jonathan this time, that Laura's severe formality began to give way. As she realised how much they knew of her past life, and realised that despite it all they had come to acknowledge her as friend and family, her amazed disbelief gradually softened to joy. The huge Negro footman had appeared during the tale with a scalloped-edged silver tray bearing madeira, glasses, and small sweet biscuits, but she had waved him to leave it and go, allowing Jonathan to finish uninterrupted. Now she offered them all refreshment before taking up the story herself.

She looked up at Jonathan with her great dark eyes.

'First you must understand that they swore to me that you were dead when I called out your name on that dreadful night at Thwayle, when they came and told me I was to leave with Count Vilnius.

'There was no one else left at Thwayle then who cared one jot for me. All the uncles and cousins would have preferred me to have conveniently died of a fever and spared them my share of the inheritance without further exertion on their part. But I obstinately lived on, and they found a doubly useful part for me to play, paying off their gambling debts as well as deserting my share of Great-Grandfather's so-called fortune. How I laughed when I heard there was nothing left! But I digress.

'That night, when they came, and I said that I would write to you, and you would come for me as you had always rescued me through childhood, they told me that you were dead. They swore that they had known for weeks, that it had slipped their minds to mention it to me, and such casual cruelty was so typical of them that in my despair I was driven to believe it as truth. That is why no childish scrawl arrived on your breakfast table in Madras.

'For the rest, you seem to know my story until the arrival of poor Jeremy's irate and blustering father on the doorstep in Eleanor Street. After that I worked for a while in company with Millie.' She smiled wryly. 'We made a sufficiently contrasting pair! Then, by a lucky chance, I met a man who became the dearest friend I ever had. I will not tell you who he was; he is dead now'—she gestured at her gown—'and his wife would not set him free to marry me as he wished. Instead, he bought me this house, and furnished it with me,' she smiled fondly about the room, 'and we had several happy months, here and on the Continent, before he became ill. His doctors gave him little time to live, but he defied them for years, and used his money and the time spared to him to help me set up my business in the other house. He was not keen at first, but I told him I would prefer this way to the small pension he could otherwise leave me, that could be queried, perhaps claimed back, by his family. So we spent the money, and set up the house, and I figured nowhere in his will.

'It was better that way. He liked to help me recruit my girls. It amused him; he was very strict in his standards; and he found Jacob, who admitted you, and his brother Abraham, who protect me and the house most efficiently.' She looked apologetically at Jonathan. 'It has served me well,' she said. 'I find I have a talent for business management, and I enjoy making money, even money from such a source as this. I have made a life at which I am a success, and when Basil eventually died he knew my comfort was assured.'

'So my first aim in finding you,' Jonathan began, 'which was to offer you relief and escape from the poverty-stricken desperation I imagined to be your life, is ludicrously unnecessary!' He grinned, looking appreciatively around the room.

'And could you have done?' she asked, curiously. 'For you too were thrown out with barely sufficient to feed yourself on the ship to India, so I was told, let alone support yourself upon arrival.'

Henrietta looked at her love in quick concern. *That* he had not told her. He only laughed, however.

'Quite true, Cousin, but I soon discovered that I too, like you, have a remarkable flair for business, and the opportunities even on board ship, and then particularly out in the east, are many and varied. I could say that I have every reason to be grateful to my family's brutality! I doubt I would ever have discovered my potential without it, or made myself the very comfortable fortune I now enjoy.'

Laura stared at him for a moment, then she began to laugh, leaning back helplessly in her chair, shaking with mirth.

'And only to think,' she gasped, 'of all their faces when at last Great-Grandfather died and that ludicrous will was read. When they discovered that for all their scheming and conniving they had inherited an equal share of his debts! It is too much!' She wiped her eyes with a pretty lace handkerchief. 'And here we both are, abandoned to our ruin, now quite disgustingly wealthy! Oh, dear!' She turned to Alnstrop and Henrietta. 'I am sorry, you must think me most unfeeling——'

'No, indeed!' Henrietta said, firmly. 'I have the liveliest distaste for all your family apart from yourself and Jonathan, and join wholeheartedly in your amusement at their fate. Incidentally, did you hear about your insufferable cousin Justin and his heiress?'

Laura had not, and when that tale had been told the four of them were hooting with laughter at the thought of his discomfiture.

'Oh,' Laura exclaimed, wiping her eyes again, 'maybe I shall begin to believe that Providence works with purpose after all! Perhaps I should offer financial support to his wife! Poor girl, I can find it in me to pity her!'

Jonathan looked at her in surprise.

'I can see that you and Henrietta are destined to be friends!' he said ruefully. 'She has already suggested as much to me. I spoke to Justin briefly when I saw him at White's recently. He suggested that the donation of a sum that will enable him to set off with his wife to seek his fortune around the gambling tables of Europe would fulfil his only ambition. I have agreed to the arrangement providing he remains out of the country for at least five years, and he has grudgingly accepted. Hopefully they will be gone within the month.'

'Jonathan! You never told me!'

'Oddly enough,' he said, smiling at Henrietta, 'it had quite gone from my mind until today. I have had so much else to think of! But it seemed a satisfactory arrangement.'

'Far more than he deserved, I have no doubt,' put in Laura tartly. 'You were always generous to a fault, even as a boy.'

'Apart from resuming our friendship,' Jonathan asked her, 'is there nothing more I can do for you? Especially now you are alone.'

Laura began to shake her head, accustomed to her independence, then she suddenly paused, and looked thoughtfully at Jonathan, then at Henrietta.

'Well?' Dane queried.

She shrugged slightly.

'No,' she said. 'I think it is not something I should ask.'

'Tell us, Laura,' Hetta put in impulsively. 'Let us judge if we can help.'

Laura sighed. 'I have a daughter——' she began slowly.

'Good grief!' Jonathan exclaimed. 'How could we have forgotten? We knew of her from Sarah. How is she? May we meet her?'

His cousin smiled at his outburst.

'She is very well. A delightful child, in fact, though I speak with a mother's partiality. But she is now ten years of age, and no matter how much I shield her the restricted life my circumstances force her to lead here is not what any parent would wish for a child. I would like her, one day, to take her place in Society, for despite her parentage she will be a very considerable heiress, and much can be overlooked in the rich.

'I privately use the surname of Lascelles now. It was one of the family names of my dear Basil, and I have adopted it for Patience also, for she thought of Basil as a father. I would dearly like to find a family with whom she could live as a daughter, and grow up a loved and healthy country child. When she is of age, I could retire from this business and go with her to live somewhere on the Continent. Then, perhaps, we could both put the past behind us, and she could marry at an acceptable level in Society...'

Laura's voice trailed away. She sounded sadly vulnerable in her hopes and dreams for her daughter.

Henrietta instantly ran over to her, and Jonathan, meeting Robert's eye, gave a quiet chuckle, for he knew exactly what was coming next.

'Would you allow her to come to us?' Hetta was asking. 'Not that we have a house in the country yet, but as soon as we are married we shall find one, and we would dearly love to give Patience a home.' She gazed at Laura earnestly. 'Wouldn't we, Jonathan?' she asked, as an after thought.

Jonathan smiled. 'Certainly, Laura, if you feel you could entrust your daughter to our care we would be very happy to have her. I dare say we will need a little Patience in the house! I make only one proviso.'

Hetta turned on him angrily.

'How *can* you make a proviso on such a matter!'

'I *insist*,' he continued calmly, 'on marrying my spitfire wife and spending a little time with her first! Perhaps...' he turned to Laura, who was regarding them with amusement '...a move in a few months, when the better weather begins at Easter, would suit Patience, for then she would have all the outdoor pursuits to distract her from the upset of changing home.'

Laura's looks spoke of her relief and delight.

'Oh, indeed,' she said. 'Such a plan would be more than I had ever dreamed.'

They did not stay very much longer. Patience was brought down to meet them, a small, shy child with her mother's huge solemn dark eyes, who caught Hetta's heart immediately, and Dane promised to call again the following day.

'I hope,' he concluded, 'to be able to invite you to our wedding!'

Once more in the carriage, Jonathan ordered Hudgell to St Dunstan's Street.

'But why?' Hetta cried. 'What of poor Meggie?'

'Because, my dear girl,' pronounced her beloved, in tones that would brook no argument, 'You will, very properly, be married from your own house. *I* will retrieve Meggie. *You* will return to reassure your staff, and apprise them of the impending happy event. And if, as I plan, I can gain a special licence immediately, I hope we can persuade your brother to remain in town to attend the event, and, doubtless with a sigh of relief, to give you away!'

'Yes, Jonathan,' she said.

CHAPTER TWENTY-ONE

HENRIETTA, perverse as ever, insisted they be married at the same little stone church under the yew trees that had witnessed the sad events in the tale of baby Dickon.

Sitting in her cosy back parlour at St Dunstan's Street, they had been discussing where to live, for Robert had told them of a particular house for sale. An extraordinary house, it had been built a century ago as a vast folly on the edge of his estates by the then Lord Kintrove, whose lands ran alongside those of Alnstrop House. It was a crazy house, four octagons of wedge-shaped rooms linked by low connecting apartments to form a square about a central courtyard. It resembled an ancient castle, and Henrietta had loved the house ever since she had visited to play there when she was a very small child. Now the present Lord Kintrove was at a low ebb, and desirous of finding a purchaser for the property. Jonathan, intrigued by the sound of the house and keen to please Henrietta, had agreed to go with her to look at it. They were to travel back to Alnstrop some time after the wedding, and hopefully, if all was satisfactory, have any necessary work put in train while they travelled on to spend some time on the Continent. That decided, they had returned to the question of where to celebrate the wedding.

'I have to go back to Lockchain Terrace *anyway*,' Henrietta said decisively, 'to make my farewells to Mrs Crabbe, her Billy who brought up the coal, Dora, and Collette—oh, and all the Perkins family of course, not to mention Sarah, and Mr Tupp! In fact . . .' she warmed to her idea as she spoke '. . . I should like to invite them *all* to the wedding!'

'Henrietta!' Jonathan, regarding her down the length of the sofa, was torn between amusement and exasperation, and he gave an exaggerated sigh. 'I have already arranged for everything to be cleared from Lockchain Terrace. You have no real need to return. I believe your true aim is to further torment the unfortunate Reverend Mr Smith. What has he done to deserve this?'

Hetta chuckled.

'He *cannot* object to marrying us! What could be more proper? Surely he will be too busy rejoicing that he has led us into the paths of righteousness to be able to disapprove!'

'I suspect,' said Jonathan, drily resigned, 'that you underestimated Mr Smith!'

And Jonathan was proved right. Special licences did not figure largely in the work of Mr Smith. He took the offending document, and studied the stiff square of parchment with its dangling seal as if it offered him a personal affront. A desire to avoid the reading of the banns he regarded as automatically suspect. What honest man, he reasoned, could wish to resort to such indecent haste and subterfuge? He reluctantly agreed, however, unable to think of sufficient excuse to avoid the duty. He would perform the ceremony the following morning. He looked forward to relishing his disapproval of the entire proceedings.

The weather, miraculously, had held fair, each morning dawning bright and clear, the sky a high, high dome of the palest blue above the city. If they were out on the hills above Alnstrop, Hetta thought, as she stepped out from the carriage at the church, gulping this air, so clear and sharp, would be like gulping white wine, sparkling and chilled. Even through the dirty city atmosphere the autumn leaves on the pavements glowed golden, and the red bricks seemed rosy through their grime.

She went quickly with Robert to see the tiny mound of earth still raw and new under the yew trees, and silently laid a bunch of white roses on the damp, dark soil. She looked up briefly at the soundless gargoyle above them, then with a little mental shake she smiled, at peace, put all those thoughts behind her, and took Robert's arm.

'Take me into the church now,' she said.

They were all there. Mrs Crabbe, magnificent in a monstrous bonnet festooned with every type of fruit, and some which defied even nature's ingenuity. Billy, the coal dust ruthlessly scrubbed from his gangling frame, had been crammed into a tidy suit, wrists and ankles sprouting, buttons straining. Dora and Collette, their bonnets all ribbons and flowers, nudged and simpered and giggled together, while Sarah and Mr Tupp gazed at each other, improbably dewy-eyed. The Perkins family had been mustered, all in Sunday best, and stood beaming their approval of events.

Sam, just when he had thought he must lose his regular supply of pennies from Mr Dane, had had a request to join the Dane establishment, when they had acquired their house in the country, as stable-lad. Mr Perkins had agreed. Sam stood, dreaming ecstatic dreams in which Sam Perkins, head groom, figured prominently.

Mr Smith's dubious regard of this motley selection of parishioners had lightened at the arrival of an impeccably dressed lady, obviously a wealthy widow of good family, accompanied by a charmingly demure little girl. His smile of condescending approval wavered and collapsed, however, as he watched Sarah, with a cry of delight, run from her pew and embrace this lady, who responded with every sign of affection. He sniffed audibly, and turned away, tapping his fingers impatiently until the bride—he sniffed again—appeared in the doorway.

Hetta advanced confidently, her hand lightly resting on her brother's arm. Even the two old crones, the witches, were there, she noticed, lurking at the side. With a spurt of amusement, she gave them a beaming smile and a little wave of welcome, and startled back two toothless grins.

After the ceremony, while Mr Smith was still shaking his head, wringing his hands and gazing in disbelief at the signatures, especially that of the bride's brother, that now graced his register, the rest were making their way back to Miss Perkins' coffee shop, where Jonathan had ordered liberal celebrations and general merrymaking.

He and Henrietta could not stay past the first few toasts, however. They were to travel to Alnstrop, with Robert, that afternoon. Only that morning he had received a note replying to his hasty letter to his wife.

The note congratulated him on so rapidly discovering Henrietta—not that Louisa had ever thought it would prove a problem for him, of course—and informed him that he was now the proud father of a daughter of outstanding beauty! He was commanded to return at once to admire her, on no account forgetting to bring Henrietta, who would certainly be desolate if she could not immediately view her niece! Naturally, they were all to leave at once.

'A kiss for the bride! A kiss for the bride!'

The chant was set up with much chafing and laughter as Jonathan led Henrietta to the coffee-shop door after they had made their round of farewells. Henrietta looked up at her beloved, her eyes dancing.

'It is not quite our accustomed venue of a public house, of course,' she said demurely, 'but I dare say that, if you were no gentleman, I *could* be unladylike enough to oblige!'

'Oh, I dare say!' he said, gravely.

So he wasn't, and she did!

Lord Alnstrop was collecting his baggage from White's, where he had put up during his London stay, thinking happily of his wife, son and baby daughter.

Crossing the coffee room upstairs, he recognised, with distaste, Justin Dane. As was his almost daily habit now, Justin had withdrawn to the club, and was immersing himself equally in brandy, contemplation of the wrongs dealt him by fortune, and the morning paper. It was the paper he was concentrating upon as Lord Alnstrop crossed the room. A wedding announcement had caught his attention.

"The marriage has taken place," he read, "between Lady Henrietta Cairshaw, widow of Sir Edward Cairshaw, of St Dunstan's Street, London, and Mr Jonathan Dane, late of Madras, India, cousin of Lord Grimsett of Thwayle. The wedding was celebrated quietly, the bride accompanied by her brother, Lord Alnstrop, of Alnstrop House. The bridegroom's cousin, Mrs Laura Lascelles, and niece were also in attendance."

'Well!' Justin sat back in amazement, shaking the paper out delicately with his long white fingers, and staring at the passage again. 'Well, I'll be damned!'

'Oh, probably,' Robert agreed with satisfaction, giving a small, polite bow as he passed behind where Justin sat. 'Very probably!'

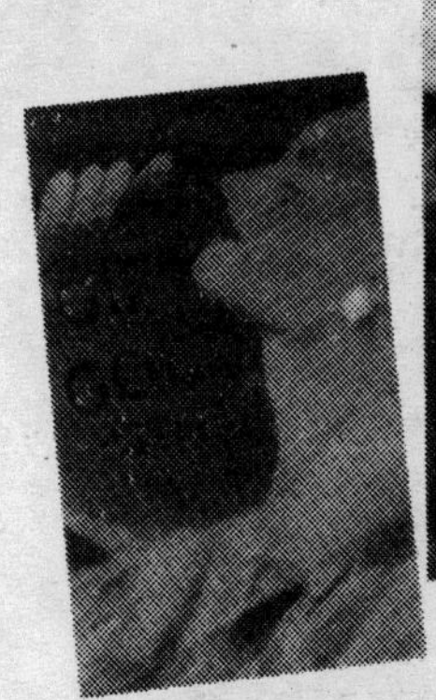

A WILD
WIND